REJUVENATION 3

The Rejuvenation Trilogy

Byddi Lee

Byddi Lee
Visit my website at www.byddilee.com

Printed in the United Kingdom

First Printing: Oct 2020
Castrum Press

For Daddy
Always remembered...

CONTENTS

CHAPTER 1

The old nightclub was the best and the worst place to have a meeting. Situated at the top of the cruise ship, it had room for everyone, but the threadbare velvet seats, arranged in semicircles around glass-topped tables, looked sad and tired. Some of the tables and seats were broken or gone, causing gaping holes, like in a mouth with missing teeth. Bobbie imagined the room in its heyday: lights bouncing, music pulsing, people dancing, couples embracing.

A fist of grief tightened in her chest. Would she ever feel Hicks' arms around her again? How could she convince the people in charge of operations that getting Hicks back was a priority? That they all stood to gain from rescuing him for the Personality Augmentation and Rehabilitation Center, the PARC, if only they knew which PARC Belus were keeping him in now? Bobbie reckoned Belus would have moved him after that last failed attempt. She dragged in a breath, counted to three, and released it. She couldn't think about what Belus Corp might be doing to him back at the PARC. Her anxiety wouldn't set him free. Only action would do that, and this sad nightclub might be where that plan to free him would take shape.

If only she could focus on what lay ahead rather than what had happened. Her escape from the PARC, Hicks' failed rescue attempt, the encounter with the Belus agents – killing them, and Joy killing Jimmy, populated not only her nightmares but sent chill tentacles of dread through her waking thoughts.

Bobbie raked her nails along her forearms, raising bright pink parallel lines. Every part of her body itched, even the soles of her feet: symptoms of detoxing from the drugs they'd pumped into her at the PARC. She folded her arms tightly against her torso, looked out the window and into the tangle of trees on the cliff, so close she could nearly pluck a leaf. The first ray of the morning sun broke over the ridge. Bobbie followed the path of golden light along the deck to where it illuminated reflective white lettering on an orange emergency buoyancy aid – *Ocean Spirit*.

Bobbie sighed. On top of everything else, she felt sorry for this damned ship. How ridiculous was that? This ship was lost not at sea, but on land. Its name was a mockery.

Neither on the ocean nor with much spirit, the cruise ship had been carried into the labyrinth of valleys of northern Norway during the tsunamis induced by the Melters' attack. It had been wedged upright, high and dry above the newborn fjords, budding off parent-fjords as the sea level rose – but not high enough to free the *Ocean Spirit*. Cloaking technology kept the ship hidden from the alarmingly close new populations that had sprung up in Norway's pleasant climate.

Bobbie turned her back on the window and watched her sister at the front of the room – Joy was in her element, tweaking cables, engrossed in setting up a portable intepanel to play back video footage. Bobbie chose a seat at a table where her father sat next to Mo, Slade's son. It would take some time for Mo to recover from his partner's betrayal. Bobbie reached for compassion for the young man, with his gaunt face and haunted eyes, but she couldn't push away her anger at his stupidity and blind faith in Jacob.

Slade appeared in the doorway and stood looking out along the corridor to the deck. Bobbie noticed she still had one arm in a sling, but Slade's posture was upright and commanding.

"Hello, Bobbie," Slade said. "How are you feeling?"

Bobbie shrugged, breaking eye contact with Slade, confused by the mixed feelings she had for the woman. Slade had used Bobbie to determine which PARC Hicks was in. Bobbie didn't mind that so much since she'd wanted to find him too. She understood that Slade couldn't let her in on the plan because of the truth drugs they used in the PARC, but the echoes of that moment when Bobbie had thought Slade had betrayed her by handing her over to Lisette Fox haunted Bobbie. It had been too easy, and Bobbie felt foolish at her own naivety.

Bobbie held a grudging admiration for Slade: for the soldier she was, for her skill in subterfuge, and for the power she had with the Candels. Slade had set up Bobbie's rescue from the PARC and had blown her own cover in the process. They were on the same side. Slade and Bobbie might want the same things, but Bobbie wondered if it was for the same reasons. She and Slade had always been adversaries, but right now Bobbie needed Slade on her side to find Hicks.

Bobbie crossed her legs, folded her arms, and clenched her fists, resisting the urge to scratch at already delicate skin while she waited for Joy to present the footage from the ONIV they had taken from the dead Belus guard after Bobbie's escape. Joy wanted to commandeer this ONIV to replace her own, which had been damaged during the electric shock treatment Bobbie had used to destroy nanobots in Joy's body.

"I'm ready to go now," Joy said, looking around the room. "Do you want me to wait?"

"No, we don't know exactly when the Fjord's Leaders will get back," Slade said. "They've had to delay their return flight because there are Belus hovercrafts too close by. We're hiding behind shields, and those can't be lowered for entry at the moment.

Belus have increased their sweep patrols after they found the base at Yosemite. I reckon the discovery has helped them enhance their search algorithms. They uncovered the Alaska group."

No-one spoke for a few long moments as their thoughts turned to this.

"We lost good people there." Luke broke the reverie. "I spent time there a while back."

"It's a loss, alright." Slade sighed. "But Fox is hopping mad. I feel as though your talk to the medical board has been the first time we've really gotten to her. You did well, Bobbie, and if Fox feels under pressure, she's more likely to make a mistake."

Bobbie had been searching her blink feeds for news of the medical board ever since she'd escaped from the PARC. When they'd broken Granny out, the media had reported that Bobbie was a mass murderer, along with Joy and Hicks. She had proved to the medical board that that was a lie. While she'd been in the PARC, the board had spoken out against Rejuvenation, which had led to a few street protests that Belus had extinguished. Now all Bobbie saw in the media feeds were reports on new Belus health initiatives that justified their use of biosensors, and an article waxing lyrical on the societal benefits of Rejuvenation, with a special interview with an "expert" who discussed how many elders had taken themselves off traveling to enjoy their new lives. There were the usual local crimes that had successfully been dealt with by the 'gentle yet firm' law enforcement officers of Belus Corp. Another in-depth report on the achievements of those treated for criminal behavior by the PARC system had come to light just as Bobbie had escaped. There had been no mention of her escape, and she realized Slade was right – she'd made Belus look bad. That gave her a strange satisfaction.

"Run the footage, Joy. It will do no harm to get an advance screening of this, at any rate." Slade stepped inside, letting the door swing shut. She took a seat by the door.

Bobbie had fought through the first brutal days of withdrawal in her cabin, with only Joy and her father for company and hadn't met any of the group based on the ship yet. She wasn't sure she was ready to meet new people, wasn't sure if she would ever be ready for anything again.

"Alright," Joy said in front of a blue screen. "This is footage from a mark two ONIV found in the Belus guard. It's one of the early ones that caches data for twenty-four hours. I was able to retrieve this data as a four-eyes file."

Joy had nicely sanitized how they'd chopped off the Belus guard's head. She didn't refer to how they'd dug out the ONIV; no mention of how the guard, less than a month ago, had been an innocent ultra-elderly person no different from Bobbie's geriatric patients. Like her Granny, Lisette Fox had experimented on this woman against her will and turned her into a youthful psychopath. And as had been the case with Granny, Bobbie had had to kill her to save Joy's life.

The screen flickered, and they were looking out through the first-person view of the Belus guard's eyes. The first image showed fingers pressed to a biometrics pad. Spinning fast enough to make Bobbie woozy, the image settled on a door sliding open. Sunshine cast a glare. By the time the light sensor had readjusted, the guard had gone through the door and was walking along a narrow path with waist-high walls on either side. The first-person view swung out over the countryside on one side, showing rolling fields, with skyscrapers on the horizon and a castle on a hill in the middle distance.

France? Maybe Germany?

The guard appeared to be on top of a perimeter wall of some kind as the image scanned the path again and swung down, lifting Bobbie's stomach in a swell of nausea. Four-eyes got her every time.

The yard below looked like a prison. This didn't make sense to Bobbie. All prisons had been abolished since criminal behaviors were treated only in the PARC system now. About a hundred people shambled below without any apparent direction: many lay slumped over picnic benches. Everyone wore the non-color-coded grey sensorfabrik tunic and trousers, like a uniform. They all seemed to be around the same age, mid to late thirties, and all were underweight, some painfully thin.

What the hell was this place?

The audio of shouts, aggressive commands, and running feet grabbed the guard's attention. The footage shimmered as the ONIV processed quickly shifting eyes. The first-person view settled on a fight in the top corner of the yard.

"Hey!" The volume of the guard's yell made everyone watching in the nightclub jump.

The speakers popped, obliterating the first few words the guard shouted into the yard, but the rest came out in a garbled command: "...before they damage each other. Fox is gonna..."

Bobbie strained to understand the few coherent words from the crackle of white noise.

More swiftly changing scenes forced Bobbie to close her eyes. From the heavy breathing coming over the speakers, she could tell the guard was running. Bobbie forced her eyes open to watch the juddering images. The guard was racing through the yard, shouldering people out of her way.

Bobbie strained to get a closer look at the people in the holding area. All had orange eyes – Rejuvenees. All had empty expressions, seemingly docile and unperturbed. All had similar features – most of the males resembling Davitt, but not quite clones of him. At least, not in the same way the women looked like exact clones of Lisette Fox. None of them turned to look toward the disruption. No-one lifted their heads to follow the guard charging past them toward the fracas. Anyone the guard bumped into either fell over and stayed there or wobbled, righted themselves, and continued to amble without direction.

Why was Belus keeping them here? Who were they? Was this the army Fox was creating? If so, it hardly seemed useful. Or were these victims of the nanobot release that Fox had no use for?

The first-person view rested on other security personnel holding a man down. Neither of the men in staff uniforms had orange eyes. They looked frightened. The prisoner screamed and flailed, battering the staff. His agitation was fueled by more than anger: the poor guy foamed at the mouth, his face screwed up, eyes squeezed shut. Sweat poured off him.

"She stole my pop," he screamed, bucking against the hands holding him. "I need it."

The first-person view swung to a woman lying against the wall. Her face twisted in a laugh, more of a leer. She gave the guard the finger before her hand flopped to her lap as she passed out.

"I need my pop." The frenzied man continued to scream in the background. "It hurts. Oh God, help me, please."

"Fuck sakes," the guard's voice boomed in the room around Bobbie. The audio was out of whack. The first-person view swung to the screaming prisoner, and the guard said, "You have to watch these losers more closely. Someone go get him a dose."

Off-screen, a voice said, "Yes, ma'am," and footfalls faded among a burble of voices.

One of the uniformed men holding the prisoner shifted enough to allow the prisoner's hand to break free. His eyes shot open, glowing orange. The crazed man clawed at the uniform still holding him. The guard reached for his taser.

"No!" The man's scream splintered the air.

The frenzied man bucked, rigid, as the current coursed through him. He collapsed, limp. His skin turned slack and grey.

Bobbie turned away, not needing to be reminded of Granny's death, nor the five guards she'd killed in a similar way only days ago.

For Mo, though, it was the first time he'd seen the effect of an electric shock on a rejuvenated person. Bobbie sensed him holding his breath and heard the subsequent gasps of horror as he watched the man's flesh disintegrate into a jellied mass, with the bones protruding through the skin in places.

The screen went blank.

"Sorry to have to show you that," Joy said from beside the screen. "There's no way to describe this. There's more footage of the compound, but it's mostly views of walking through corridors. The unedited twenty-four hours is available for anyone who wants to see it."

Bobbie didn't care to watch. She knew this tape ended with the last hours of this woman's life – up to the point when Bobbie had killed her. She was grateful Joy hadn't shown that.

"There's one more thing you need to see," Joy said. Her dark eyes gave nothing away.

Bobbie reached for her father's hand and held on.

The screen blinked to the first-person view inside a massive warehouse, looking down a row of cages. At first, Bobbie thought it was a server room. A deep hum filled the air. Each cage had columns of wide, flat shelves, stacked six high. As the light adjusted on-camera, she realized with horror that the shelves were makeshift bunk beds, and people were lying on them. The hum, Bobbie now could discern, was the collective murmuring, moaning, and groaning of hundreds of people, so drugged they could barely move. Bobbie thought of her years of tending to the elderly, and she couldn't bear to think that their lives were now reduced to this.

"Je-sus Chr-ist," Luke said on a long exhale beside her.

The blink icon appeared in the top corner of the screen. The guard opened the message.

All hands northern region to crafts now. PARC escape in progress. Intercept and return to PARC.

Bobbie felt the chill of sweat on the back of her neck. She'd been that escapee. Would there be further blink messages to tell them anything about Hicks?

The view tilted and swung, shuddering as the guard jogged. Blurred pictures and fuzzy black and grey screens made watching painful for Bobbie, but the picture smoothed out. The first-person view was in a hovercraft lifting off.

Bobbie swallowed.

The screen tilted, an optical illusion, as the first-person viewer swung the hovercraft around in a tight circle and looked out over the compound. It stretched for a couple of miles: more yards with hundreds of people wandering listlessly, interspersed with warehouses that likely housed more makeshift bunk beds.

Bobbie's heart plummeted. How many people were Belus keeping there? And why?

The first-person viewer looked away, and the screen filled with blue as the guard flew away – to her death.

Joy cut the feed, and the room plunged into gloom for a few seconds before the intepanels flickered to transparent, letting the afternoon sun spill through. None of them seemed able to speak at first. Joy moved first, touching symbols on a control panel, her chin quivering. Luke stared at the floor.

Bobbie caught Slade mouthing "You okay?" to Mo.

He nodded. "But I've to get back to work. They're expecting me to fly out on a scouting mission."

"I'll see you later, then." Slade watched her son leave.

"I suppose each time he leaves; you wonder if he'll come back?" Bobbie said, flinching at her own insensitivity, but wanting Slade to see her parallel thinking.

The very idea that Hicks might never come back curdled Bobbie's stomach and she needed Slade to feel that too.

Slade pursed her lips and held Bobbie's gaze for a second before breaking eye contact. "Good work on getting that ONIV footage, Joy," she said.

Joy shrugged.

They'd witnessed so much yet had not a single clue that would lead them to Hicks. Bobbie wanted so badly to know that he was still alive. Rolling her hands into fists, she focused on the bite of her nails into her palms.

"Well, there's nothing there we can't share with the Norway team," Bobbie said. The urge to do something filled the void left by Hicks. *I'm ready*, she thought, *I am ready*. "Where are they? I thought they'd be here by now."

"They'll be here when they get here," Slade said. "We're their guests."

"They're lucky to have us," Joy said. "It's not like this is actually a cruise." She looked at the filthy, cracked windowpanes. "The service leaves a lot to be desired."

Bobbie felt an encouraging glow, loving her sister for her refusal to be cowed and her black humor. As if reading her thoughts, Joy threw her a wink, like Gracie might have done when they'd been kids.

The door of the nightclub swung open. All heads turned. Slade jumped up to meet the man entering. Her height, slim build, and straight black hair were in stark contrast to the rotund little man sporting a fuzz of white hair and a bushy beard.

"And you told me Santa wasn't real," Joy said in a stage whisper to Bobbie.

"Shush," Luke said. "He's the boss around here. Think of him as Nordic Slade."

"My dear Ori, you and your team are welcome," the man said to Slade, shaking her hand.

"Thank you, Niclas, we appreciate it. Let me introduce you."

Luke stood and faced the man, his hand outstretched. "Luke Chan. Pleased to meet you."

"Niclas Koslov." He shook Luke's hand, eyes waning to slits as he smiled. "And you" — Niclas turned to her — "must be Bobbie."

Bobbie grasped his hand. Niclas squeezed her fingers together, then put his other hand over the top and drew her closer. "I've heard so much about you. You're the image of your father, but that red hair, very unusual in Asians."

"The red hair gene *is* rare in Asians, but it does lurk. And then, of course, my mother—" Bobbie's voice caught, but she pushed on. "My mother was Irish."

"I'm sorry for your loss."

Bobbie nodded. "Thank you." She cleared her throat. Had it only been a couple of months since her mother had died? It seemed like a lifetime ago. She pointed to Joy. "This is my sister—"

"Ah yes, Joy. We've met before, in Foureyes."

"I won't tell if you don't," Joy said, before turning to Luke and Bobbie. "I was testing his blink security protocol."

"Thankfully, I knew to expect you. You did a great job. Good to have you on the team."

Joy dropped her smile and turned back to her work. A draught whistled through a crack in the window.

"Niclas and the leadership team have just returned from a week-long mission," Slade said. "We can bring them up to speed when... Ah, here comes April."

April seemed to float through the door, wrapped in acres of cream material that flowed over her ample bosom and hips. Her chestnut skin glowed with vigor; her face framed by long thin braids bound with beads that clacked as she moved. She lifted her arms from the folds of her robe and put her hands on Slade's thin shoulders. "How are you settling in?"

"Well, thank you." Slade did another round of introductions and said, "We've got some footage from an old ONIV we took from a Belus guard to show you."

Bobbie had the uncomfortable sense that April's stare lingered on her a moment too long. Bobbie ran her tongue over her teeth in case she'd left some lunch there. When April broke eye contact and nodded at Niclas before settling down to watch the footage, Bobbie felt as if she had fumbled a catch, and now something important had tumbled from her grasp.

As Joy replayed the ONIV footage, Bobbie watched for anything she'd missed the first time around. There were fewer guards than she expected, and the ones with orange eyes were relatively well disciplined. With huge numbers of people affected, variation was bound to produce some Rejuvenees that were more stable than others.

Or perhaps it was only a matter of time before the Rejuvenees acting as guards became too mentally unstable to work. Jimmy had seemed well for the first few weeks, but in the end, he'd succumbed to psychosis. Jimmy hadn't asked to be rejuvenated; none of these people had. The psychosis, a terrible side effect, wasn't their fault either. They weren't responsible for any of their actions while they were under the influence of the nanobots. They weren't evil, just ill. She had to help these people, but how? The truth was, she was new to nanotechnology. She had so much catching up to do, and if she were lucky, she could figure how to make anti-nanobots that would dismantle the nanobots gently, without killing the host, but she couldn't rely on luck.

"We had no idea it was this bad," Niclas said when the footage ended. "Our undercover people living in Belus land reported that some of the ultra-elderly facilities had closed. They thought it was because finally the dependency laws were having some effect, that the population standard deviation curves had finally shifted toward a younger mean age."

"Wishful thinking," April added. "Bobbie, what else can you tell us? You're the authority on Rejuvenation – at least, while what's-his-name's in a coma."

"We were the first geriatricians to discover it in our patients and follow it up to discover that nanobots caused it. So if that makes us the leading authorities, then I guess we are, but our knowledge is limited to what Davitt was able to share with us before his attack." Bobbie hated how simple that sounded, how it glossed over how much she'd lost. She added, "My partner, Hicks, and I have been working to stop the virus that was used as a vector to spread the nanobots. But Hicks was taken captive by Belus Corp–"

"Yes, we know that." April interrupted with a wave of her hand.

Bobbie clenched her teeth. "Why don't you tell us what you know, then."

"I'm sorry my second-in-command is so impatient." Niclas glared at April from under bushy white eyebrows. "We know that Doctor Davitt Hanson is in a coma, and therefore of no use for the present."

"But what can we do to stop this?" asked April.

"Good question," Luke muttered.

Bobbie stood up, adjusting her chair behind her as she gathered her thoughts. "We need your labs to finish producing a vaccine so the virus can no longer spread the nanobots." She stopped. "Judging by the footage, a lot of people have already been exposed. So we need to develop the anti-nanobots."

"How long will that take?" April said.

Bobbie shrugged. "Weeks, months, years – I don't know."

"We can't wait that long," Slade said.

"We might have to. I need to start from scratch. However, it would go much faster if I had Hicks helping me."

"That's the other doctor?" Niclas asked. "The one that Belus has in the PARC?"

Bobbie nodded. Her throat tightened.

"What doesn't come across in the footage is how crazed a Rejuvenee can be," Slade said. "That one prisoner you saw, the one tased–"

"Poor bastard," Niclas mumbled.

"That's nothing," Slade said. "These rejuvenated people are violent, strong, and have absolutely no moral code. They're sociopaths. Belus controls the ones you saw by making them dependent on narcotics."

"Addiction?" Niclas said, his eyes round. "But we've a cure for addiction. Christ Almighty, she's using it on purpose."

"If we can fix the side effects of Rejuvenation, we can administer the anti-addiction therapy protocol to these people," Bobbie said. "I'm hoping that's why they've kept them alive."

"Fox is building an army. That's what's happening," Luke said.

"To fight who?" Niclas asked. "Us? I hardly think so. We're too small beside Belus Corp as it stands. No. I think it's something else."

"Slaves," Joy said. "For the Melters. She's in cahoots with them."

"Defeating the Melters was the only good thing Fox did," Niclas said. "I don't think she'd go into business with them, even if they'd stuck around after she'd flattened them."

"So where did they go?" Joy looked to her father, but Luke stared at his hands.

Bobbie cringed. She'd heard Joy's wild theories before but wheeling them out in front of Slade and April left Bobbie feeling embarrassed for her sister.

Joy looked away.

A few awkward seconds stretched out before April changed the subject. "The taser did that to the prisoner?" She shook her head, beads clicking around her shoulders as she swiveled to point at where the footage had played. "How?"

"The nanobots are like scaffolding around the DNA, correcting faults that have occurred over time. They base the repairs on templates from donor DNA," Bobbie said.

Niclas nodded. "That's why they all look alike."

"Exactly. But the nanobot circuitry is sensitive to electrical charges," Bobbie explained. "When the current surges, the nanobots are destroyed. Without support, the DNA disintegrates, and the cells fall apart."

"We could fight back with an EMP," April said, sitting forward.

"An electromagnetic pulse?"

April nodded.

"We can't kill all those people." Bobbie flung her arm toward the intepanel. "Rejuvenees are still people. We need to help them recover. Never mind that an uncontrolled EMP blast will wipe out anything with electronics in it and send us all back to the Stone Age."

Luke stood beside Bobbie. "Bobbie's right. The only way to beat Rejuvenation is to expose Lisette Fox. Discredit Belus Corp. Force them to stand down."

Bobbie held up both hands and said, "Wait!" Her heart pounded. This might never work, but she had to try. "If you want this solved, I need Hicks' help. You've got to help me find him."

"What? Don't be ridiculous," Luke said. "You're the only one we have left who can fight Rejuvenation now."

"Dad, are you protecting me or protecting the cause?"

"What happens if you die?" April asked, almost casually. "The whole world becomes psychopathic? Tears itself to pieces? Just because you miss your boyfriend?"

Bobbie squared her shoulders and faced April. "If you're not sending me because I'm the expert, consider this – Hicks is the only *other* expert in Rejuvenation. Without his help, it will take even longer to develop anti-nanobots. We have to find him, and not just because I fucking miss him." She slammed her fist down on the table. A crack, already in the glass top, grew into a web and spread outwards, held together for a second, then the whole tabletop crashed to the floor in a cascade of glittering cubes.

Joy stared at the pile of broken glass. "Wow."

"Look," Bobbie said more evenly, "Everything I know about Rejuvenation, I have already told Slade and the medical board. Any doctor who is a quick study will be able to do as good a job as I can do in the same time span. I'm not a nanobiologist – Davitt is."

"Your value isn't just your medical skills, Bobbie." April leaned forward. "Your identity is known to Belus, but more importantly, to the medical board. You stood up to Belus and showed those doctors the truth behind Rejuvenation."

"And I showed them what happens to someone who sticks it to Fox – I landed straight in the PARC! Not very inspiring."

"But Slade got you out. That's the thing. And we want to use you to raise awareness of the threat from Rejuvenation, show the world Belus is flawed and recruit new members–"

"No, that's not what I do. I'm a geriatrician!"

April held up her hand. "You'll do it. We'll make clips of your messages about Rejuvenation and send them to people's blinks–"

"Belus will close that down straight away."

"I think I can work something around that," Joy said from where she worked packing up the portable intepanel. "I'm working on one of the detention centers. Bobbie just needs to do the voice-over."

"Anyone could do that!"

"No, Bobbie," Luke said. "It has to be you."

"Bullshit! One person is never the be-all and end-all of any organization, nor should they be. You can do without me, but Hicks can't. Dad, it's worth me risking my life to get him, and I'm the best one to do it, since I know the PARC system. I know the layout, the protocols, the people. When we find Hicks, he'll need my help, or the drug withdrawal might kill him."

Bobbie looked at the people sitting around the shattered table. Niclas met her gaze and held it, his blue eyes calm, giving Bobbie no clue as to what he was thinking. April shook her head slowly. Luke scowled and looked away. Slade stared at the broken glass on the floor – Bobbie expected no help from that quarter. But she caught in Joy's eye a flicker of shared rebellion – would her sister back her up?

"Just think – if you want to play me up as a hero..." Bobbie rolled her eyes and took a breath. "...You could film me rescuing Hicks. We could expose what's going on in the PARC."

April pursed her lips, looked at Niclas, and raised an eyebrow. But Niclas' face remained expressionless.

"If you don't at least help me to find Hicks, I won't help you at all." It was blackmail, and Bobbie knew it. But if they called her bluff and didn't help her, could she morally refuse to fight Rejuvenation?

CHAPTER 2

To Bobbie's astonishment, Slade said, "Bobbie has a point."

But then again, Bobbie thought, the last time Slade agreed with her, Bobbie had ended up in the PARC. She knew that Slade's support might be a thorny stick to walk with.

April shook her head. "You're going soft, Ori."

"I'm not saying yes yet."

"There's nothing soft about discussing our options," Bobbie said in a rush. "We've barely had a chance to draw breath since we left Belus Corp. All we've done is react to whatever's been thrown at us. Let's sit down, talk this through, and take the time to make a plan."

"That sounds fair," Niclas said. "But let's move to a different table."

As they moved to the next intact table, Bobbie considered apologizing for smashing the last one, then decided, fuck it. She wasn't sorry. Her finger dug at a scab on her arm, the result of a self-inflicted wound from scratching too much. A red bead rose on her skin, and she pressed down with her thumb.

"Soft," Slade muttered, sitting down next to April. "I'll give you soft, bitch."

"Yeah, yeah, so you keep telling me. I used to think the softest thing about you was your teeth." April suppressed a smile. "Prove me right."

"Now, now, ladies," Niclas said. "Enough sweet talk. We've business to do."

Joy left what she was doing and joined them, settling in beside her father.

"Our problem is that Hicks may have been transferred to any PARC facility around the world," Bobbie began. "If he's in the PARC system." *If he's even alive*, she thought but didn't dare say.

"Right, but we need to start with some assumptions," Niclas said. "So let's assume, for now, that he's in the PARC."

"Can't we Foureyes hack his ONIV and see where he is, like we did with Granny?" Joy asked.

"Everything is blink-blocked inside the PARC, and even if we could Foureyes hack him, all the PARCS are identical on the inside. I wouldn't be able to tell which one it is." Bobbie pressed two fingers to her temple.

"How many PARC facilities are there in operation now?" April asked.

"Two months ago, there were eleven," Bobbie said. "Two in Europe, two in Asia, two in the Arctic sector countries, two in Antarctica, one in Chile, one in South Africa, and one in New Zealand." She didn't want to consider that they might have been amalgamated with the awful detention centers for the Rejuvenees.

"Do we have any operatives still active in the PARC?" Luke asked.

Slade looked weary. "We had Janet, but..."

Bobbie thought of the nurse who'd helped her escape from the PARC and couldn't block her mind's eye flashing up the image of Janet lying, throat cut, eyes staring. Fatigue crashed down on Bobbie so quickly she had to lean her elbows on the table and cradle her forehead. She felt her father's hand on her shoulder. Its warmth spread to her taut muscles.

"We had an operative in the PARC system for years," April said. "A doctor, but he's gone dark. The last message we had from him was a couple of months ago. He said Belus had assigned him to a classified project. We haven't heard from him since." She and Niclas exchanged a look.

They think he's dead, Bobbie thought. Would they give up on Hicks too? Terror slashed through her. She needed to give them something to work with, a place to start so they wouldn't give up on him.

Bobbie sat up. "I know how to start looking for Hicks."

"Okay, so how?" Niclas asked.

"At the end of each shift, every member of the medical staff has to transmit their notes on a patient to the central database. For approximately twenty minutes every eight hours, there's an open window. The staff blinks will be on. There's an opportunity for two points of access. Foureyes-hack the staff, which may not yield much since patients are referenced only by their biosensor UUID, but we could grab a copy of the file that's being transmitted."

"UU what?" Luke asked.

Joy interrupted. "It's just a long-ass serial number. I can cross-reference with Bio Sense to pull the names. Go on, Bobbie. You want to intercept the patients' files?"

"Yes, but the file is encrypted for the transmission." The look on Slade's face made Bobbie stop. "What?"

"Breaking the encryption could take centuries using our computers," Slade said. "There's about a hundred staff in each PARC, and who knows how many patients. That's thousands of files to decrypt."

"Joy, what do you think?" Bobbie turned to her sister. "Could you hack the files?"

"Slade has a point. I'd have to use brute force decryption and try each combination one by one. On our computers..." Joy narrowed her eyes.

Bobbie knew that look – Joy's brain was working faster than her mouth could keep up with.

After a moment, Joy wagged a finger in the air. "A quantum computer could break the encryption in minutes rather than centuries."

"How do we access that?" Slade said.

"We need a physical presence, but no-one's ever been able to break into the HQ to get near the quantum computer. Not even Ori, when she was undercover. But I've been working on something... Bobbie." Joy turned to her. "Do we just need a decryption key? Or would each file need a separate treatment?"

"If we're lucky and there's just one key, we can use the same key to decrypt all the files. But if they use a different key for every file–" Bobbie began.

"–we'd have to hack each file from scratch," Joy said.

"So which is it?" April asked.

Bobbie's excitement drained as suddenly as it had surged. "We won't know until we try."

"Where is this quantum computer?" Luke asked.

Wind vibrated a loose windowpane. Joy chewed her bottom lip, then said, "Belus have one in their Swiss HQ."

"Christ," Luke hissed. "Can you hook in remotely?"

"No," Joy said. "It's off-grid. We'd have to go in person."

"You want to break into Belus headquarters!" said Niclas incredulously. "I can't let you–"

"Dad," Bobbie said, "it's not up to you."

"Your father has a point," Slade said. "But what's the point in arguing about who's going where until we have the files? How many do we need? What is the timeframe, Bobbie?"

"Shifts change every eight hours. Usually, every patient will have had contact with a medic at least once a day, so let's gather the files from four consecutive shifts." Bobbie's skin itched, and a flash of heat made sweat break on her top lip.

"Joy, how long do you think it would take you to set up the intercept?" Slade asked.

"A day or two. Sooner if a little project I'm working on pans out."

Three days, minimum, to get the files, and they still had to hack the encryption and plan the rescue after that. God only knew what Hicks would suffer during that time.

"There are eleven different sites," Bobbie said. "So we can prepare in parallel – build a rescue plan for each site while we figure out the files."

Slade beamed. "Your girl is learning fast, Luke. You should be proud."

"Oh, believe me," Luke said, his eyes glinting. "I am."

Bobbie swallowed hard and looked past him at their reflections in the windowpanes as they sat hunched forward, faces as brittle as the glass they appeared in.

#

Light seeped in a yellow line under the door from the hallway, but otherwise, the cabin was dark. Tomorrow they'd have the last of the files. Bobbie hoped that in twenty-four hours she'd be on her way to the quantum computer. She'd worked all day setting up the lab and training medical students on the finer details of producing a vaccine. Now, bone tired yet unable to rest properly, Bobbie twitched and turned in the small bed. She could do nothing for now except battle through the last dregs of her detox and wait.

"Would you quit wriggling." Joy's voice came through the darkness. "You're keeping me awake. For God's sake, if you can't sleep, get up and go somewhere else to scratch."

Every muscle and tendon in Bobbie's shoulders tightened. An ache bloomed at the base of her skull. She turned again, carefully this time, but the bed squeaked beneath her.

"Shush," Joy hissed.

"I'm sorry," Bobbie whispered.

"Don't be sorry. Be quiet!"

Bobbie lay ramrod still, annoyance at her sister's lack of empathy rattling in her skull and inviting dark thoughts. Sure, Joy was grieving too – the loss of a child, her fertility, her ONIV, her lover – but hadn't Joy brought her woes upon herself with her wild behavior? Bobbie asked herself.

I didn't ask for any of this.

Hicks had been taken from Bobbie when all they'd been trying to do was stop evil being done unto innocent people. The injustice of it rampaged like a firestorm in Bobbie's chest.

Bobbie held her breath and listened. Joy's breathing had deepened, and Bobbie decided it was safe to move again. She turned on her side. The bed groaned.

"For fuck's sake, Bobbie!" Joy snarled from her bunk.

Bobbie's patience snapped so hard she thought she could feel the recoil against the insides of her skull. "You know something, Joy? I'm sick of your shit." She sat up and faced Joy's bed. "You're not the only one going through a tough time."

"Oh, boo hoo, poor Bobbie. It's alright for you. After you've detoxed, you'll be back to what passes for normal for you."

Joy's sheets rustled and her bed creaked.

"What the fuck's that supposed to mean?" Bobbie felt flung back into teenager mode. Christ almighty, would they be doing this when they were ultra-elderly? The way things were going, they'd never grow old – they'd be rejuvenated and crazy, if Belus didn't kill them or if they didn't kill each other first.

The light blazed on. Joy sat on the twin bed facing Bobbie. Their knees almost touched. They glared at each other, nostrils flared, breathing heavily.

Joy looked away first. "I need sleep." She opened the drawer in the bedside table between the beds, pulled out a box of medipatches and held them in the air, as if she were raising a toast. "What do you say?"

"Go ahead," Bobbie said, "but only one." She didn't add that they wouldn't help Joy escape her nightmares. She'd heard her sister's mumbles turn to screams every night since they'd landed. Joy might say she had no regrets about killing Jimmy, but Bobbie knew otherwise. Jimmy had infected her with nanobots, which had lost her both her uterus and her ONIV, but Joy had loved him.

"Want one?"

"No." Taking something to help her sleep would only set back Bobbie's withdrawal. It was a case of pushing through to the bitter end. She'd survive, but that was little comfort to her when all she could think about was what Hicks was going through now. "I'll ask about getting us separate rooms."

"No," Joy said. "How much longer will your detox take? I'm sure we'll be fine when you're better." Joy examined her hands in her lap. She was thin: all shoulders, elbows, and knees. Lilac smudges embossed the skin beneath her eyes.

"We will, li'l sis." Bobbie reached across and patted Joy's knee. Joy caught Bobbie's hand and squeezed it. They sat for a moment looking at their joined hands until the urge seized Bobbie again to stretch her legs, wiggle her toes, and just move those agitated limbs.

Bobbie slipped off the bed, stood up, and pulled a tunic over her nightclothes.

"I'm sorry, Bobbie," Joy said. "I'm exhausted with the file retrieval set up."

"I know. Thank you."

"And I miss him too," Joy said softly.

Bobbie stood with her back to Joy. She didn't trust herself to speak.

Outside the cabin, the dim hallway stretched in both directions in a repeated pattern of doors and carpet. It was enough to spark hallucinations without the PARC drugs, Bobbie thought. Most of the corridors looked the same to her. She still hadn't fully gotten her bearings, other than knowing that when she reached the ripped carpet on the landing, she was on her floor – Deck 5.

Bobbie rounded the corner into the stairwell and nearly bumped into Slade.

"Found you." Slade's hand went to her injured arm.

Bobbie sprang back. "Is your arm bothering you?"

Slade shook her head. "Davitt woke up."

"When?"

"A couple of hours ago."

"You should have told me straight away." Bobbie started walking up the stairs. "How is he?"

"He's got post-traumatic amnesia."

"How far back?"

"He thinks he's still working on Rejuvenation for Fox." Slade huffed out a brittle laugh. "And that you're still a couple. So that makes it what? Two, three months' regression?"

"Shit!" Bobbie felt queasy. "Well, I'm happy to put him straight on both counts."

"Although–" Slade stopped at the top of the next flight of stairs and scrunched up her face.

"No way," Bobbie said as the penny dropped. "I'm not pretending to still be his–"

"We need to make him believe he's still in Fox's good books. I always felt he was holding out on us. You kidnapped him, after all. He wasn't exactly going to be a team player."

"I can't do it. He'll see right through me."

"I wonder when he started sleeping with your grandmother."

Bobbie threw Slade a dirty look.

"Sorry."

Bobbie curtailed an impulse to shove Slade down the stairs.

"Still," Slade added. "I'm pretty sure it wasn't until Gloria rejuvenated, so –"

"Jesus, give over, would you?" Bobbie snapped. "I know what you're doing."

"But wouldn't you like to play the weasel? Find out what he really knows?"

Bobbie clenched her fists. "This is why you didn't come to get me straight away."

"It's complicated. When the doctor on duty determined Davitt's cognitive function, we–"

"We?"

"Your father and I. We wanted to talk with you. Plan our approach with you first."

"It sounds like you've already made up your mind. Where's Dad?"

"He's on guard outside Davitt's room. We just want to press the advantage – if there is one."

"His memory, or parts of it, could come back at any time, you know." Bobbie sought out doctor mode, the black and white of medical fact, but even that was nuanced, especially in the case of a brain injury.

"We need you on board," Slade said.

"On board?" Bobbie stopped at the door to the medical wing. "I was prepared to kill myself back at the PARC rather than give away any information that Belus could use against us."

"So let's get our stories straight now."

"Until he remembers."

"If he ever remembers," Slade said with a look that sent a shiver snaking through Bobbie.

Was this a tactic to keep her at the base? If she were play-acting girlfriend to Davitt, it would delay her departure for the quantum computer, and every hour she delayed would put Hicks through another hour of torture. But with Davitt awake, they'd have a nanobot expert and no need for her, especially if he was well enough and willing enough to help.

"Who's his doctor?" Bobbie had only met the nursing staff on the brief visit she'd made to the medical center the day they'd arrived.

"Niclas," Slade said.

"Niclas? He's a doctor?"

"He's a neurologist."

"Handy," Bobbie said, taking note of Slade's gaze hugging the ground. Bobbie didn't know exactly how to read the woman, but she was beginning to recognize the signs of trouble.

Deck 4 was the medical wing. It felt like a teaching hospital, with groups of young people standing around three more senior medics. Their proximity to population centers allowed more equipment and blink access.

Slade led Bobbie through the main medical wing of the deck, through a portal and along a dimly lit narrow corridor. Luke sat on a metal chair, arms folded, head back, eyes gazing unfocused on the ceiling, reading blinks.

Slade cleared her throat, and Luke zeroed in on them. "Bobbie, darling, how are you feeling?"

She hugged him without answering. What was the point?

Bobbie nodded and flicked her eyes at the door to Davitt's room, then back at her dad, raising her eyebrows in a question. Her father led them several paces from the door, then said in a low voice, "The doors are pretty thick, but let's move up the corridor just in case. I can keep watch from there."

Bobbie and Slade followed him down the corridor.

"Niclas is with Davitt now," Luke said. "He's asking questions, but he's severely confused. Before you go in, Bobbie, we need to ask a favor."

"I'll do it," Bobbie cut in. For now.

"I know it's tough for you, especially with—"

"The very idea disgusts me. It'll be a struggle to keep that from him."

Slade held Bobbie's gaze. "You can do this."

Something that had been wound deep in Bobbie loosened a notch. Could Slade actually be human?

"I'll play along as Davitt's girlfriend," Bobbie said, "but he's going to know time has elapsed, so we need a story. Some way to keep him thinking about manufacturing the anti-nanobots, but I think I know how."

CHAPTER 3

I n the two weeks since Davitt's surgery, his shaved head had grown a stubby carpet of black hair covering all but the jagged red scar at the crown of his head. A memory flared in Bobbie's mind of her gloved fingers punching a needle through blue-white skin under violet sterilighting, Hicks by her side as they worked together to save Davitt's life. She pushed the image away.

Davitt's pale face lit up when he saw Bobbie, his smile triggering a spiral of confused emotions. There was a time when she had welcomed that smile. Now she craved Hicks' smile, and his absence burned with unbearable ferocity.

"Hi," she said with fragile levity, moving to Davitt's bedside. His fingers stretched toward her. Taking his hand felt clumsy and awkward.

"What happened?" he croaked and licked his lips.

Bobbie lifted a beaker of water and held the straw to his lips. "Shh, focus on getting better."

"Please, Bobbie. No-one will tell me anything."

"What do you remember?"

"Nothing."

Here goes, she thought, and took a deep breath. "There was an incident with one of your s-subjects." She hated to blame an innocent, and technically Jimmy hadn't been a subject. He'd caught the virus when she'd dropped the vials.

Davitt's eyes widened. "You know about my subjects?"

"I do now. It's okay. Slade filled me in on everything," Bobbie said. He'd fallen for this before, so why not try it again? "The rejuvenated subjects got out of hand and tried to escape the research center. One hit you over the head."

"What? Even with them being dosed with..." Davitt missed a beat. His eyes scanned the room. "Why can't I get into my blink?"

"We had to turn off your ONIV – you've suffered a serious brain injury. It's a precaution."

"Where am I?"

"We're in a medical facility near the research center. Do you remember the research center?"

"In Ireland?"

Bobbie almost nodded but held back as Davitt frowned and bit his lip.

"...Or Switzerland?"

There was another one in Switzerland? Where?

"Switzerland," she said, a little derailed. If he was double bluffing, they were sunk, but she didn't think he'd be able to pull it off. And why would he pretend? "Can you remember the address? We need to test your cognitive function."

"It's ... it's near Belus headquarters, but the exact address..." He winced as if it hurt to think.

Bobbie patted his hand. "It's okay. It will come back."

"But we aren't there now, are we?" Davitt tried to sit up, paled and flopped back down, scanning the corners of the room with wild eyes. "This doesn't look right."

He's frightened, thought Bobbie. "You're safe here."

"Switch on my ONIV, Bobbie." His eyes narrowed as if something was materializing just outside his reach.

Bobbie stood up. "I'll ask the neurologist."

"No, don't go." He gripped her hand. "Not yet. Just read me the news from your feed. Just the headlines. What have I missed?"

Bobbie sat, weakened by a flush of relief. Davitt had always been a news addict. He hated not knowing what was going on in the world. She scanned through her blink, looking for a news item that might work, but not wanting it to seem like she was picking or choosing.

"Well, there was a strange sighting of an extra-terrestrial drone that had sparked panic in the general public yesterday."

"Melters?"

Bobbie shrugged. The report had alarmed her too, but Belus had dealt with it, and their increased patrols searching for more drones had conveniently coincided with more pressure on the Under-Rad camps to conceal themselves. A month ago Bobbie would have believed this report, but now?

"Belus have successfully dealt with the threat and have intercepted any off-planet telecommunications," Bobbie said.

"I miss my blink. Maybe you should ask the doctor?"

"I don't know. You're so important to the project, Davitt. We've fallen behind already. We don't want to jeopardize your recovery."

"I can't quite..." Davitt scrunched his eyes shut and rubbed the skin between his eyebrows, his exhalation a prolonged hiss. He lifted his hand to the wound on his head and touched his fingers to the scar, pulling them away as if the skin burned him. "A subject did this?"

"Yes."

"What did Lisette say?"

Lisette Fox? Bobbie cast her mind back. Davitt had always claimed he didn't know who was behind the project when they were back at Yosemite. He'd said he didn't know the source of the DNA samples, that he had added his own to work on the project. He'd already been in the coma when Bobbie and Slade had run the facial recognition software that led them to Lisette Fox. The bastard had been withholding information.

"Lisette is interviewing the Rejuvenees. She's talking to Granny at the moment." Bobbie let that settle.

Davitt said nothing. Could he remember that he'd slept with her grandmother? His face didn't flicker. Bobbie reminded herself that he was good at lying.

"We had a meeting with Lisette yesterday," she said. "She brought me in on the project as soon as you were injured–"

"How long?"

Bobbie hesitated.

"How long have I been unconscious?"

"A few days." Vague was better. "Now that the Rejuvenees are getting out of hand, she's having second thoughts. She wants to develop anti-nanobots."

Davitt's face relaxed, and he smiled. "Oh, I'm way ahead of her. I have it already."

Bobbie paused in disbelief before gushing, "Oh my God. That's brilliant. Davitt, you're a genius."

Slick bastard hadn't shared that in Yosemite either.

Davitt puffed up. "Jesus, Bobbie, it's the first thing I did when I saw the psychological effects the nanobots had. Especially when she made me work on the virus to deliver them faster." His hand found hers. His thumb moved in circles over her knuckles. "I'm so glad you're here. I recommended you for this project so many times. I knew you'd be interested, you know, because of Gracie. Just think how this might have helped her."

Bobbie swallowed back the bile that rose in her throat. He didn't know her at all if he thought she'd have condoned his approach to this project. It was all she could do to maintain eye contact and smile – a small price, she told herself, for a ticket to help Hicks. "So the anti-nanobots? Where are they?"

"The prototypes are here, in the lab."

"Here. In Switzerland?"

"Yes. How handy is that? Good job they brought us here." Davitt's eyelids closed slowly. "I need my ONIV." He opened his eyes, and his gaze bore into Bobbie.

She nodded. "Sure, as soon as we can." She offered him another sip of water. "Can they dismantle the nanobots slowly to allow the Rejuvenees to survive the effects of nanobot withdrawal?"

Davitt pursed his lips. "No, not if the nanobots have been working on the subject long enough to make a difference."

Subject...

Davitt seemed to pick something up in her expression even as she fought down her rage. "Jinko's been working on a gentler version, but it's not finished yet," he said. "If I had my ONIV–"

This changed everything, Bobbie thought, saying, "Jinko? The guy who used to steal your matter streamer credits in the lunchroom?"

"Yeah, bastard!"

Bobbie didn't think Jinko was the bastard here. "I thought you guys hated each other. Weren't you rivals?"

"Yeah, he's a dick, but Fox put us both on this project. I got the nanobots working first, though." Davitt smiled and squeezed her hand. "I guess that's why he went off at a tangent and started working on taking them apart – always was an obtuse fucker."

"So has he managed to do it yet?"

"Do what?" Davitt's brow furrowed.

"Make gentle anti-nanobots?"

"Huh – gentibots, he calls them. Hard to say." A yawn buckled his face, and he raised his free hand to cover his mouth. "Sorry. Why don't you just ask him?"

"I will." Bobbie took her hand back from him. So maybe Jinko didn't have the gentibots, but at least he was working in that direction. She had to get to Jinko before April set off the EMP. "You need to rest."

"Kiss?"

Bobbie's stomach flipped over, but she bent and gave him a peck on the forehead. As she stood up, he grabbed her hand again.

"Stay with me," he whispered.

"I should go ask about your ONIV."

He hesitated, then gripped her hand. "No, don't leave me yet."

His little-boy-lost routine that had suckered Bobbie so well in the past tugged at her, stirring a bed of emotions she thought she'd long buried. The unfairness of comforting this toe-rag while Hicks suffered God only knew what made her grind her teeth together. Or worse, Hicks might be... She couldn't let her mind go that route.

She took in Davitt's droopy eyelids and pale face. The last twenty minutes had taken their toll on him. She sat beside him and prayed he'd fall asleep quickly so she could escape him, update Slade, and plan her trip to Switzerland.

Bobbie backed out of Davitt's room and closed the door as quietly as she could. She looked up the corridor. Mo had replaced her father on guard duty.

"You were brilliant! You were so convincing." Joy's voice behind her made Bobbie jump.

"Don't do that to me!" Bobbie placed a hand over her heart. "Wait. How do you know? Are there cameras in the room?"

"There are..."

Of course there were. Slade and her father were probably upstairs watching and had seen it all already.

"But..." Joy danced on her tiptoes. "I was using Foureyes."

"Whoa there, li'l sis, back up. You didn't..."

Joy nodded with a triumphant grin.

"You got that ONIV from the severed head to work?" Bobbie suppressed a shudder as she remembered Joy chopping off the disfigured head.

"I sure did!" Joy turned her left-hand palm up. Attached to the pad of her little finger was a black box the size of her fingertip. A blue light blipped. Dried blood crusted the edge of the box where it sat against the skin.

"How?" Bobbie took off walking at a brisk clip toward the stairwell.

Joy walked with her. "I already had augmented ONIV connectors in my fingertips for added peripheral articulation. I was able to take the ONIV that we extracted from... from Mont St Michel and merge it with some of the circuitry. Offline, over time, I can use that as a conduit to repair my broken ONIV."

"And you've just stuck it into circuitry that's integrated with your neural pathways to your brain?" Bobbie rubbed her hand down her face. Joy never seemed happy unless she was dicing with death or playing with technology – combine the two, and she was truly in her element.

"It's fine. Really, it is." Joy wiggled her finger at Bobbie. "Pinkie swear."

"Why didn't you get a new insertion instead of using the one from the guard?"

"I'd rather fix my own, have my own backup, and run it as close to what it was beforehand as I can. A brand new ONIV isn't as good. Basically, Bobbie, they don't make them like they used to."

Bobbie smiled at the words her grandmother had often used. "Know what?" Bobbie turned to her. "I think I preferred the 'need to know' protocol. Aren't you supposed to be intercepting the last of the files from the PARC today?"

"All set up and running," Joy said. "We'll have them all downloaded by midnight."

Excellent, thought Bobbie. If they left at midnight, Davitt wouldn't notice her missing. She could tell him she'd had to sleep in her own cabin – hospital rules, or something like that.

"I need to practice Foureyes hacking to test out this ONIV," Joy said.

"But you hacked mine already."

"Yeah, you were too easy. I need a challenge."

"Hey!"

"Ah, come on, big sis, you know what I mean."

Bobbie, warmed by her sister's bright eyes and flushed cheeks, rolled her eyes but smiled. "I need to find Slade. Why don't you hack her Foureyes and tell me where she is?"

"Oh, that's a brilliant idea. I'll be able to check out the holes in Slade's security, and if I can hack Slade, I can hack anyone. She has the best AVD I've ever seen."

"AVD?"

"Attack Vector Detection. It's pretty damn amazing!" Joy shook her head as though she could hardly believe it herself.

"Really? Who did her security?"

They reached the stairwell and Joy headed up the stairs, taking them two at a time. "Me."

"God, you're modest," Bobbie said, slightly out of breath as she trotted behind Joy.

"And really good. That's why Belus had to send in Jacob."

"Well, then, what are you waiting on?"

"It's better if I'm outside."

They reached Deck 7. Heavy double doors led out to a lower deck known as the promenade. Humidity hugged her skin, and Bobbie squinted against the glare of the low-hanging sun. The latitude here made it feel like late evening, even though it was only halfway through the day. The subtle drop in temperature reminded Bobbie of walking with her mother on autumn evenings in Ireland before the Melters.

"Want patched in?"

"No, just get on with it." Bobbie was more worried about the interface between the antique device and Joy's optic nerve causing damage than being caught spying on Slade, but Joy's self-worth depended on her being back in the saddle with the technology.

Joy's eyes took on a soft, out-of-focus stare. "Bor-ing," she said.

"Well, what did you expect?"

"I dunno."

Joy fell silent, watching, tapping her fingertips. Enhancing the hack, Bobbie presumed.

"So, where is she? I need to talk to her."

"Oops – something's gone wrong with the feed. It's all blurred." Joy's fingers twitched and tapped together. "Nope, can't clear it. Oh my God, that's why it's blurred – is she? No!"

"Is she what?"

"She is, she's crying. Holy shit!" Joy gasped and clamped her hand over her mouth.

"What?" Bobbie asked.

"No way–"

"*What?*"

"Can't be," Joy whispered.

"Jesus Christ, just tell me, would you?"

"Slade's looking at a photo of herself with Fox and..." Joy swallowed hard. "...and Jimmy."

"No way!" Bobbie said. "Wait. Describe the picture to me."

"They're near Notre Dame Cathedral, and... that's weird." Joy's eyes narrowed, even though it wouldn't make her Foureyes view any clearer. "There's a beached whale in the background."

"It's not Jimmy!" Bobbie said, excited but not sure yet why. "I've seen that picture. It's Gustav, Slade's brother."

"But it looks just like Jimmy."

No! The realization hit Bobbie up the face. She'd seen that same picture in Slade's apartment and had recognized Gustav's face, but hadn't been able to put her finger on who it had reminded her of. Joy was right; Gustav looked like Jimmy.

"Slade doesn't have a brother," Joy said.

"She told me he went missing in action during in the War. Presumed dead, according to what Fox told her."

"Why is he holding hands with Fox?" Joy asked.

"They were an item, according to Slade."

"Is he related to Jimmy? How come they look so alike?"

"I bet he's the other DNA donor," Bobbie said as the pieces of the jigsaw fell loosely into place. "Davitt told me he'd been given DNA from a cryogenic source, but it was damaged, so he augmented it with his own. Of course Fox would use her lover's DNA. Clone him, never lose him again. The bigger question is, if Gustav went missing in action, like Slade said, how did Fox get Gustav's DNA?"

"And how come Slade didn't see the resemblance between Jimmy and her brother before? Or if she did, why did she stay quiet about it?" Joy's voice trailed off as her eyes went off focus.

Bobbie got the blink too.

Foureyes security breach registered. Joy you're in deep shit. And if this wasn't you, Joy, we're all in trouble. Both of you to the Bridge NOW!

Joy chopped her hand sideways in front of her throat, tilted her head and stuck her tongue out the side of her mouth before saying, "She sounds cross."

"And for good reason," Bobbie said. "If Gustav didn't disappear during the war, either Fox has been lying to Slade since the war, when they were supposed to be good friends, or Slade is at best up to her old tricks telling us half-truths, or at worst, playing a double game we don't know anything about."

CHAPTER 4

The ship's bridge was now the Operations Centre for the Fjord group. Floor to ceiling windows ran halfway around the room in a semicircle. Rain fell like pebbles on a roof that jutted farther out than the floor, slanting the intepaneled windows inwards at the bottom. Despite the tilt, drops of water lobbed against the windows by the breeze smeared Bobbie's view of the fjord. Some intepanels set on display extended the workspace beyond the consoles inset into the countertops. Other intepanels, switched to transparent, allowed light in and enabled people to see out.

"Welcome to the bridge, big sis," Joy said as they entered together. "I've a workstation over here. It's open-plan, but we'll be tucked out of the way." Joy showed Bobbie through the room as people working at the desks looked up. One guy stared and nudged his partner as the sisters walked by. Bobbie squirmed beneath their scrutiny.

Luke worked at a terminal on a desk in the center of the room. He tipped his head to the girls. "Slade's on her way. She's in a foul mood."

"I sent her an update on her blink security." Joy pulled a face but couldn't mask the glint in her eye.

"I'll be over to you in a second," he said with a frown, returning his attention to the display in front of him.

A buzzer sounded from the center of the semicircle, and a woman—in her late twenties, Bobbie reckoned—spoke into a headset. "Hovercraft Lima-Alpha-Delta-Alpha-Eight. Ocean Spirit Tower. Security code confirmed. Wind, two-one-zero at five knots. Quebec-November-Hotel, one-zero-two-two. Confirm de-cloaking code received."

The woman paused and listened before she continued, "Incoming hovercraft Delta-Alpha-Eight, clear to land on port Charlie."

"Busy day?" Bobbie said, taking in the twenty, or more, workforce bent over consoles in muted conversation.

"Nah, I get the impression it's been quiet lately – apart from us landing in on them. Though it's amazing how the ship can absorb 2 hundred people so easily," Joy said. "Belus have increased their patrols, code red on some suspected Melter scout-drone sighting. It means we have to ground our hovercrafts."

"That's a pain in the butt."

"But necessary." Joy pointed to the last terminal on the counter. "Over here, we'll have privacy."

Bobbie followed her. "These look like antiques."

"They are." Joy stroked the grey plastic casing. "But they work."

The door to the bridge slid open. Slade marched straight to Joy.

"I suppose I should thank you for finding the flaw in my AVD." Slade sent Joy a withering look. Bobbie saw the strain tightening Slade's jaw.

Joy smiled broadly. "Don't mention it."

Slade's eyes narrowed. "If you ever do that again without my permission, I will personally see to it you never touch a piece of tech again."

Joy's smile disappeared. "I'm doing my job! You're the one withholding vital information."

"Don't be a child!" snapped Slade. "Withholding sensitive information is part of my job. Imagine the damage Jacob could have done if he'd known everything."

Anger roiled in Bobbie. "Like the fact that it's your brother's DNA that Fox is using?"

Slade pressed her lips together. Muscles flexed in the skin below her temples. The moment swelled, like a bubble growing before it popped.

Bobbie bit her tongue.

The anger leached from Slade's face. "I should have noticed Jimmy looked like my brother," she said in a scraped, dry tone. "When we watched the footage, I saw one of the detained Rejuvenees and thought..." Her voice caught. "I thought he was Gustav."

She drew in a breath, tipped her head back, and exhaled. Her fingers rubbed circles in the material covering her sternum as she continued, "I've spent decades catching glimpses of him in crowds, only to realize it's not him. So I put it down to the same thing."

"But Jimmy–" Joy began.

"Jimmy had a lot of Davitt in him too. I guess it's like how everyone says Mo looks like me, but I don't see that at all. I didn't see the resemblance until I looked at that photo...of us... together. Lisette lied to me, but I can't put my finger on how...or when."

Bobbie's gut instinct was to believe Slade. Something about her rawness triggered Bobbie's pity as she felt the pain rolling off Slade. Grief haunted Slade's red-rimmed eyes, and Bobbie understood well grieving for a sibling.

"Don't beat yourself up," Bobbie said. "We've had a lot to keep us occupied, and Jimmy's change was gradual. When you first met him, he was a white-haired old man."

"I remember Jimmy from way back, when he was a friend of your grandfather's," Luke said, joining them. "And now that I think of it, he had brown hair as a young man, not blond."

"So if Gustav is the frozen donor..." Joy worked on the terminal in front of her as she spoke. "How? And why?"

"Fox wants to be young forever," Bobbie began. "All this is about her staying young and fit and in charge – forever."

"But why clone the whole world to look like you?" Luke said. "That part doesn't make sense."

"Maybe she didn't set out to do that initially," Bobbie said. "Her primary goal was to develop an anti-aging technology that would work for her. Eventually she might have even extended it to work for others, but for now, the biotech is still not perfect. She needs a huge sample number. Infecting all these ultra-elderly patients served as a large-scale clinical trial for her own treatment. To keep the variables down, she only needed to use her DNA."

Luke nodded. "I'll buy that, but clone Gustav? It's not actually going to be him."

"Yep, that's where the science gets weird. Can you imagine living forever without the person you love by your side?" Bobbie stopped. She'd hate to be young forever without Hicks.

The others waited for her to continue.

Bobbie stared out through the windows, watching the birds dip and wheel around the bow of the ship. She sighed and continued, "Fox was madly in love with Gustav, right?"

Slade glared; lips pressed tight. "Is this relevant?"

"Maybe, if we..." Bobbie began.

"More to the point, how did Lisette get Gustav's DNA?" Slade snapped, her fingers fidgeting with the clasp on her sling. The clasp sprang open.

Bobbie sighed and moved to Slade's side, adjusting the sling and closing the clasp.

Slade tapped her foot and looked up at the ceiling. Bobbie rested her fingers at Slade's wrist.

"I'm okay," Slade said.

Bobbie stepped back. "I know. Look, we're on the same side here. I'm really confused about the timing of this too. Fox gave a sample of Gustav's DNA to Davitt twenty years after the war ended – how could it be?"

Slade shrugged.

"If you can tell us what you know about the relationship... Anything?"

"Gustav was very private. So was Fox."

"Is it possible they were working on Rejuvenation as far back as before the war? How much time did they spend together? Were they in love?" Bobbie asked, hoping she'd eventually ask the right question.

"Why do you keep coming back to that?" Slade said wearily.

"Love?" Bobbie sensed a change in Slade's defenses. "Because love can be the most motivating emotion of all – or the least, if you lose love."

"Yes, they were in love. They spent all their together," Slade said with a huge sigh. "Lisette hadn't known much love in her life. Her mother died when she was young, and by all accounts, her father was a cruel brute of a man, so yeah, Gustav was everything to her, everything."

"I heard about her father," Joy said. "He lost everything after a chemical accident cost an employee his life. The board of health and safety ruled against the company's procedures. He really became a monster at that point, apparently. Word is, Fox drove herself nearly as hard as he had done, so that she could graduate quickly and escape him."

"How do you know that?" Bobbie asked.

Joy tapped her nose. "I have my sources." She turned to Slade. "How did they meet? Had she already set up Belus, or did they do that together?"

"She hired him. She'd already started Belus," Slade said. "But that's not the point."

Bobbie nodded. "Yeah, the point is, how did she have his DNA?"

"I know I've been lied to," Slade said. "I just don't know how or when."

"Maybe he didn't die in the war," Joy said.

"He wouldn't have done that to me, or Lisette," Slade said. "And to what end?"

"Oh, people died in the war who didn't *die*, Ori. We all know that." Bobbie met her father's eye.

Luke shook his head slowly. "She has a point, Ori. Either he died in different circumstances, or he didn't die at all."

Slade swallowed hard, her features a mask.

"Either way," Bobbie said, "Lisette Fox wants to use his DNA to create a world of clones of herself and Gustav so they can not only be young together forever, but that everyone will be them, together and young forever. We'll all eventually turn into what Fox sees as love's young dream."

"More like a narcissistic megalomaniac's dream," Joy said. "Her daddy would be so proud." She handed Bobbie what looked like two clear plastic butterflies set on an indigo metallic disk.

"What are these?" Bobbie examined the butterflies. They fit side by side on her palm, their wings open at 45° angles.

"Watch – hold these to the screen."

Bobbie set one on the screen. Joy touched a folder in the top corner, and it moved across the screen to sit beneath the butterfly. Its wings pulsed red and pink.

"It's uploading the encrypted files that we intercepted from the PARC. It pulses purple and blue when downloading, and yellow and green when uploading, so you know what it's doing."

"How does it know what you want it to do?" Bobbie asked.

"I can either preload or blink the commands. In this case, I've preloaded them and the quantum computer will know what to do. The real beauty is that it leaves no trace of having copied the folders and the files in them. It leaves everything exactly as it found it." Joy folded her arms and leaned back against the counter, looking at Slade, and said, "So what do we do?"

"About what?" Slade said, watching the butterfly.

"About our narcissistic megalomaniac?"

"The plan doesn't change. Rescue Hicks, find Jinko, expose Lisette," Bobbie said. "It would be better if we could confirm our suspicions scientifically. We can run a DNA test on the rejuvenation tissue samples we have in the lab with Ori's DNA, to test for a sibling relationship. If it comes back positive, we'll know Fox used Gustav's DNA." She shivered.

"We should assassinate Fox," Joy said.

"No," Slade and Bobbie said together.

Bobbie cocked an eyebrow at Slade. "Go on."

"Lisette has done great things for humanity. Without her, we'd never have defeated the Melters."

"I agree," Bobbie said. "Maybe Fox's premise of Rejuvenation was to benefit everyone, to begin with. The government was spending so much of its resources maintaining the ultra-elderly. But power corrupts—"

"Amen to that," Luke said.

Joy lifted the butterfly and set its metallic disk over the box inserted onto her pinkie finger. "There are 4 thousand encrypted files on this one. When we finish later this evening, we'll have a total of nearly 10 thousand files over both butterflies to take to the quantum computer."

"How long will it take?" Bobbie asked.

"Five minutes." Joy chewed her lip. "No, make that ten. Yes, ten, for sure."

It wasn't like her to be flaky in these matters. Bobbie tried to catch Joy's eye, but her sister looked away, smiled, and set the other butterfly on the screen, then turned her back as she said, "I still think we need to kill the bitch."

Luke put his hands on Joy's shoulders. "Killing Fox is not the way forward. We have to expose her. We have to show the world that she's instigated Rejuvenation, and how bad it is. We can't be judge, jury, and executioner. We don't have that right."

"But all those people could die. Isn't it better to kill one dictator than let Fox—"

"Technically," Bobbie jumped in, "as far as we know, I've killed as many people as she has."

"But all those people in the detention centers?"

"Joy, I agree that Fox has placed thousands of lives at risk. But they're not dead."

"Yet. And what about the test subjects? Ayushi, your old teacher? And Granny's not dead because of you. She's dead because of the actions that Fox initiated. And Hicks–"

Slade said, "Killing one individual will achieve nothing. She has support. There's a hierarchy of people who hold her in high esteem, who believe in her. If we take her out, someone who shares her values will emerge to take her place. Her successor would use the assassination as an excuse for further repression. And Lisette may have more to offer –"

"Who's really going to think that developing a strategy to get younger is so bad?" Joy said. "That hierarchy you're trying to win over might never believe us."

"The medical board believed Bobbie," Slade said. "They started protesting."

"And now they've all disappeared. There's no word of the protest after only two weeks."

"Fox controls the media," Luke said. "She has done for decades. She can make up any story she wants and broadcast it, and people will believe it."

"We need more hard evidence," Slade said, looking at Bobbie. "And someone to present it."

Bobbie met her gaze. "Sure. So we go to headquarters to use the quantum computer, and from there break into Fox's inner sanctuary. If we can gain control of her systems, the news output–"

"Bobbie, don't you think we've tried that already?" Luke said.

"We need to try again."

"No – too dangerous."

"Dad, we agreed–"

"Actually, Bobbie, no-one agreed to anything yet."

He was right. Bobbie had to focus on one objective at a time. She chewed her lip. "If you send me to headquarters, to the quantum computer, the research facility is close by – we can go there too. I can try to find Jinko and make him come back with us."

Slade narrowed her eyes. "Make him?"

"Davitt says he's a dick, but I think the fact that Jinko went ahead with the gentibots shows his humanity. I can convince him to listen. Isn't that my thing? Isn't that why you're threatening to keep me safe?"

Slade sighed. "Bobbie, you can't go. Period. Your face has been sent out in every security report since you escaped from the PARC. They're saying–" Slade bit her bottom lip. "Belus are telling their security that you're insane, that you were taken to the PARC for personality augmentation but that a glitch allowed you to escape, and that you're on the loose and dangerous. They haven't disclosed this to the public because they don't want to admit that someone escaped the PARC or the procedure they claim you were midway through. But if you go to HQ, the first guard you encounter will recognize you."

"I can wear a disguise."

"blink automated facial recognition is too good –their blinks will process faster than their eyes can see. They don't even need personnel. The cameras all around the facility will pick it up. If you wear a mask, same thing." Slade's voice softened, but not her words, which she delivered looking Bobbie straight in the eye. "Short of plastic surgery, there's nothing we can do."

"Actually," Joy said, unable to hide her smile, "I've been working on a new toy." Turning to Bobbie, she said, "Your crazy, brilliant sister might just have something that could get you past the guards and into Belus headquarters."

CHAPTER 5

hree electrodes tingled against Bobbie's skin – one under her chin and one behind each ear. Bobbie scratched the skin by her collarbone to relieve the prickling sensation but feared touching them would disrupt whatever electronic magic Joy hoped to work. The itching from the PARC drugs' withdrawal had abated, but this provoked fresh torment. All things considered; she'd take it on the chin – quite literally – if it would get them closer to finding Hicks.

Bobbie sat facing a screen that beamed back an image of her. Her ginger mane, scooped into a ponytail, exposed more of her haggard face than she'd like, showing her sallow skin and red-rimmed eyes. After another night of sleeping badly, if at all, she looked like shit, and she looked like herself – which was more of a problem.

"Almost ready," Joy said. Her bottom lip blanched where her teeth bit. "Press the pinkie implant on your right hand to any of the facial electrodes until you hear a short, high-pitched sound."

Bobbie chose the right ear electrode. The loud chirp made her jump. When she opened her eyes, a woman in her fifties with streaked brown-and-grey bobbed hair looked back at her. When Bobbie shook her head, the bob swung about the image's ears. Bobbie ducked in for a closer look, and the image moved closer to the camera, narrowing round grey eyes above peachy cheeks. Bobbie felt herself smile, and the image smiled back, crow's feet deepening at the edges of unkempt eyebrows.

"Oh, my God, that's amazing," Bobbie said. "This is what you see when you look at me now?"

"Yep. It's what everyone sees. Everyone with an ONIV."

Bobbie twisted to see a different angle, but the image flickered. Bobbie's face appeared as a ghostly overlay, then settled into a hybrid of Bobbie and the other face.

"Shit!" Joy touched her index finger to the electrode at Bobbie's chin. It vibrated, tickling against Bobbie's skin. "That should help, but you have to try not to move your head from side to side."

"Side to side?" Bobbie turned from Joy to the screen slowly. The image of the other woman was steady again — no trace of Bobbie.

"The projection has to catch up with the head moving in that plane. Forward to back is fine but be careful of up and down too. Just move slowly." Joy handed her a square of sensorfabric. "Keep the electrodes dry. Sweat can make them glitch too."

The very thought made Bobbie 's skin clammy. She took the material.

"It would take a fair bit of sweat, but just to be on the safe side, you know?"

Bobbie nodded. "Is this image from someone real?"

"Carlotta Benson – she's a technician at HQ. I used her because she typically comes to work, sits in her office, eats at her desk, keeps to herself, and doesn't interact much with her co-workers. She passes all security protocol, so as her, you can access the quantum computer."

"What if she decides to change her routine? What if I bump into her?"

"I'll be monitoring her, so I can warn you if she moves. It would not be good if you both showed up in the same place at the same time."

"Like Gracie's two-headed kittens," Bobbie said.

"What do you mean?"

Bobbie had never shared that many stories about Gracie with Joy. By the time Bobbie had moved past her grief at losing her twin and her resentment at Joy for being the 'replacement' baby, she had boxed up her happy memories of Gracie and tucked them away in her own heart. It had been both selfish and self-preserving, and Bobbie realized that she now needed to fully share who Gracie had been with Joy.

"When we were seven, we were on holidays in Galway. Gracie made friends with a farmer's daughter. Gracie made friends with everyone. She attracted a lot of attention because she had progeria, you know? So anyway, this girl's cat had had two pure white kittens, and the girl offered them to Gracie. Mum said she could only take one. When the day came to go home, the girl gave Gracie a large cardboard box with holes punched in the top. Gracie wouldn't let anyone open it, saying that the kitten might escape and they'd not be able to catch it."

"Gracie was smart, wasn't she?" Joy said, patting Bobbie's forearm.

"Yes, like you." Bobbie looked at Joy and smiled. "Anyway, she got home and took the cat box out to the back shed to release the kitten, but insisted she go alone, claiming the rest of us would scare it. No easy feat – she was using crutches at the time, but she struggled out and came back happy as a lark. We got used to seeing the white kitten around the back yard. But one day Mum saw the kitten standing along the top of the back fence. At first, it looked like the kitten had two heads. Then she realized that it was actually two cats facing opposite directions. Gracie had secreted both kittens home, knowing we'd mistake them for each other so long as we only saw one at a time."

Joy turned off the screen and faced Bobbie. "Well, big sis, we'll be putting Operation White Kitten into action tonight."

"Joy, this is...ingenious, but wouldn't Belus already have some way to combat this tech? It just seems too easy."

"Oh, I'd say they would have – if they knew about it."

"How is it possible Belus don't know about it?"

"Jeez, and there's me thinking I was the pretty sister and you were the smart one. I invented it. This is my baby."

The last word hung awkwardly, until Bobbie gave Joy a nudge with her elbow and nodded to her new image in the intepanel. "Wow, that means right now you're the smart one *and* the pretty one."

"Like there was ever any doubt," Joy said, nudging Bobbie back. "Let's go to the canteen to try this out."

The canteen was busy with dinner. A bank of matter streamers along one wall hissed and gurgled as they dispensed food to lines of people. A supervisor stood at the top of a line of children, arguing with a kid about his choices. The ship had a lot more children than Bobbie had seen at Yosemite. The supervisor snatched up a tray from the matter stream and pressed into the child's hands. The kid took it and stomped off, his bottom lip pushed out and his brows low.

Bobbie took her place in a shorter line for adults. The smells of the food mingled to create a meaty fug, making the air damp. Would it be enough moisture to affect the electrodes? No-one gave her a second look, and she found herself enjoying her anonymity.

An extensive menu flashed up on her blink. Under 'experimental food,' she spotted "salmon leg," described as "the perfect meal for those who enjoy leg meat and fish." Her gaze must have lingered too long on that item, because the matter streamer in front of her served up a plate with what looked like a chicken leg, except the meat was pink and flaky, almost falling off the bone. Potatoes and carrots joined the salmon leg. Bobbie lifted the plate, her mouthwatering at the smell, even if the presentation was odd.

She looked around the dining room, hoping enough time had passed for Joy to have gotten served and seated. Bobbie spotted the blue tips of her sister's hair where she sat with Niclas, April, and Slade at one end of a long table. Bobbie took her tray and walked to a free seat at the other end. She nodded at the empty seat, afraid to use her voice.

"Please, sit," Niclas said.

April stared. Bobbie thought the game was up. She sat down as slowly as she could without it seeming odd. She watched April. She was the security supervisor for the Fjord group, and she'd want to know everyone on board the ship. April's eyes took on the soft out-of-focus stare of a blink reader; then they refocused on Joy, and the two exchanged a smile. April speared a carrot and continued with her meal. Bobbie was impressed that April had so easily sussed out the stranger at the table.

"So, Slade, what do you really think about Bobbie going on this mission tonight?" April asked. "Is she up to it?"

Slade glanced at Bobbie, but her gaze didn't linger long. Bobbie reckoned that Slade didn't expect to know all the members of the Norway group. Slade gave April a raised eyebrow and tipped her head in Bobbie's direction.

April flicked her hand. "You can speak freely. Everyone in earshot is vetted."

Bobbie stared at her food. From the corner of her eye, she saw Joy suppress a smirk. April had a strange sense of humor, and Bobbie enjoyed how she and Slade ribbed each other.

"Once Joy can prove her disguise tech works, I'll be more comfortable. Bobbie's resourceful and determined, but she hasn't had time to train in combat, and that has me worried." Slade took a mouthful of stew and chewed.

"Worried? Is she that valuable?" April asked.

"Yes, she is – she's a good doctor. The medical community will respect that. If we can keep momentum with them, the public will start to listen. We've a lot of propaganda to combat."

"Good point," Niclas said. "The public is polarized. There are those who believe nothing unless they know the data origin, and then those that believe everything no matter how ridiculous. Bobbie is a firsthand witness, with the data to back her up. She's believable to everyone."

"And she's Luke's daughter," Slade said. "I used to think she was a stuck-up goody two shoes–"

Goody two shoes?

"– more jobs-worth than sensible –"

Bitch!

"– but the past couple of months have opened my eyes," Slade said, turning to Joy, who could barely hold back her grin. "I'm glad you find that funny, but I've grown attached to that sister of yours."

"She'll be glad to hear it," Joy said, taking a sip from her mug and glancing at Bobbie.

"Oh, Jesus, don't tell her! It'll go to her head, and she'll be insufferable," Slade said.

Joy choked on her drink, spluttering and coughing.

"Are you okay?" Niclas passed her a napkin.

Joy nodded and flapped the napkin.

April turned to Slade with a sweet smile and folded her arms. "Anyway, you were saying?"

"Nothing," Slade said, giving Joy a curious look.

"I'm worried about Davitt," Niclas said. "If he takes a turn for the worst, we'll be down a doctor."

"You can handle it, surely?" Slade said. "Neurology is your field, not hers."

"But I only–"

"You only nothing, you're a good neurologist," April cut in. "You know your way around a nervous system."

"Of a macaque!" Niclas said. "There's a difference."

Bobbie froze, afraid to look up and seem too interested. She remembered Slade had seemed shifty when she'd first mentioned Davitt's neurologist. Typical Slade, to hold back the details.

Slade waggled her good hand at Niclas. "It's close enough."

"What will Bobbie think when she finds out I'm not much more than a monkey doctor? Have you told her yet?"

"No, but it won't change anything for her," Slade said, picking up her fork.

Slade was right, Bobbie thought. A primate neurology researcher was still better qualified than she was. As a trained veterinarian, he'd be as good as any doctor: better, since he could figure out what was wrong with his patients without them talking. But why hadn't they told her the truth? Perhaps they thought she still had feelings for Davitt.

Slade looked at Bobbie and blinked hard.

Bobbie felt sweat trickle down the side of her face. She blotted with the sensorfabric, prayed it wouldn't interfere with the electrodes. If it stopped working now, they'd never let her go to the quantum computer. But Slade looked past Bobbie and smiled. "Here come Luke and Hang. Niclas, April, have you guys met Luke's son yet?"

"Our half-brother," Joy added before the thirteen-year-old reached the table.

That Joy felt the need to make this distinction pleased Bobbie. Bobbie had only met him a few weeks ago, and still wasn't sure how she felt about her father having another child. Hang, on the other hand, was delighted to have big sisters. When he reached the table, he wrapped Joy in a hug that she returned, her eyes softening.

Luke didn't notice Bobbie at all, but sat down beside April, who watched Luke until she seemed satisfied that he didn't recognize Bobbie.

Hang released Joy from his hug and turned toward Bobbie, arms outstretched. "What are you doing sitting a way down there?" he asked, moving to her side and wrapping his arms around her neck.

Bobbie froze. Could Hang see her? Of course. He hadn't yet had an ONIV implanted, so he had no blink. She hugged him back, inhaling the tang of sweaty teenager hair.

"Hang, what are you doing? How do you know this lady?" Luke asked sharply.

Hang's eyes widened in innocent bewilderment. "It's Bobbie."

"Put your left pinkie to any electrode," Joy said to Bobbie.

She did as she was told.

"Holy crap! That's awesome," Luke said.

"What? What?" Hang looked from his dad to Bobbie, utterly confused.

"Don't worry, honey," Joy said. "It's a blink thing."

Hang frowned and sat down in a chair next to Joy. "When will I get my ONIV implant? All the other kids my age have one."

"We'll talk about that later," Luke said.

Slade glared at April, her face blazing. "You knew, didn't you?"

"I noticed something weird when she nodded." April couldn't keep a smug smile from her face. "I knew she wasn't one of ours, and when you didn't introduce me, I knew she wasn't one of yours. So, I searched her using facial recog. and when it came up with an engineer at Belus HQ, I figured it was Joy's disguise tech. It's good, isn't it?"

"But something malfunctioned when Bobbie nodded." Slade looked at Joy. "It made me look twice at her."

"But why didn't you say anything at the time?" Joy asked, leaning in and resting her chin on her hand.

"In fairness, I thought it was my ONIV misfiring or just tired eyes or something." Slade sat back and pursed her lips. "Even with the weird shimmer, it did get past me. It's new tech, your design?"

Joy nodded.

"Then Belus guards won't be on the lookout for that. I guess if you can tighten up the glitching—"

"I will. I'll work on aligning her electrodes better," Joy said. "And Bobbie just needs a bit more practice moving with the electrodes. It won't be a problem. We need to get her to that quantum computer."

Slade arched an eyebrow. Joy held her gaze.

"I can manage it," Bobbie said.

"Didn't work for Hang, though," Slade said darkly.

"Everyone at Belus will have ONIV. That's a certainty." Joy leaned forward on her elbows. "How many adults do you know without ONIV? And if they don't have ONIV, they'll certainly not have received any information about how Bobbie is a crazed escapee from the PARC."

Slade pursed her lips and sighed. "Okay, I'd say it works, then. Niclas, what do you think?"

April began, "I think—"

Slade glared at April. "I asked Niclas. He's your commanding officer, I believe."

"Ladies, enough," Niclas said. "Joy makes a very convincing argument for using the tech; now let's get the job done."

"Tonight?" Bobbie asked.

"After you've spent a bit more time being the dutiful girlfriend to Davitt, then yes." Niclas stood up and lifted his tray. "You can leave after all the files have been uploaded to Joy's butterflies. What time do you expect that to be, Joy?"

"Zero one hundred hours, latest," Joy said, standing also.

"Luke, you'll go with her," Slade said.

"Copy that." Luke smiled at Bobbie. "We'll find Hicks soon."

"We'd better," Bobbie said, a band tightening across her chest. She didn't add that if they failed, she didn't know how she'd keep going.

CHAPTER 6

The side-entrance gate of Belus HQ opened into a dim corridor. A trickle of night-shift workers filed in on one side of the turnstile. Some gave a nod to those leaving on the other side, but most kept their eyes down and walked in silence. It felt so normal, and the feeling she'd had as they flew over Europe to get here revisited Bobbie. Even though her world had been upended in the last couple of months, the outside world, at least the areas governed by Belus, had remained largely unchanged. Even as Lisette Fox held the Rejuvenated elderly in concentration camps, the people in the cities got on with life. No-one paid any attention to their hovercar zipping through the traffic. The media reports on ONIV didn't mention any more news about the ill effects of Rejuvenation. Belus controlled the minds and opinions of the population. As they flew over the towns and cities to get to Switzerland, Bobbie had realized that their biggest battle would lie in changing that.

She kept the figure in front of her in her line of sight, worried that she might have trouble picking her father out in a crowd, especially from behind. A fourth electrode at the crowns of their heads covered the back angle of their disguises. Bobbie's lips twitched as she watched the ample backside of her father's disguise wobble back and forth as he walked, a tad too nimble for his stature.

Slow down she blinked.

Sorry, as he turned to her, his jowls quivered and chins piled into a fleshy cleavage. He slowed his pace. *I'm surprised this woman's not in the PARC for sugar addiction.*

"Dad," Joy's voice sounded tinny in Bobbie's ear, "you've been a woman for five minutes, and already you're moaning about your body image. Just don't walk close to anyone – we don't want them walking into your hologram projection."

Why didn't you give me a slimmer identity? Luke blinked both women.

"Because," Joy said, sounding impatient. "There wasn't anyone else on the night shift that suited. I've got you on the security cameras. Just remember – keep your heads as still as possible, so your images don't glitch."

They gave their hand signals – Bobbie's a balled left hand clasped in her right, like the type of nervous tick Carlotta Benson would have. Luke pulled at the clothing on his shoulder. Bobbie wondered if he realized it looked like he was hitching a bra strap, and reckoned Joy had devised it that way.

"Good, the visuals are coming in clear," Joy said. "There's a staffed security desk coming up. I won't talk to you again unless I have to until you're past that point, just in case."

Just in case what? Bobbie wanted to ask, but decided not to. Joy would have told her if there was anything she needed to know. She was in her sister's hands now.

In front of them, a tall young woman drew the guard's gaze. He hardly gave Bobbie and Luke a second glance. Joy was right. Belus workers were complacent – confident, perhaps, that they were stronger than the Candels. Their so-called heightened security had a weak point: pride.

"Dad, your doppelganger is having her break in the canteen. That gives us about forty-five minutes before she moves. She likes her grub," Joy said.

So I believe, Luke gave Bobbie a wry smile.

"Bobbie, Carlotta might be problematic. She's left her office for the restroom at least twice. Fortunately, that isn't on your route. She hasn't settled down to work yet, so I'll keep an eye on her."

We'll make this as quick as possible, Bobbie nodded at Luke and they picked up their pace.

Slade's injured arm had prevented her from coming, even though she knew the facility well. Her diagrams seemed accurate. The building's old facade, built against the mountainside, was in keeping with the ski chalet style of the surrounding building. Lisette Fox had maintained the illusion that this was a small building from the outside, but as soon as Bobbie and Luke passed through security, the building opened into a huge atrium. Clever use of light from intepanels gave the illusion of a sky, dark with stars, overhead, and Bobbie guessed that at dawn there would be a simulated sunrise.

Muted lighting in the atrium gave way to a brighter, more work-appropriate illumination as they moved into the corridor Slade had indicated in her drawings. Bobbie had a pretty good head for maps, but her father had an almost photographic memory. She followed him into the deepest recesses of the mountain, where the granite would protect the quantum computer from the bombardment of particles from space.

Twice they met other members of staff, and each time Bobbie kept her head rigid and her eyes down. Luke walked slowly and gave the people around him a wide berth. The other employees hardly noticed.

"Guys." The urgency in Joy's voice tensed every nerve in Bobbie's body. "Carlotta Benson is on the move. She's coming toward you. There's a utility closet at the end of this corridor. Get Bobbie into it now."

Luke took off and reached the door moments before Bobbie. Cleaning supplies packed out the small closet. Luke dragged a few boxes out into the corridor, and Bobbie squeezed herself into the tiny grotto.

"I'll stay outside the door," Luke whispered, his voice augmented by the electrodes to sound feminine.

"I'm fine. Go." Bobbie widened her eyes, forcing them to adjust to the darkness, but all she saw were the flimsy shadows of retina ghosts dancing over the blackness. Her heart pounded in her ears. A line of light seeping in along the bottom of the door pushed her panic aside. If light was getting in, so was air. She breathed deeply but quietly. A tickle at her temple made her realize she was sweating. Joy had warned her about keeping the electrodes dry, but the space was too small to lift her hand to blot the moisture. She tipped her head back, hoping gravity would pull the beads of sweat into her hairline.

"You there," said a voice. "What's your name?"

After a beat of silence, Joy's voice in the earpiece said, "Dad, your name is Martha."

"M-Martha," Luke said. The cupboard blocked his electrode's broadcast, so Bobbie heard him speak in his real voice, but higher pitched. Was he trying to sound like a woman? Thank God, Joy had built in the voice augmentation. He sounded ridiculous.

"Well, Ma Martha, I need my office cleaned better."

"Certainly."

"Today. It's so dusty, it's aggravating my allergies."

"Sorry to hear that."

"You're sorry? You should be. It's a disgrace. I don't know what you people do all day. I can't work there. My biometric readings for histamines are far too high. I'm going home, and that office better be spotless when I come back."

"It will be."

Bobbie heard Carlotta stomp away, but felt glad to get rid of the woman. Maybe they'd have free rein if she went home.

"Folks, we have a problem," Joy said. "When Carlotta Benson leaves, she'll electronically check out, which means I can't use her access codes to get you into the high-security areas. You have to stop her."

Bobbie heard her father call after Carlotta in his falsetto voice.

"Excuse me, Miss Benson? I think you might be sensitive to some of the chemicals we're using. Would you like to come and take a look at the supplies?"

Bobbie took a sedative jet from her pocket. She didn't want to hurt anyone if she could avoid it. Better to drug the woman than use the small laser gun Bobbie had strapped to her ankle. She opened the door a crack so she could look for something to tie Carlotta up.

We'll stash her in the closet. Loop the footage from before I got into the closet to cover it up.

43

"Copy that," Joy said in her earpiece. "They're right outside the door. I'm blocking her blinks. Hurry!"

Bobbie grabbed a roll of plastic bags to tie the woman up and a stack of towels for a gag. It wasn't perfect, but it would give them enough time to get to the quantum computer and get the files decoded.

"Cheap materials, cutting corners. It's always the workforce that suffers," Carlotta was saying.

Bobbie stepped out from the closet. Carlotta stopped dead in her tracks; her mouth dropped open. She backed up. Luke clapped his hand over her mouth as Bobbie delivered the sedative jet. Sweat dripped down Luke's face. When he looked at Bobbie, his features shimmered between his own and Martha's.

Carlotta clawed at Bobbie's face, dislodging one of her electrodes. Judging by Carlotta's horrified expression, Bobbie guessed her disguise was flicking between faces too.

Carlotta gurgled behind Luke's hand, then went limp as the sedative kicked in. Luke caught her, lowering her to the floor.

"What an old trout!" Luke whispered, putting Carlotta into the closet. "No wonder her workmates have nothing to do with her."

Bobbie's heart hammered as she tied Carlotta up. She suppressed a crazed urge to laugh. The old trout was going to have a very strange story to tell whoever found her. "Do we need to gag her?"

"Stuff some wadding in her mouth. Let me – it would be my pleasure," Luke said, blotting his face with a spare towel. "God, I'm sweating. How's my disguise? You need to sort yours out – you're a bit spooky-looking."

Martha's image flickered every few beats, but it held. Bobbie found the dislodged electrode, dried her chin, and reattached the electrode. The adhesive felt slimy, but it held.

She signaled a thumbs up to her father and blinked to Joy, *How do I look?*

Joy's voice was upbeat. "That was awesome! Yeah, you are glitching a little bit more than usual when you move your head, the alignment might need to be adjusted, but it should hold for security cameras. If you meet anyone, keep your chin down and steady, okay? But it's late – with a bit of luck, you two spooks won't bump into anyone else."

"Luck? We're due some, alright," Bobbie said in a hushed voice turning to Luke. "Let's get her in the closet. We'll pile these boxes up on the outside. Joy, what do the corridors look like?"

"It's pretty clear. Night workers stay at their consoles, and Dad is the only cleaning staff in this area."

"Let's go." Bobbie took off down the corridor until she heard her father loudly clear his throat. She looked back to find him pointing in the opposite direction.

"I think we'll do better this way."

"Shit! Thanks, Dad. I'm a bit turned around."

The corridors sloped, and Bobbie felt pressure in her ears. They were going underground. As they moved through each set of security doors, the hum of electronic panels lessened. Bobbie realized that strings of LED lights lit the hallways. "Joy, why no intepanels?"

"No need," Joy's voice crackled with static. "The quantum computer isn't connected to networks. It's completely isolated."

"You're breaking up," Luke said.

"It will get worse. We might lose ... after...okay?"

"Please repeat," Luke said.

Only static.

Bobbie whistled out a long breath. "We're on our own, Dad. Let's get it done."

They rounded the corner. There it was, exactly where Slade's diagrams had said it would be: a scooped-out cavern, deep within the mountain, with a room-sized glass chamber housing a bank of computer cabinets that twinkled with flashing blue, red, and green LEDs.

"I'll stay here," Luke said, tucking himself against the wall by the door. "I can watch the entrance and you from here. And I might get some connection with Joy."

"Will it make much difference? Here or behind the glass?"

"Don't underestimate that glass – it's designed so that not even radio waves can get through," Luke said. "Go quick."

Carlotta's image reflected from the glass. Even though there were no blink connections, her blink receptors still translated the electrode transmitters. Good job, too; if they came across other staff in this area, she had to continue to look like Carlotta Benson – and not just to them, but to the quantum computer as well.

A work console nestled in the center drew Bobbie like a magnet. As she approached the door to the glass cubicle, the A.I. voice interface – Mage, Joy had said its name was – greeted her in a smooth female voice: "Good morning, Carlotta, how are you today?"

"Hello, Mage. I'm fine; thank you." Bobbie heard her voice as Carlotta's, harsh and arrogant. "I have work for you."

"Your voice sounds different today," Mage said.

Bobbie had hoped the electrode voice augmentation would have been enough to fool Mage, but Joy had warned her how accurate the computer was. "I have allergies."

"I'm sorry to hear that. I need to use a visual security protocol. Please step in front of the retina scanner."

Bobbie's hands balled into fists. The muscles in her necks ached as she held her head stock-still. Joy's disguise electrodes had to be able to project the downloaded biometrics containing the details of Carlotta Benson's retina well enough to fool Mage. Bobbie's nose itched, but she resisted wriggling it. If the computer didn't give them access, all this risk would be for nothing. They would never get the files decrypted, never find out which PARC Belus was holding Hicks in. She would be adrift in a life without Hicks. He was her anchor, the place she went to for comfort and strength.

A trickle of sweat crept toward the electrode on her temple.

Hurry up, Mage!

Bobbie didn't breathe until Mage said, "Identity verified. Please continue, Carlotta."

A door-sized panel slid open. Relief left Bobbie euphoric. They were in.

She set the butterflies on the console and heard the hiss of the door closing behind her. "Mage, please follow the instructions on this device."

"Certainly. One moment, please."

Bobbie smiled at the idea of "one moment," given how long this job would take without Mage. She felt a surge of affection for this machine. Did Joy feel like this about all her gadgets?

The butterflies pulsed purple and blue – downloading. A green progress bar popped up on the screen, displaying, 13% Complete.

Bobbie's pulse pumped in her ears. It felt like it had taken several minutes to get this far. If she multiplied that by ten, or even eight, to get to one hundred percent, she would be standing here for another twenty minutes. It was fast, but would it be fast enough to get the job done and get them out before Carlotta raised the alarm or before anyone else happened upon them?

The progress bar displayed 37% Complete. The smooth hum of the machine frazzled Bobbie's nerves. The colors on the butterflies changed to green and yellow. It seemed too soon to be uploading, but maybe Joy had broken the job into segments.

Decrypting the PARC messages and locating Hicks was going to work, she told herself, and she would be on her way to rescue Hicks within twenty-four hours, and with any luck, they would be working to stop Rejuvenation as soon as possible.

Bobbie looked for her father on the other side of the glass. Barely visible, he stood with his back to the wall, watching the corridor, ghosted by the reflections of the lights blinking and flickering from the quantum computer. She wiggled her fingers at him. He tipped her a nod. She went back to watching the green bar, willing it to move faster.

53% Complete.

The butterflies pulsed with purple and blue again. Somewhere in all that digital data lay the answer to Hicks' location. It felt like Mage was counting down to the rest of Bobbie's life.

73% Complete.

The devices were uploading, and Bobbie watched them turn green and yellow.

Footfalls in the hallway chilled Bobbie's blood. Heart thundering, she turned to look, but couldn't see clearly past the reflections of light on the glass. Luke had pressed back into the shadows. She couldn't make out his expression, but saw he had one finger on his lips, the other hand making a stop sign to her.

The outline of a figure loped into the cavern. A man's voice said, "Stop what you're doing."

"Why?" Bobbie said, channeling the commanding tone of Carlotta. "I'm working. What do you think you're doing?"

"Please come with me, ma'am," the man said. His voice sounded vaguely familiar, like a harsher version of someone she knew, but she couldn't concentrate on that yet.

"Absolutely not. This is a very delicate procedure," Bobbie said, "and you're interrupting it. I'll report you. What is your name?"

"Please cooperate, ma'am," the man said, and moved closer. The reflections in the glass obscured his face, but she could see the blue tunic with the double stripe up the sleeve, the Belus guard uniform.

97% Complete.

Bobbie knew Carlotta was a pushy woman. She could use that. "On whose authority are you here?" she asked. "I'll have you disciplined."

99% Complete.

Come on, come on!

"Ma'am, step away from the computer."

Bobbie angled her body to hide the display from the guard. "You can't order me away from my work. I'm Carlotta Benson."

"Job complete," Mage said.

"Right now, ma'am," the man said, still on the other side of the door.

"All right, all right, I'm coming. But I *will* be reporting you." Bobbie scooped the butterflies into her pocket, keeping her head and face as motionless as possible. "Goodbye, Mage," she said as she faced the door to the glass cubicle.

The door slid open. Bobbie looked at the man. The glare of the pinpoint lights inside the cubicle left floating black spots in her vision. As her eyes adjusted, her jaw dropped, and air whooshed from her lungs. No wonder he'd sounded so familiar.

"Hicks?" Bobbie whispered. Elation swooped through her.

He looked healthy, stocky even. Certainly not tortured or beaten.

Of course! He saw Carlotta.

"Wait." She put one hand up. "I'm going to touch my chin slowly." She turned off the disguise. "It's me, Bobbie."

"What the fuck!" Hicks stared, his eyebrows pinched together in a frown.

Bobbie waited for him to recognize her, but his expression remained angry.

She wanted to run to him, but as she stepped forward, Hicks raised his laser-gun with both hands. "Don't move."

"Hicks?" She reached for him. He stepped back. The LED lights from the hallway lit up his face. His eyes glowed orange.

Bobbie's stomach flipped. She couldn't breathe.

Hicks kept his gun aimed at her forehead.

A shot whizzed from the shadows. The laser struck Hicks' temple and seared a slice off his skull. His orange eyes popped in surprise. Pink gobs of brain dropped onto his shoulders. His legs buckled. Hicks fell at Bobbie's feet.

CHAPTER 7

Tears dripped off Bobbie's face as she felt in vain for Hicks' pulse. His eyes stared vacantly, orange and remote.

"Bobbie, I didn't–"

Her father's lips moved, but she couldn't hear him, wouldn't listen to him. He'd killed Hicks.

"Oh, God no," she moaned. She cupped Hicks' face in her hands, but stopped short of kissing his lips. He didn't smell like Hicks. Perhaps it was the nanobots. The odor was sour, as if he'd been sick for a long time.

"What did they do to you?" she whispered. Her mind flashed back to a four-year-old's shy smile that even then had crinkled the corners of his grey eyes when he sat at the table with Bobbie and Gracie that first day of school. A carousel of memories detonated – sunlight dancing in his tousled ten-year-old hair; him holding her hand at Gracie's funeral so tightly the pain helped distract from the pain of losing her twin; his warm hug soothing her broken heart; his face strained and tense, melting into jubilation as they opened their college entrance exams and found they'd be going to the same school; eating two bites of matter-streamer pizza, throwing it aside, then buying the real thing and groaning as the taste swamped their tongues – moments stolen from a life of moments.

Hicks was lost to her now. Even had there been a heartbeat, his skull lay open. He would never have survived such an injury. She couldn't move. Grief scorched her lungs with every breath. Tears burned her eyes.

"Bobbie, we have to go. Now!"

Her father's words penetrated, releasing her from her paralysis.

"You killed him!" She flew at him, pummeling him with her fists.

"I didn't." He caught her by the wrists and pulled her to him.

She writhed, trying to pull free. "How could you? I loved him. I could have cured him. He was there for me when you weren't!" Sobs wracked her.

"It's not him!" Luke turned her to the body. "Look closer. This can't be Hicks. This man was the same height as me. Hicks is taller."

Bobbie focused on the body. The corpse's pale skin shifted to grey. Part of his face had caved in – not a huge amount – but Bobbie understood that with death, the nanobots had no power supply, causing them to dysfunction. But their breakdown shouldn't be that catastrophic, because Hicks was young. Yet the subcutaneous tissue was already collapsing, as it had done in the older Rejuvenees. This man had been old before Rejuvenation.

"Bobbie," Luke shook her shoulder, "now!"

She stared at the hands. They were all wrong. Hicks had square-palmed farmer's hands, like his father. Bobbie pulled away from her father and knelt down, stretching her own trembling hand beside the dead man's hand. They were almost the same size. Her father was right about the height too. This man was shorter than Hicks. She clasped her hands to her chest to control the tremors coursing through her.

"Bobbie, please," Luke said, tugging her arm.

"I'm sorry. You're right," Bobbie whispered. "The nanobots haven't had time to change the length of the bones in the limbs."

Luke raised his gun. "More people are coming."

Two figures emerged from the hallway, both with features identical to Hicks, both armed. Bobbie scrambled to her feet.

Luke fired rapidly, shooting both as they entered the chamber.

Bobbie stared in horror at three versions of Hicks, all lying dead. She tried to speak but couldn't. Leaning forward, hands on knees, she gulped in air and shivered. Luke slung the strap of one of the dead men's laser rifles across his shoulders and another over Bobbie as she straightened up.

"I'm going into shock, Dad," Bobbie said huskily. "If I can't treat myself–" She dragged in a lungful of air. She had to get as much oxygen into her system as possible to combat the symptoms. "I might lose consciousness. If that happens, go without me." She took another deep breath. "Get these butterflies back to Joy."

"It won't come to that." He removed the power unit of the third man's gun and put that in his tote bag, saying, "But we do have to get out of here before more come."

Adrenalin rocketed through Bobbie, driving up her respiration and heart rate. The doctor in her applauded. It would keep the blood flowing, delivering oxygen to her muscles, and keep her moving.

"I'm right behind you," she said, and followed, stumbling into the dark recesses behind the quantum computer.

"The way we came in is the only hallway out." Luke reached back and grabbed her hand. "But I noticed on the schematics there's an air-conditioning duct behind the cube. It should lead us outside, probably to somewhere in town. When we get higher, we'll probably reconnect with ONIV and Joy, and we can get the hovercraft to pick us up on self-drive."

A metal grid in the ceiling covered the opening to the air-conditioning duct. It was wide enough for a person to climb into, with enough room to bring a bag of tools along. Luke reached up and gave the handle a tug. The grid swung open, hinged along one side. Luke ran to another similar opening in the wall, yanked it open, and left the cover lying on the floor below it.

"That one is the warm air outflow. Hopefully, the guards will think we went that way. It might buy us some time. Now, quickly." He bent over and hooked his fingers together into a stirrup. "Reach for the rungs when I give you a leg up."

Bobbie found a rung. When she put her weight on it, a metal ladder slid down, landing her back onto the floor with a thud and rattling her joints. The duct had been built for easy maintenance. Bobbie scrambled up the ladder, high into the pipe. Above her, it went so far up that she couldn't see where or how it ended. Darkness had fallen outside, thwarting her attempts to gauge the length of the shaft.

"Keep going," Luke hissed from below.

Bobbie got her arms and legs moving up the ladder. Below her the clunk of metal and diminished light let her know her father had closed them into the duct. It wouldn't take long for their pursuers to figure out where they were. She pushed herself to climb faster, heart bursting. Sweat trickled down the side of her face. Her limbs shook as she hauled herself up, up, up. She focused on breathing deeply, on keeping oxygen feeding her muscles.

They'd been climbing in darkness for about five minutes, with no light for their eyes to adjust to at all. The top of the duct seemed as far away as ever.

Below, voices rattled up the shaft, all of them sounding enough like Hicks to tear strips off Bobbie's sanity. Someone directed a search of the outflow shaft in the wall that Luke had left open as a decoy. How long before they'd look up?

Bobbie's hands felt a gap in the vertical shaft – an intersecting duct running horizontally. She peered into the space and spotted a dim light source along it, some way off – or maybe not that far away. The perspective was distorted. Her hands explored the perimeter of the opening.

"There's another shaft running horizontally to this one. It's big enough for one person to crawl down," she whispered. "Where does it go?"

"I don't remember seeing it on the charts, which is weird considering how wide it is. They'll be checking the up shaft any minute now. Let's get into that side duct. If it's not on the plans, maybe they won't know about it. Maybe we can hide there. Go. Quiet as you can."

Bobbie eased herself from the ladder into the side duct and crawled along it to make room for her father. She sat with her arms wrapped around her knees.

The grid to the vertical shaft opened, and light flooded into it.

Luke pulled back, but aimed his gun at the opening. Bobbie froze, praying that when the guards looked up, their lights were strong enough to make them believe it was empty but not strong enough to pick out the side duct. If their pursuers climbed up, they'd easily find them. Luke could shoot the first one – another Hicks lookalike. Christ, could she bear it? He'd fall back on the others coming up the ladder behind him, but how long would that give them? The chase would be on, and they had no idea what lay at the end of this side duct.

"Nothing in here," said a voice so like Hicks that Bobbie had to force herself not to groan. She froze, afraid to cover her ears in case she made a noise.

"Get your ass up there to make sure," a guard said.

"Fuck that, shoot a laser up it in case they reached the top and we can't see them."

Green light flared, so intense it hurt her eyes and left floating black lines swimming like eels in her vision. A shower of sparks fell past the opening. Bobbie heard the clatter of metal bouncing off the sides of the shaft and falling past them.

"That's a job for maintenance."

Hicks' laugh made Bobbie clench her teeth and squeeze her eyes shut. It sounded of home, of comfort, yet tortured her with its falsehood, multiplied by at least three voices.

She longed for the real Hicks. *Her* Hicks.

"All clear," a Hicks voice below rang out.

The metal grid slammed shut.

Luke held up one hand. Metal clanged as the guards replaced the grid. Bobbie shifted a fraction forward, but Luke grabbed her forearm, one finger to his lips.

The voices below receded.

Bobbie felt weak with relief. Her muscles quivered. Bending forward, she placed her forehead on the cold metal.

"It's alright, Bobbie," Luke said in her ear as he massaged between her shoulder blades. "Deep breaths. In..."

He rubbed her back. "...and out."

Bobbie followed his instructions. The shakes subsided. Her heart felt like it might not explode.

"Bobbie, take a minute. That, back in the room." Luke squeezed her arm. "That was intense."

"How...how did you know so quickly it wasn't him?"

"Hicks would never point a gun at you. When you revealed who you were, and he kept the gun on you, I knew it wasn't him."

Bobbie had wanted it to be Hicks so desperately – had wanted to believe so much that she had missed the truth.

"We should go." She wanted to get back to Joy, find Hicks' location.

"I know, but I'm guessing they don't know about this side shaft. If I were in charge, I'd send someone up right away to check the outlet of the vertical shaft. When they don't find us there, Belus might think we never came this way at all. Thank God they were too lazy to climb up here." Luke took her chin and looked into her face. "Can you hang in here for a little while longer? Just to give them time to check where that outlet exits and leave?"

Bobbie nodded, saying, "You should rest too." She shuffled along to make more room for his legs to stretch out. "They must be using his DNA. But why his?"

"To fuck with you?"

"But how would Fox know I love–" Then it hit her. "The PARC. I must have said something when they drugged me. Shit! That's why they're using him."

"Don't go taking the blame for this. You know what those drugs are like. You couldn't have fought them. But it looks like Fox sees you as her biggest threat right now." Luke settled in beside her. He wrapped an arm around her shoulder and pulled her to him. "Are you warm enough?"

She rested her head on his chest and willed her heart to match the steady *pa-dump* of his. Her father's word rang true. She couldn't be held accountable for what she'd said in the PARC, but it didn't feel that way.

"They've had him for two weeks, and managed to program the nanobots with his DNA already," she said after a moment.

"Seems like they're making adjustments in the nanotech."

Bobbie said nothing, not wanting to put words to the idea that Hicks might not even be at a PARC now, that getting the staff-note files decrypted might have been an utterly futile exercise.

Luke crawled to the opening, looked down into the vertical shaft, then twisted his body so he could see up it. "Do you hear that?" he asked.

Bobbie listened, but only heard her pulse pounding in her ears.

They sat in silence for a few seconds, then she heard it: a whirring sound with a click every second or so. "What is it?"

"It's a fan at the end of the main duct. They damaged it, but it's still revolving. We have to get past that to get out."

"Maybe we'll find something to jam the fan?" She tipped her head toward the dim light at the opposite end of the duct from where they sat. "Better than sitting here while we wait for them to check the outside of it."

"Exactly," Luke said. "I hope it's a tool store for maintenance. Are you okay?"

The concern in his voice grabbed Bobbie and dragged her back to her childhood. "I..." Words jammed in her throat. She rested her forehead on Luke's shoulder and felt his hand rubbing her back. She could have been five again.

"Don't bottle everything up, darling," Luke whispered. "This might not be the best time for a heart to heart, but I want you to know you'll always be my little girl. I love you."

Bobbie choked over a sob as she said, "Love you too, Dad."

"It's okay," Luke soothed. "I never told you this, but when you were small, after Gracie was diagnosed and especially when she was really frail, you got me through her illness."

Bobbie lifted her head, incredulous and looked at him through blurry eyes. "Really?"

Luke nodded. "Your mother was consumed with caring for Gracie. It was like...like Gracie was her child, and I had you. You were a gift to me. We were a team. You pulled me through, until–"

"Until Gracie died," Bobbie said. A lump lodged in her chest.

"Then you turned in on yourself. After that, I think Hicks was the only one who could reach you, and even then..."

"I'm sorry."

"No, no, don't be. That's how you found your strength. And God knows, you've needed it...but I'm here for you now. You can talk to me."

"Thanks, Dad."

They folded into a hug. Bobbie clung to her father, feeling timeless, lost in decades of longing for this embrace, drawing strength from him.

"I'm good," she whispered after a while. "Let's keep going."

"That's my girl." Luke gave her a squeeze before he released her. "Lead the way. But stop short of the hatch, so we can listen to see if anyone's there."

"Of course." As quietly as she could, Bobbie crawled toward the dim light. She adjusted the gun Luke had given her – the one he'd taken from the guard – so it didn't knock against the sonorous metal lining the duct. She counted her "steps" – every time she crawled forward on her right knee, she added one. Every twenty steps she tried to hail Joy on the blink, but made no connection. "It feels like we're going deeper into the mountain. I still can't reach Joy."

"I get that feeling too. It's odd. What would you keep deep in the bowels of the earth... apart from the quantum computer?"

"Storage?"

"Sure, but it's well-vented. Why would storage need to be vented?"

"If people are going to be there at all, I suppose it needs ventilation." Bobbie lost count and started again.

"True, but not to this extent. And storage would be better off near where it might be needed, right? No, a duct this big feels odd."

"We'll know soon enough." Bobbie dropped her voice to a whisper. "We're getting close."

Light flickered through the grill in regularly-spaced stripes at the end of the duct. The grill was screwed on from inside the room. Bobbie peered through, but couldn't see anything. They listened and heard nothing.

"I think I can get my fingers through, but we need something to unscrew it." Bobbie searched her pockets, but all she had were a few more sedative jets and the butterflies, which she didn't want to risk breaking.

"Try this." Luke's hand reached from behind. He pressed a little silver cross into her hand. "Might work as a screwdriver."

"This was mum's." Emotion stampeded through her chest as Bobbie remembered it hanging on a chain around her mother's neck years ago.

"Yes, she gave it to me when I went to war."

"You've kept it all this time."

"It's all I've had of her for a very long time. Now use it to get us out of here."

Bobbie's hands felt too large, too clumsy. The cross, small and angular, slipped and twisted in her fingertips as she tried to orientate it. The first screw rotated with a squeak and eventually came loose. Drawing her fingers back in, she massaged her wrists. Her hands were covered in red-brown dust.

"Rust," she said remembering the gleaming equipment in the quantum computer chamber. "So I'd say this isn't a new area."

There were two screws on each side. The second came out. Bobbie had freed one side, but it hung under its own weight, creating tension on the two remaining screws. When Bobbie tried to unscrew the first screw on that side, it stuck halfway. It refused to move. She adjusted her position. Using fingertips only, she turned the silver cross to a different angle, but it slipped. Before she could react, it fell from her grasp. "Shit!"

"Move aside," Luke said.

Bobbie squeezed past him and moved back to give him room beside the hatch.

Luke peered through the grill. "It looks like an empty room. I'm going to have to risk making some noise." He curled his body up and turned himself around so that his feet were over the grill. He slammed his boot down, and metal twisted and bent back from the ceiling beneath where Bobbie had unscrewed the first screw. He gave it another kick. The rusty screws snapped. The grill fell with a crash to the floor below.

"That was loud," Luke said, taking aim with his gun through the opening.

Tense seconds passed as Bobbie listened above the ragged sound of her breathing for people approaching.

"There's no-one there," Luke said, and disappeared through the hatch, landing below with a soft thud.

Bobbie unfurled her legs, muscles aching, as she lowered herself to the floor. Light bounced and flickered around the room from an LED candle on a shelf high up on the wall. The silver cross glinted on the floor. She snapped it up. "What the hell is this place?"

They were in a large room with old-fashioned kitchen units and a counter along one side, and a bed against another. A third wall housed cabinets and computer equipment. Against the fourth wall, beneath the candle, a white cuboid metallic chest took up most of the space.

"It has no matter streamer. Wow, I haven't seen a kettle and a stove since the twenties," Luke said. "And that's an LED TV – it's like a museum in here." He stood facing an old television set hanging over the foot of a day-bed. Sheets covered the bed. Even in the dim light, Bobbie could see that a layer of dust had turned the white to grey.

"Cotton?" Bobbie said. "Everything's so old. No intepanels either. I wonder, does the tech still work?" She pointed at where the kitchen counter turned a corner into what looked like a lab setup. An old LED monitor connected with cables to a keyboard spewed more wires to a black box, all covered in a layer of dust. "So many cables."

"And switches." Luke pressed a switch in the wall at shoulder height. The room lit up. "That looks like a router," he said, squinting. "It's how they used to connect to the internet."

"I remember that." Bobbie tried her blink again and got nothing. "Could we use it to connect with Joy?"

"No, unfortunately. ONIV uses a different protocol. I could rig something up, but it would take time we haven't got."

"Right, let's get out of here. This place is creepy." Bobbie walked to the door and tried the handle. "It's locked mechanically. An empty keyhole only on this side. And even if we get out from here, where do we go?" She saw her footsteps in the dust leading from the center of the room to the door. "There's been no one in here for months, maybe years."

"Check those cabinets, see if you can find anything we can use to get out past the fan." Luke began opening cabinets. "Jeeze, they've enough food here to last a few years."

"It reminds me of those old nuclear bunkers from the last century," Bobbie said.

"Urban legends." Luke opened another cupboard and whistled through his teeth. "Or at least, very few people actually had them, but they did feature heavily in popular fiction. I've seen many movies with this kind of thing, but I've not seen it for real before. This ... this is astonishing."

Bobbie pulled open a drawer with scalpels and saws. The drawer below had gauzes, sterile pads, and an extensive first aid kit with an array of drugs. "Whoever was planning on holing up here wasn't counting on any help from the outside world for a very long time." She heard a click and a buzzing sound, and turned to its source. The white chest beneath the candle vibrated.

"I think that's a fridge." Bobbie shook her head. "No, actually, it's a freezer." Hairs tingled on the back of her neck. Bobbie pulled the handle, but hardly moved the heavy lid. "Dad, help me open this."

With her dad's help, she hoisted it open. White mist swirled as cold air met warmth. As the vapor cleared, Bobbie saw a man's naked body folded, knees to torso, a bleak parody of a fetal position. Discolored skin, cream to red and black in places, showed frost burn at the very least, possibly bruised, Bobbie reckoned. One arm ended in a ragged stump.

"Jesus Christ!" Luke said.

Contorted as the corpse's face was, Bobbie knew this man. "It's Gustav. Dad, we've found Slade's brother."

CHAPTER 8

Bobbie lowered the freezer lid. What was this place? The burning candle made it feel like a twisted shrine to Gustav. No wonder the DNA had degraded. Fox hadn't taken much care with the cryogenic freezing. Maybe she hadn't the time or resources to dehydrate the body first? But she'd had the resources to set up this bunker.

"How did he die?" Luke asked, lifting the lid off the freezer again.

"Perhaps that big hole in his back had something to do with it." Bobbie pointed out the black oval shape visible through the transparent polythene wrapped around the corpse.

Luke gave her the stink eye.

"Sorry. Not the best bedside manner," she said.

The plastic crackled and flaked, fragments of hair stuck to it as Bobbie removed it from the corpse's face.

"It's well kitted out for performing an autopsy." She threw a nod to the cupboard in the laboratory section. "But we don't have time. We need to get these butterflies back to Joy."

"This is probably the safest place right now. I don't think security knows about this place."

"What makes you so sure?"

"They gave up so easily at the ventilation duct. If security knew about the side shaft, they would be here by now."

"Maybe only Fox knows about this room." Bobbie looked around the dust-covered room. The only footprints were theirs. "She hasn't been here in a long time."

"No need – she has his DNA. She doesn't need anything else."

"But the candle?"

"It's electric."

A shiver crept over Bobbie's skin. "Fox kept his body, kept a candle burning for him, but didn't tell anyone she had his remains. How did she get them in the first place? The war department would have contacted Slade as his next of kin."

"Unless Fox killed him."

"But she loved him."

"And she's crazy. Look, his eyes have been glued shut, his mouth too." Luke turned to Bobbie. "Why would anyone do that?"

"Maybe he died with both open? If Fox loved him, maybe she couldn't bear to see his face like that."

"Or it's symbolic – see no evil, say no evil. If only we knew what he saw, what she doesn't want him to say." Luke pulled the lid down.

"Wait." Bobbie put her hand on his arm. "There might be a way we *can* see what he saw. How old would he be now?"

"About the same age as me, sixty-five, maybe more."

"Did you have your old ONIV taken out? The one that saved data before uploading it?"

"No, but..."

"...Most people didn't, right?" Bobbie ran to the drawer with the dissection kits. "Joy can extract the data as she did before, with the guard."

"But that means you'll have to–"

Bobbie turned to her father, saw in hand. "Yup."

"Can't you just take out his old ONIV without cutting off his head?"

"I don't want to risk damaging the circuitry." Bobbie held the saw up. "This is quicker and safer."

"Okay, okay. You do the ... the needful," Luke said. "I'll find a container."

"There are bin liners." Bobbie pointed toward the kitchen as she strode to the freezer.

"Isn't there anything better? This is Ori's brother."

"No time, Dad. He'll defrost, and that's going to be a mess. No part of this will be easy for Slade. Let's just get it done."

Bobbie set the blade against the back of the neck between the second and third cervical vertebrae. The flesh was frozen. She had to work harder than when she'd taken the guard's head. It took long minutes of sawing, keeping the blade between the vertebrae. When she felt the handsaw bite into softer tissue, she switched to a scalpel and scissors to cut through the muscle and skin at the front of the throat.

"Bag, please." Bobbie lifted the frozen head. Already the defrosting process had produced a slimy surface, and she nearly dropped it as she put it into the bag. "Double-bag that. Do you think it's safe to climb out that shaft now?"

"I'd say so." Luke held the bag with Gustav's head with arms straight, elbows locked, as he lowered it into another bin bag. With a loud exhale, he rolled and tied the neck of the bin bag.

"It doesn't smell," Bobbie said, lifting the bag.

Luke was a bit green around the gills. "I wasn't going to take any chances."

Bobbie and Luke used stools to climb into the maintenance shaft. Fox would know that they'd been here and how they'd gotten in, just from the patterns in the dust. There wasn't much point trying to disguise that. Who knew when Fox would even return to this bunker, anyway?

Armed with screwdrivers and a crowbar, Bobbie and her father crawled back to the vertical shaft. The climb up drove Bobbie's tired limbs until every part of her throbbed. Gustav's head, tied to her back, felt heavy and cumbersome. She winced as if she were inflicting pain on the dead man every time she whacked the bag off the sides of the vent. She hoped the dampness on her back was simply a mixture of condensation and sweat. She couldn't bear the thought of the bag leaking as the flesh inside thawed.

Light appeared in the vertical shaft suddenly, sputtering through the movement of the fan.

"Sunrise," Luke said.

The dawning of a new day – the thought gave Bobbie hope. Today she'd find Hicks. She tried blinking Joy but couldn't connect.

Luke, climbing first, reached the fan. Bobbie couldn't see past him, but she heard him grunt as he shifted position to tackle stopping the blades.

Metal squealed against metal. Light flickered, then steadied, as the fan stopped.

It's going to be a squeeze, Luke blinked. *There might be a guard posted. Don't move if I don't come back for you. Give it as long as you can, then proceed out carefully. Okay?*

Bobbie nodded, sick at the idea of her father getting caught.

Luke climbed into the gap. Bobbie pushed away the gruesome thought of the crowbar slipping with him halfway through. His feet were the last thing to disappear through the opening. Then his head appeared, blocking the light as he looked back in at Bobbie. He reached a hand to her, and she passed him the bag with Gustav's head. She climbed out, helped by Luke grabbing her under her arms and pulling her to a standing position beside him.

They were halfway up the side of a ravine. Sheep tracks crisscrossed the valley sides. A stream gushed along the bottom and disappeared into thin air. The roar of a waterfall provided the backdrop to the buzz of insects. Alpine flowers, bunching grasses, and stands of giant hogweed in full bloom covered the slopes.

Bobbie shaded her eyes and pointed to where the sun spilled over the mountain. "We should be able to connect with Joy if we get to the ridge."

The ravine was steep. They were both bathed in sweat by the time they crested the ridge. On the other side, a vast sprawl of buildings lay below them in a broad flat valley. Sunlight reflected off the solar glass covering most of the structure. It reminded Bobbie of the research facility on the west coast of Ireland, where Belus had kept Granny.

"Hello?" Joy's voice in her ear made Bobbie jump.

It's so good to hear you, li'l sis. Now they could blink, she didn't have to risk talking.

"Where the hell did you guys go? I've been worried sick!"

Long story, but we're okay now. Can you figure out our coordinates so we can send for the car? Bobbie joined her father, hunkered behind a rock.

"Forget about your hovercar," Joy said. "It's been impounded. I'm sending April and Slade as far as Scotland. The self-drive will be in range from there, but it can't pick you up from the ridge you're on. Those buildings are a research and development lab. How did you end up there?"

There's a shaft that connects the two. I know this facility. Davitt worked here with Jinko.

"I'm sending coordinates for the pickup point to your locator b-app. The hovercraft will be there in three hours."

Luke moved his head from side to side, then stopped. The locator b-app produced an amber arrow in Bobbie's blink. She looked in the same direction as Luke. The arrow changed to green, telling her they had to walk along the ridge.

I'll bet she wants us up on that high point there, Luke pointed at a peak in the distance.

How long do you think it'll take to get there? Bobbie looked from the summit back to the research facility. Jinko worked down there.

One hour. Two tops. Luke followed Bobbie's gaze down the mountain. He turned to look at her, pursed his lips, and nodded.

Bobbie was torn. She wanted nothing more than to get into the hovercar and go back to Norway so they could get on with finding Hicks. But Jinko held the key. If he truly had the gentibots, they could send those out in a recreational virus and stop Rejuvenation without killing the thousands infected.

Joy, can you get eyes inside the research facility? Bobbie asked.

"Yes... why?"

Can you find Jinko?

"I can find out if he's electronically signed in. It would take me a fair bit longer to actually find him by sight. I don't know what he looks like... but I can find pictures. It'll just take more time. But Bobbie, what are you thinking?"

Jinko's been working on the gentibots. I want to try to get him to come with us.

"Why would he come with us?"

If I can make him see what Fox is doing, he might. He's different than Davitt. He has ethics. It's worth trying, now we're so close. Get the footage we took from the Belus guard's ONIV ready to share.

"But you can't go in there. Both your disguises are blown, they're looking for you."

But they aren't looking for me, blinked Luke, *At least, not as me, Belus doesn't know my face. Even if Jacob has told them everything about the Yosemite camp and they figure out who I am, the most recent pictures they have of me are from before the war. I know how we can do what Bobbie wants and get back in time to catch that lift.*

CHAPTER 9

Fifteen minutes of scrambling downhill through bushes and scrub took Bobbie and her father within a hundred meters of the research facility's loading bay. Any closer, and they would trigger the AI nanosensors embedded in the solar glass and paint covering the walls.

Bobbie had hidden Gustav's head, along with Joy's butterflies, near the top of the ridge under a pile of brush and marked it with rocks. She blinked an image of the hiding place to Joy, knowing it would have the exact coordinates on the image's metadata. If they didn't make it back, at least April and Slade would be able to find Hicks and investigate Gustav's death.

On the way down the mountain, Bobbie and Luke gathered up as many leaves and twigs as they could. Now she piled them beside larger pieces of wood. Luke fired his laser into the tinder, and the flames licked up through the pile in ribbons of orange and yellow.

She held up a handful of damp moss. Luke counted down silently on his fingers, then pointed at the flames. Bobbie set the moss on top of the small fire. White smoke billowed from it.

"They're coming. Two men, unarmed," Joy said. "The AI will have informed them there's smoke outside. I've blocked their blinks."

Bobbie and Luke crouched out of sight and watched as men in security uniforms approached the fire. One carried a fire extinguisher, and the other a shovel.

Ordinary in-house security. Luke blinked.

That's a good sign. Means they haven't brought Belus guards into the research facility yet.

"Some asshole must have left a glass bottle out here," said one of the security men, shoveling dirt over the fire.

"Don't be stupid. That looks like it's been set on purpose," said the other, blasting it with the fire extinguisher. "Damn kids shouldn't be in this area."

"I'm not getting through to control." The guard stopped shoveling dirt and tapped his fingertips together.

Luke stepped out from the bush with a gun in each hand. "Don't move, either of you."

Bobbie slunk out from the other side of the bush, creeping up behind the men.

"I won't hurt you if you don't make me," Luke was saying.

Bobbie swooped in, a sedative in each hand, and applied the jets dual-handed to the guards' necks in one action. The guards swung toward her, confused and staggering. She scurried back, hoping Luke wouldn't have to shoot them. One of the men tried to speak, but no words came as he dropped his shovel. The other blasted the extinguisher. The water hit Bobbie in the stomach, winding her, the combined pressure and cold water making her gasp. She reeled back, arms spinning for balance.

Luke ran between the men and Bobbie, but she could see there was no need to shoot as first one man then the other dropped to his knees and keeled over. Luke hurried to the one closest to him, pulled off his boots, and undressed him. Luke pulled the tunic over his head, but he stuck halfway in.

"Give me a hand. It's too small."

Bobbie yanked the tunic down his arms and eyed the sleeping men. "He didn't look that much smaller than you, but the other guy is huge."

"It'll have to do." Luke stripped the other guard and climbed into his uniform. The crotch of the trousers hung halfway to Luke's knees.

"Come here. Let me roll those up for you. The tunic will cover the bulge."

Luke waddled to her.

"That looks better," she said when she was finished.

Bobbie knelt beside the smaller security man and fixed her disguise electrodes to his face and pressed her pinkie to it. His face took on a grotesque version of the woman Luke had been disguised as at Belus Headquarters, but with the distortion, it was hard to discern if this face was male or female, or if it were even human. Bobbie moved to the bigger man, who was now naked but for his underpants, and she attached her disguise electrodes to him and activated the Carlotta Benson face. It too was grossly disfigured and glitching, but that didn't matter. Later, when the security staff were found, the disguises Luke and Bobbie had used in Belus HQ would buy them more time.

She stood up, wringing the excess water from her tunic, and hoped the fast-drying properties would have her looking close enough to normal. Her father looked the part, dressed as a security guard.

Bobbie put her hands in the air. "Shouldn't you be pointing a gun at me or something?"

"That's a bit much. I'm escorting you for an appointment," Luke said, taking her by the arm.

"The AI saw two leave, and won't raise any flags at two returning," broke in Joy's voice. "But to be on the safe side, Dad, you should keep closer to the building, so the AI nanosensors build a picture of the uniform first. It's likely the person supposed to be looking at the footage is one of the guys snoozing under that bush where you left him, but just in case. There are a lot of people inside. You're going to have to sell your story."

The glass door reflected Luke and Bobbie's approach. Shorter strands of Bobbie's hair had loosened from her braid, giving her an aura of desperation. Her tunic clung in places where it was damp. Luke was convincing in his uniform; Bobbie took comfort from his swagger as they walked up to the doors.

Luke's uniform had a black and red pattern over the right breast and an identical one on the top of each sleeve. He angled his chest so the design was in plain sight, and the door swooshed open. The lobby bustled with people striding from hallways to elevators, past a desk where three women bent over consoles.

The woman nearest the door lifted her head. Her gaze went out of focus as she read her blink update, and then her eyes widened as she refocused on Bobbie.

"C-can I help you?" Her eyes flicked to Luke, then back to Bobbie. The other staff members didn't look up from their screens.

"I'm to take this patient to see Doctor Jinko in Nanobiology."

"That's a secure area, sir." Her eyes never left Bobbie.

"Didn't you get the blink from Belus HQ? They've just arrested this criminal. You've seen the blinks, I'm sure?"

The woman shook her head, her brow wrinkled in confusion.

Luke sighed and put his hands on his hips. "Totally inept!"

What happened to the blink hack? Bobbie kept her head bowed to mask the fact she was blinking.

"Look, I need to get her to the nanotech lab. I dunno why. That was my orders. I'm just the delivery guy!" Luke was really selling it, but Bobbie hoped he wasn't overdoing it. The woman on the desk seemed flustered. After the lies Belus had spread about Bobbie's violence, she'd be nervous in the same position.

"I'm working on it." Joy's voice hissed in her ear. "Jesus, these things aren't just snap-your-fingers magic, ya know. I need you to look directly at her ID. The black and red pattern on her tunic shoulder."

Got it.

"O-kay," Joy said. "Getting there. Hang on."

"I-I don't have any instructions, sir," the woman on the desk was saying to Luke. "Perhaps I should call security to help you."

"I am security!" Luke hissed through clenched teeth. "Let me tell you, this order comes directly from Lisette Fox. It's high security. Perhaps you don't have clearance?"

"I certainly do have clearance."

Bobbie glanced up and guessed the woman was in her late twenties – young enough to be insecure about her position, but old enough to think she deserved better treatment.

"Dad," Joy said. "Get her to go back in and check her blinks – I set up one marked as 'read' in her inbox."

"Then you must have overlooked the blink," Luke said. He turned his back on the woman and walked away, running his hands through his hair. "Jesus Christ, this is ridiculous! Do I have to call and get them to resend the order?"

"No." Her frown smoothed as she tipped her head. "I found the order." Her eyes narrowed on Luke's ID badge. "I've given your badge temporary clearance and blinked you directions to the lab. Just follow the instructions."

Joy, where the fuck is that blink going? Luke asked.

"She sent it to Sleeping Beauty outside."

Shit! Luke stepped back from the desk and placed an arm on Bobbie's shoulder.

"Where are we going?" Bobbie asked, pulling back from Luke, not needing to add too much to her pretense of being scared.

He grabbed her arm, making it look more violent than it felt. "Just tell her already. I'm sick of dealing with her!" Luke said.

"Please." Bobbie poured as much pathos as she could into her expression, but the woman was concentrating on her screen again.

"Let's go." Luke pulled her after him. *Joy, can you get that blink?*

"Trying to, but you're in with full security clearance. Just walk to the elevators and get in the first one that opens," Joy said. "Your clearance is only temporary. She probably only gave you a few minutes to get to the floor and scan in."

Some non-security personnel had turned to stare at the small commotion Bobbie had caused as she tried to get the directions, but now that she was subdued, they ignored her.

In the lift, most floors had labels, but none identified the nanobiology lab.

Let's just start at the top and work down the list of levels with no tag. Bobbie checked the time. They had two and a half hours before the hovercraft arrived. They would need at least an hour to climb the ridge too. Luke's clearance was temporary, but the details of how much time they had were in the blink they couldn't access.

People entered and exited the elevator on each floor, making the journey to the 12th floor achingly long. On the 9th floor, a security guard joined them. He stared hard at Bobbie before reading Luke's ID and relaxing. He got out on the 10th floor, leaving Bobbie and Luke alone in the lift.

The doors to the 12th floor opened. The lobby looked the same as every other floor. They left the lift. The lobby doors slid back to show an enormous hoverport, with cars parked at rows of charging stations. Port exits lined the walls, and vehicles queued to take off.

Wrong floor. Bobbie blinked as she turned back to the lifts.

"I've got it!" Joy sounded pleased with herself. "8th floor. Turn right on the corridor and use Dad's ID badge to gain entry. Hurry up. It's only valid for another six minutes."

The doors to the lift seemed to take forever to open. Unsure how many seconds had already ticked by, Bobbie set a five-minute countdown timer in her blink.

"Come on, come on," Luke muttered beside her. They both jigged on the balls of their feet, ready to move, watching the numbers above the door light up and dim as the lift passed each floor. It seemed to stick at seven, then went back to moving at its usual pace until it got to twelve. The lift doors peeled apart. They dashed into the empty lift. Bobbie jabbed the button for their floor. The number eight glowed green, but so did numbers nine and ten.

"What the?"

"People getting on there," Luke said.

Three and a half minutes left.

At the 10th floor, two young women got on. One pressed the panel for the 11th as the doors were closing.

"Oh, it's going down," her friend said and reached for the 'door open' square.

Luke blocked her hand. "Sorry. Too late now, you have to get out on 9 and take another lift."

He shrugged, smiling at her. She scowled.

The lift set off. No-one spoke or made eye contact. Seconds later, it settled on 9, the doors opening too slowly for Bobbie. Forty more seconds had clicked off the timer. They were heading for the two-minute mark.

The women exited the lift. A middle-aged man on a carebot got on. "8th floor, please."

"8th selected," the lift auto-voice said.

The man lifted one leg and adjusted its position. Bobbie reckoned he was going to the nanobiology department for treatment.

The lift stopped with fifty seconds remaining on Bobbie's timer. Luke positioned himself between the carebot and the door. It took the door three long seconds to open wide enough for Luke to squeeze through.

"Excuse us," Bobbie said, squeezing past the carebot.

They turned right and charged toward a set of glass security doors with intepanels down one side.

With seconds to spare, Luke presented himself.

An image of a revolving circle in one of the intepanels indicated that something was happening, then the words flashed up, "System update in process. Please wait."

"What the...?" Luke hissed.

Bobbie's counter hit zero. She felt like crying.

The intepanel flickered and then posted the message. "Identity verified."

Bobbie sighed with relief.

"Doctor Jinko is on his way," said Hicks' voice from a speaker above the intepanel.

Bobbie clamped a hand over her mouth. Her father's hand on her shoulder steadied her as Hicks' voice continued, "Please take a seat."

A section of the wall opened, and a bench slid forward. Bobbie sank onto it with Luke beside her.

Bobbie swallowed hard. "Do you think they have Hicks clones working there?"

"Probably," Luke said. "I can't see Hicks working for Belus."

Bobbie nodded. As much as she wished the real Hicks would appear at the door, it would mean he had sold them out. That would be too much to bear.

"Jesus, Bobbie, that's brutal." Joy's voice was like a soft breath in Bobbie's ear. "It was one thing having you fill me on the details, but to hear it myself... oh my God."

Bobbie's eyes prickled. She shoved her self-pity aside — no time for that. No energy either.

Luke and Bobbie looked up as the security door opened.

"Bobbie!" Jinko had lost weight. Looked like he'd aged ten years, though she'd last seen him only months ago. "What are you doing here?" His gaze flicked to Luke and again to Bobbie.

"We need to talk," Bobbie said, tapping her finger on her temple. "In private."

"Private?" Jinko arched an eyebrow. "Patient confidentiality private?"

"Exactly," Bobbie said, pleased he remembered a discussion they'd had with Davitt at the Genetics faculty social dinner about a year ago. New guidelines about patients over seventy not being permitted to mute their blinks during medical consultations had pissed Bobbie off. Davitt had sided with Belus, saying it was helpful for the elderly to have a record of the discussion, but Jinko and Bobbie had felt that if a patient wanted privacy, they should have it. That included turning off the surveillance in the examination room.

"But that's just futile," Davitt had pointed out. "Since Succor Tech had a record of everyone's biometrics through their biosensors, and that's available to Belus."

"But the patient might want to discuss sensitive topics – like E.P.," Jinko said.

Ultra-elderly patients were under immense pressure to consider Elective Passing, since the Dependency Law only permitted a couple to have a child after a death in the family. Bobbie agreed with Jinko that the ultra-elderly should have the right to discuss their options privately with their doctor.

"But doctors aren't permitted to discuss EP with their elderly patients." Davitt sat back and folded his arms, smug with the knowledge he had the law on his side of the debate.

"Exactly," Jinko had said, tapping his finger to his temple.

At that moment Bobbie had admired Jinko's humanity and had hated Davitt, but as the conversation drifted on, she told herself he would say anything to oppose Jinko. They had been colleagues, but also bitter competitors.

"We can talk in my office," Jinko said. "But I can't guarantee 'patient confidentiality.'"

The security doors closed behind them. Bobbie sensed Luke looking back.

There's no way to open the doors manually, Luke blinked to his daughters, *I hope we aren't trapped.* He gave Bobbie a sidelong glance.

"I'll work on that from here," Joy said through the vibro implants.

Bobbie looked at Jinko a few steps ahead of them. Their fate rested with him, and the future of humanity rested on Bobbie convincing him that they were the good guys in less than an hour. If she couldn't convince him that they were the good guys, how far she was willing to go to get the gentibots? Her hand closed around the last sedative jet in her pocket.

Byddi Lee

CHAPTER 10

Intepanels displayed rainforest views on the walls of Jinko's office, making it feel more spacious than it was. The chirps of birds harmonized with the clicks of cicadas in the background. An intedesk set up as a standing workstation against a wall left room in the middle for a small sofa and tub chair arranged around a low intedesk with an integrated matter streamer.

"Make yourselves comfortable." Jinko waved at the sofa, then clasped his hands to his chest and curled his fingers into white-knuckled fists. The thin elbows poking out under the short sleeves of his tunic, coupled with his mop of black hair, cast Bobbie's mind back decades to Mowgli from the *Jungle Book*. Gracie had loved the story, but Bobbie had always been too frightened for the little lost boy to enjoy the tale. Jinko sparked the same fear in her now.

"Can I offer you a drink?"

"Water's fine, thanks," Bobbie said, realizing her throat felt dry. She sat on the sofa.

Luke sat beside her. "Same for me, please."

Bobbie looked around the room – only one way in and out. If Belus realized they were here, they'd be trapped.

Joy, are camera transmissions blocked? Bobbie blinked.

"I've been filtering out your presence since you entered the building. It won't raise any flags, but if anyone decided to look at the output from that research facility, they'd know something was up. We're depending on sloppy human-screen interaction."

Jinko handed out glasses of water from the matter streamer, then settled in his chair across from where they sat on the sofa while Bobbie slugged down half the glass. She had to get this right on the first go. Jinko didn't have an inflated ego like Davitt, so she could be honest with him, but his extreme unease worried her. To be fair, her turning up under security escort might have triggered that. She leaned forward and set down her glass on the low intedesk between the sofa and tub chair.

"Jinko, this is my father, Luke Chan."

"But I thought your father–"

"No, not dead." She gave him a quick smile. "It's a long story, but many things are not as they seem."

Jinko lowered his eyes. His hands clasped and unclasped in his lap.

Panic fired in her chest. If he blinked Belus, Joy would know.

"We don't have much time," Bobbie said. "We're here about Rejuvenation."

Jinko's eyes widened, sweeping around the room. The color drained from his face. "We? Who's 'we'?"

"It's okay," Bobbie said. "We've blocked security footage. You can speak freely."

Jinko narrowed his eyes. "Is this some kind of trap?" He looked around the room. "Some kind of loyalty test? How can I 'speak freely'?"

"Because I'm a fugitive, and if Belus knew I was here, you'd notice." Bobbie poured confidence into her smile.

"You're a fugitive?" Jinko leaped to his feet. "You can't be here. I can't talk to you."

"Jinko," Bobbie said, digging deep to find a voice steadier and calmer than she felt. "You know me. You know we share the same values, the same ethos. I took the doctor's oath, do no harm – I'm trying to live by it. Belus is making that hard. How many times have we sided together against Davitt in an ethical debate?"

Jinko's eyes bored into hers. "This isn't some ethical debate. God! What have you done?"

"I'm trying to save lives."

Jinko took a step back. "Belus is too..."

"Powerful?" Luke said.

Jinko pressed his hands to his face. His ribcage rose and fell as he sucked in and blew out air too rapidly to be effective.

"We have friends," Luke said, standing up.

Jinko moved back another step.

"We aren't alone. There are more of us who can back you up." Luke stood still, his arms by his sides, palms out – harmless, welcoming.

"What's wrong?" Bobbie asked. "Talk to us, please."

Jinko glanced toward the door. His Adam's apple bobbed. Bobbie counted through long seconds, praying he wouldn't bolt.

"We can help you to fix Rejuvenation," she said.

Jinko shook his head, his brow furrowed.

"We need you, or we wouldn't risk coming here," Bobbie said.

"I have too much to lose if I get on the wrong side of Belus."

"What do you mean?" Luke asked.

Jinko looked to the corners of the room. The cameras were well hidden, but Bobbie knew they were there.

"Trust me, we have someone blocking all transmission from this room," she said.

"Trust you? Trust you?" Jinko looked on the verge of tears. "Bobbie, they have my family. If they find out you came here, God knows what they'll do to them!"

Her stomach tightened.

"Jesus! No wonder I had so much trouble patching in that fake blink to security," Joy said to Bobbie and Luke through their vibro-implants.

"God, Jinko, I'm sorry," Bobbie said. "We didn't know."

"Now you see why you have to go! Or I do. Before it's too late." He bolted for the door.

Bobbie and Luke sprang after him. Luke grabbed his arm and spun him around.

"Stop," said Luke. "It's too late. Belus will find out we came here. They'll think you're in cahoots with us."

"No!" Jinko said, wild-eyed.

His desperation broke Bobbie's heart. She reached for his hand. He snatched it away.

"We're your only hope now," she said gently. "Where is your family?"

"Last I heard, my wife and daughter were in northern Alaska. That new settlement in Kobuk Valley."

"I can send a unit for his family right now," Joy said. "You guys need to get out as soon as possible."

"I know it well," Luke said. "We have operatives in that area."

"Operatives? What are you talking about?"

"We're sending someone to get them now."

"You-you can do that?" Jinko shook himself. "I don't believe you. This is a trap. Belus sent you." He looked up into the corners of the room and spoke, "I've done everything you asked. Please don't hurt them."

"They can't hear you," Bobbie said. "We have someone blocking the footage."

"Who?"

Luke and Bobbie exchanged a glance.

"Tell me – a name – who is helping you? If you really have the drop on Belus here. If you're really that safe, then tell me who is helping you."

"Bobbie, tell him I was right about Davitt," Joy said. "We met at that crappy party Davitt had to celebrate his fellowship. Jinko will remember me. I said Davitt was full of shit. We spiked Davitt's drink with laxative, but he spilled it before he could drink it."

Luke narrowed his eyes as he sent a blink to Bobbie and Joy, *If he doesn't cooperate it compromises you too Joy.*

"I'm already compromised. Belus knows me now."

Bobbie looked into Jinko's haunted eyes and said, "My sister, Joy. She says she was right about Davitt."

Jinko's face brightened a shade. "No shit," he murmured.

Joy laughed. "That's what we said when Davitt knocked over his drink."

"Davitt didn't drink the laxative," Bobbie said.

"It doesn't prove you aren't working for Belus –" Jinko rubbed his hands over his face and paced.

Luke made to move toward him, but Bobbie placed her hand on her father's arm. "You know Joy. Do you really think–"

"Okay, okay." Jinko pushed his hair back from his forehead with both hands, elbows pointing skywards, and exhaled. "So can you really send help to my family?"

"We can," Luke said.

"Found them." Joy sounded triumphant. "I can patch a message from Jinko into his wife's Foureyes."

As Luke relayed the information, Jinko slumped into the tub chair and rubbed his face with his palms.

"Jinko, I need you to look at me," Luke said. "You can send a message to your wife on my Foureyes so she'll know to go with our people. They'll say they're Candels and that you sent them."

"Right now?"

"Yes – just talk. Your wife is looking at you through my eyes, using my Foureyes b-app."

Jinko stared into Luke's face. "Anisa, can you hear me?"

"She can," Luke said. "Ask her a question only she'll know the answer to, and she'll do the same for you."

"Anisa, what was our first fight about?"

Luke's lips twitched. "She says she didn't mean to break your Hatchimal."

Jinko beamed. "Oh, she knew what she was doing. But okay, what's her question?"

"What color was her wedding bouquet?"

Jinko narrowed his eyes. "She didn't have one."

"And what else?"

His eye lit up. "She had red roses on an umbrella instead."

"Okay, she's happy with that. Are you happy to proceed?"

Jinko nodded.

"Okay, go, she's listening."

"Listen carefully. You're in danger. Take Yasmine right now and leave the house. Do what Joy tells you. Be ready to go with people who identify themselves as the Candels. I'm sending them to you to take you somewhere safe. I'm sorry, honey. Please go with them quickly. I – I love you both."

"She says they love you too," Luke said. "As soon as it's safe to, we'll patch you into them directly."

Jinko gave a shuddering exhale and nodded.

Thanks, Joy. Bobbie said.

Jinko sat forward. "My mother – she's in assisted living in New Zealand. She needs a lot of care."

"Oh shit," Joy said. "How old she is?"

Bobbie asked Jinko, who replied, "Seventy, why?"

Bobbie relayed the information to Jinko as Joy fed it to her. "She's probably fine. She's still young. The ultra-elderly have all been exposed to Davitt's virus. But if your mother's immune system is weak, she'll have been Rejuvenated."

Jinko jumped up. "They released the fucking virus?"

"Yes! Thousands have been infected. That's why we're here."

His chin quivered. "She's one of them, then," he said in a small voice. "She had vaccine-resistant cancer last year. The last time I talked to her, she had a cold. A fucking cold? Who gets a cold now? Her immune system is fucked. Dammit!" He kicked the tub chair.

Bobbie gave him a minute, watching despair replace the anger in his eyes, then said, "Davitt told me that you were working on a nanobot that could dismantle the Rejuvenation nanobots without harming the host. That's why we need you to come with us."

"I can't leave." Jinko paced. "They pumped me full of nano-trackers. I'm not allowed off the property, or..."

"Shit!" Joy said in Bobbie's ear.

"But you do have the gentibots," said Bobbie.

"Look, Belus wasn't interested in that research. My resources are limited. I only had one test subject." He looked at the ground. "He isn't aware of the fact he's a test subject."

Bobbie clenched her teeth – another person experimented upon without their permission.

Jinko went on, "It hasn't been completely successful yet. Patient 17–"

"Patient 17," Bobbie burst out. "He's a person. He has a *name*."

Jinko frowned and bit his lip. "Sorry. You're right, but I don't know their names."

"Ask him–"

"They don't know their names."

"Jesus Christ," Bobbie said, horrified. "They? How many are there?"

"There were thirty in this study. I was only able to get the gentibots into one of them –Patient 17. I was going to see how that went and then try the gentibots with another patient, but others became too violent too quickly, and were taken away."

"Where?" Bobbie asked.

"I don't know... a secure unit at the PARC, I presume. I wasn't party to that information. I developed the gentibots before Belus decided to keep me here." Jinko shook his head, slump-shouldered. "They don't care about the gentibots. But I saw they were necessary..." Tears welled up in his eyes.

"You did the right thing," Bobbie said.

"Thanks," Jinko muttered, and fisted the tears away. "I injected all the gentibots I had in that first run into Patient 17. He remained Rejuvenated, that is, young and fit after the nanobots were dismantled, which was an unexpected outcome. Some other major issues need to be fixed, but he didn't progress to violence the way the others had."

"Why did you treat only one patient?" Luke asked, blinking Bobbie at the same time, *Half an hour and we need to split. We must get him to bring his work with him.*

"I wanted to treat them all, but I was worried about something going wrong and it killing..." Jinko pressed his lips together and shook his head.

Bobbie sat forward. "We understand."

Jinko sucked in a deep breath. "I had to try. We have to bring him with us. All the gentibots I made are inside him. I haven't had a chance to make more."

"Is it possible he has nano-trackers?"

"They can't track him. The gentibots are programmed to dismantle any nanomachinery they find."

Bobbie stood up. "Can he walk?"

"Yes, but..." Jinko struggled to compose himself. "I can't go. It's too dangerous. I still have nano-trackers. It would take too long to extract any of them from Patient 17 to use on me."

"Patient 17 – is the room set up with medical equipment? Since he's referred to as a patient, I was just wondering."

"Yes, but just the basics. No surgical equipment."

"Cardiac paddles?"

Jinko nodded. "In the first aid room next to his, but we've never used them. Why?"

"An electric charge would wipe out your nano-trackers."

Jinko's face lit up. "Of course!"

"But there's a risk–"

"I have to destroy these nano-trackers, or I can't leave." He ran his hand through his mop of hair and squeezed his eyes shut. He opened them and looked at Bobbie. "You're sure my wife and daughters will be safe?"

"Yes," Joy said.

Bobbie nodded.

"Then it's my only option. Bobbie, I trust you. You're a doctor." Jinko smiled and moved toward the door. "Zap my nano-trackers, and I'll help you get Patient 17 and go with you."

"We need to hurry," Luke said. "We have about twenty minutes."

Bobbie strode to the door. "What are we waiting for?"

Bobbie and Luke followed Jinko down the corridor and into a lab with workstations staffed by half a dozen grey-tuniced workers. A couple close by nodded at Jinko and gave Bobbie and Luke a quick glance, but no-one seemed curious about their presence. Bobbie wondered if they all had nano-trackers and families at the mercy of Belus Corp.

The intepanels in the hallway leading from the other side of the lab flicked on as they triggered the motion sensors. Regularly-spaced doors ran the length of the hall. Luke nudged Bobbie and nodded to the stairwell at the end of the corridor – an escape route.

One door had a green cross. Jinko opened it and popped his head inside. He looked back at Bobbie and Luke. "In here."

The room reminded Bobbie of the consultation rooms in her hospital – sparse, functional. Cardiac paddles hung on the wall above a narrow trolley-bed.

"Hop up," she said. "We'll leave a trace of blood here as a decoy, so the nano-trackers' signal doesn't disappear completely." She searched the drawers. "Dammit!'

"What?" Luke asked.

"There's no way to draw blood. With biosensors, there's no need to." She lifted out a tray of scalpels and scissors.

Jinko nodded at the scalpel. "That will do."

"It won't take a minute – just a scratch."

Jinko flinched as Bobbie dug the blade into his forearm. Blood oozed up and dripped into a petri dish. She dressed the cut with wound glue.

"Good as new." She smiled, leaving the petri dish tucked into the corner of the countertop. "But the next part will be very uncomfortable."

Jinko lay back. "Worth it."

Bobbie opened an intepanel data screen on the wall. "Touch your pinkie to that screen, please."

Jinko touched the screen, and his biosensors hooked into the data stream on the intepanel.

"Your vitals are healthy. Heart rate's a little high, but that's understandable." Bobbie lifted the paddles from the wall. "Dad, stand back."

Luke moved away as Bobbie opened Jinko's tunic. She lifted the paddles and pressed the "on" switch. Nothing happened - no sharp electronic whine of them charging. The red light blinked on, indicating they were drawing current from the mains, but the green light – "good to go" – didn't come on after the usual three-second wait.

"Shit! They're not working." Bobbie threw the paddles down and pulled open cupboard doors. "Look for a black case with red and yellow striped labels on it."

"Here!" Luke pulled the box out from under the trolley-bed.

Bobbie unclipped the latch and opened the lid. "Fuckit! The battery needs charged. Fuck! Fuck! Fuck!" She slammed the lid and locked the case.

"How long will that take?" Luke asked.

"Too long." Bobbie put her hand on Jinko's shoulder as he sat up. "We can take the paddles with us and zap you in the hovercar."

"Too risky. Belus will follow you and shoot us all down," Jinko said, shrugging her hand away. He lifted the hard foam pillow from the trolley bed and handed it to Bobbie. "Here, hold this. You'll know what to do."

He grabbed the malfunctioning paddles and yanked them out of the wall. He swung a hand forward and touched the back of it to the dangling wires. A bang, a shower of sparks, and the intepanels went out as the current flung Jinko across the room.

In the blue hue from the emergency LEDs, Bobbie ran to Jinko as he lay propped against the wall. She hadn't needed the foam pillow. He'd been thrown clear of the current. With bated breath, she felt for his pulse.

Nothing.

"Dad, get him flat on the ground."

Luke pulled Jinko's legs. Bobbie thumped her fist down onto Jinko's chest twice before straightening her arms and pumping to the count, "One and two and three and four."

After thirty compressions, she bent over, placing her cheek above Jinko's mouth. "Dad, keep up the heart massage exactly as I was doing."

Luke locked his elbows and started pumping as Bobbie put her fingers below Jinko's chin and tipped his head back. She held his nose, sealed his lips with hers and blew hard twice, watching his chest rise and fall with her breath.

She counted off thirty more of Luke's compressions and bent over to give Jinko two more breaths. Warm air tickled her cheek.

"He's alive. He's breathing."

Luke stopped.

Bobbie checked Jinko's pulse. "It's weak, but it's there."

"Thank fuck!" Luke sat back on his heels and rubbed his face.

Bobbie examined the burn marks on Jinko's hands. They'd heal. Her heart thundered as her fingertips moved over the back of his head and down his neck. He'd been thrown with a wallop, but nothing seemed to be broken.

She felt like hugging him as his eyelashes fluttered open and he said, "That ought to do the job." He winced and sat forward, tentatively shaking out his arms and legs.

Luke put out his hand. "You're fucking crazy, man!"

"Desperate times." Jinko grabbed Luke's hand and pulled himself to his feet. "Let's go before maintenance arrives and give us a hard time for wrecking the equipment." He took a wobbly step forward and almost fell before Luke caught him.

Bobbie held up the portable paddles. "I'll take this."

Jinko left the room. Luke followed him. Bobbie walked into the back of Luke, who had stopped abruptly in the doorway. She heard a woman's voice saying, "What did you do in there? We have a maintenance alarm."

"I'm giving a tour to a visiting doctor. It's highly embarrassing that we had an electric short circuit as I tried to demonstrate our facilities."

"Maintenance will be along right now. Jinko, you need to file a report right away."

"I'm just about to do that, Sara, but I do still have a visiting doctor. Belus want them to see Patient 17. I'll come to your office in half an hour. Okay?"

"Fine. Carry on."

Bobbie joined Luke and Jinko in the corridor.

"Who was that?" she asked Jinko, taking in his pallor but satisfied he was fit to keep going.

"She's admin, likes to throw her weight about. And is probably embarrassed she didn't know we were having a visiting doctor, and wouldn't admit it by asking who you were." Jinko walked to the room at the end of the hall and knocked on the door twice. He didn't wait for an answer, just opened the door, and said, "Hi, I've brought some visitors."

Jinko turned to Bobbie and Luke and beckoned them into the room with a curl of his fingers. Luke stepped back, letting Bobbie enter first.

Patient 17 rose from his chair to greet them.

Bobbie stopped in her tracks.

"Hello," Patient 17 said, his voice, his face, his body, his stature, the way his grey eyes crinkled as he smiled - exactly like Hicks. Was it him or another clone?

"Hicks?" Bobbie said, taking a step forward.

He locked eyes with her, and her heart skittered.

"Is it really you?" She drank him in. All the other clones had something not right about them, but this man ... everything matched, everything was him.

Patient 17 shrugged, the smile faded. "I don't know. I woke up in this room, and that's all I know."

CHAPTER 11

Patient 17 stared past Bobbie. She watched him, willing their lifelong connection to exert a force over him that would make him turn in her direction, to seek her out the way he used to.

She reached to touch his arm. He flinched.

"I would never hurt you," she managed through a tightening throat.

"Bobbie." Jinko moved between her and the man. "Go easy."

"But I know him—"

"She knows me?" Patient 17 pressed forward. "Who am I?"

"Look, nobody can say for certain," Jinko said. "It's complicated."

"So you keep telling me. I'm sick of this!"

"But—" Bobbie began.

"Let me sort this out." Jinko took Bobbie's elbow and guided her toward the door, saying in a voice too low for Patient 17 to hear, "You may know the source DNA, but all our patients look like this man – all thirty of them."

Jinko looked at the floor and hummed a tuneless tune. She'd seen him do this before when he was thinking hard. Davitt had often scoffed at Jinko's "odd way."

Bobbie glanced back at Patient 17, pacing by the bed and grumbling to Luke, "It's too much, just too much." He looked as bewildered as Bobbie felt. She longed to embrace him, melt into him, have him hold her and hear him whisper, "I'm here."

"Maybe this is Hicks. Maybe this is why he's not become violent," she insisted to Jinko. "He looks so like him – his expressions."

Jinko stopped humming. "Who's Hicks?"

Luke's voice held an edge of warning. "Bobbie, let it go. Now's not the time."

Her father was right. Jinko probably still thought Davitt was her boyfriend.

"Someone important to me," She said. "Are you certain they all look this much...look like... this man?"

"Yeah, they all look exactly like this guy," Jinko said. Bobbie's hope crashed around her. Pressure pulsed in her head. *Think*, she told herself, *what can this mean?* Where did she go from here? She pressed her hands to her eyes.

Luke said, "Sir, take your belongings and come with us."

Bobbie pulled her hands from her face and watched Patient 17 nod. Confusion creased his brow as his eyes swung from Luke to Bobbie. Her heart snagged on his expression – familiar yet distant.

He caught her staring. "Who do you think I am? Tell me."

"A doctor, Ryan Hicks," Bobbie said. "Does that spark any memory?"

Jinko whistled through his teeth, looked to the ceiling, and shook his head.

Patient 17 pursed his lips. "No." His expression darkened. He lunged at Bobbie and caught her by the shoulder of her tunic. "What the fuck did you people do to me?"

Bobbie stumbled back. "I didn't do–"

"Watch yourself," Luke growled, moving in front of Bobbie and staring Patient 17 down.

Patient 17 stepped back. "I need to know."

"You need some manners. She's trying to help you. And we need to leave now!"

"I'm going nowhere till I get answers."

Luke walked to the door. "Look, you've got two choices. Stay here with the people who fucked you over, or come with us and learn the truth."

"Dad, don't."

Patient 17's nostrils flared. His breath came in rasps.

Jinko jumped in beside him. "Calm down. Deep breaths... Like we've done before."

Patient 17 did as instructed, staring at the floor. Bobbie had witnessed Hicks have a panic attack less than two months ago. They were in the ventilation shaft at the research facility when they rescued Granny. When the hatch didn't open, he'd been seized by terror, thrashing about in the confined space, hyperventilating.

Jinko spoke softly to Patient 17. "They want to help you. Trust them. You trust me, don't you?"

"Yes."

"Then trust me. I'm coming too."

Patient 17 shrugged. "Okay."

"Let's go," Bobbie said. "We'll take the stairs. Lead the way, Jinko."

The corridor was empty. If they met someone, Bobbie wasn't sure she'd be able to hold it together. Her brain was stretched tight. Patient 17 crammed her senses. He moved like Hicks, looked like him, sounded like him. Christ Almighty, he even smelled like him, but something was missing. It was as if he'd been scoured out, and this hollowness petrified her.

This guy could be Hicks, or Hicks could be one of the thirty crazy guys in the rest of this group or another group in another research facility.

Repetition of results makes the results more reliable.

The mantra had been drummed into her at every step of her scientific education. Christ Almighty, how many other groups might there be? Or maybe Belus had Hicks on his own somewhere else. Either way, Fox was baiting Bobbie, making this personal in the sickest possible way.

They made it to the stairwell, the pat-pat of their feet the only sound as they descended eight flights. Bobbie stared at the back of Patient 17's head as she followed. He needed a haircut. The ends of the brown crew-cut flopped at his ears as he jogged. Jinko had said Patient 17 had been a Rejuvenee, but he had Hicks' grey eyes, not the orange of the Rejuvenated. This man seemed fit and healthy. No bruises, no signs of injury. Maybe the rejuvenation nanobots had sped up his healing process.

Granny's rejuvenation had seemed slower, but everything Bobbie had witnessed since then pointed to Fox tweaking the nanobiology, using new DNA and somehow speeding up the effects of the rejuvenation nanobots. The gentibots might only have dismantled the rejuvenation nanobots, but what else were they capable of? She needed a long debriefing with Jinko. *Concentrate on the science*, she told herself. That might ground her better. None of it would matter if they didn't make it out.

They reached the ground floor. The stairs continued down to basement floors, but on this level, a set of heavy fire doors led back into the central atrium of the building. Opposite, an emergency exit led outside, judging by the view through the glass. The ground sloped away as they looked down the mountainside.

Jinko checked the walls on either side of the glass doors. "There's no key code panels."

"No need. It's an emergency exit, low-tech in case the electricity is cut. Will that trigger an alarm?" Luke asked, pointing at the manual push handle on the doors.

"I guess so," Jinko answered, but Bobbie knew her father wasn't asking him.

"It will, and I can't stop it." Joy's voice came through on the vibro-implants. "It's an internally wired circuit. The best I can do is keep the cameras shut off. Once that goes off, the chase is on."

Bobbie turned on her m-app and selected the coordinates for where she'd stashed Gustav's head and the butterflies near the designated hovercraft landing point. The green arrow showed up as she looked west, into the building. "Shit. We're on the wrong side of the building."

"You're going to have to run for it," Joy said. "I have to... Look probably nothing but... I'll ...posted."

Joy? Bobbie looked at Luke.

He shrugged. *We've been lucky with comms so far... it happens. Joy will figure out a workaround.* Luke turned to Jinko and Patient 17 and said, "We need to run; can you manage?"

They both nodded.

Patient 17 began, "But why—"

"Trust them," Jinko said. "They'll help you, but first we have to get somewhere safe."

Patient 17 looked around. His eyes caught Bobbie's. She felt a jolt as his gaze softened a fraction. He nodded and said, "I trust you." He looked away and smiled at Luke, plunging Bobbie into the cold again.

Luke shoved the emergency exit open and looked back at the others, then up into the air above his head, wide-eyed in the silence.

"C'mon," he said, holding the door open. "An alarm could be going off in a control room somewhere, and we can't hear it. If Joy has the cameras blocked, they might think it's a fault. Follow Bobbie."

Bobbie led them downhill, dodging clumps of giant hogweed, scraping between scruffy shrubs, jumping over rocks and skidding on gravel. They needed to turn left, but the building was in the way. Bobbie didn't want to go too close to the AI detector paint, so she guided the others down through rough ground away from the research facility. The taller stands of hogweed would hide them from view. Her m-app calculated a new route that would leave them ten minutes late for the hovercraft.

Can you slow the hovercraft? Bobbie blinked Joy, unwilling to risk making unnecessary noise.

"Sorry, no," Joy sounded distracted.

Joy? What the fuck was she doing? Bobbie didn't know if the hovercraft would be able to land, and if it did, would it be vulnerable to the security team from the research facility? Had Belus guards been called in by now? Why wasn't Joy keeping them updated?

It's been a half-hour since we sedated those security men, Luke blinked, *If we're really lucky, they're the ones who should be monitoring the emergency exits. Or maybe they came out through one to get to us, and that's why the system didn't sound off.*

New coordinates arrived at Bobbie's m-app *Meet the hovercar here*

The new landing spot was easier to reach from this point, but a mile northwest from where Bobbie had stashed the butterflies and Gustav's head.

"Take them straight to the hovercar," Bobbie said to Luke. Not wanting to freak the others out, she blinked, *I'll go for the butterflies and the head.*

Luke rubbed his hand down his face. "Go. We'll pick you up."

The men peeled off, traversing the contour of the hill as Bobbie charged upward. Muscles in her calves and thighs screamed. A stitch niggled in her side.

She needed those butterflies more than ever now. They might mention Hicks and rule out Patient 17 as a candidate. If Hicks were still being held in a PARC, his name and location would be in those files.

Her breathing labored to keep up with her muscles. Her heart pounded. Sweat soaked her skin. Her sensorfabric was unable to keep up with wicking the moisture away. She berated herself for leaving the butterflies with the damn head. The butterflies were light enough to carry. She could have left the head behind. Slade would never know how her brother died, but in the scheme of things, Slade having that closure was a small grace.

Bobbie hadn't far to go, but the gradient steepened. Plant life dwindled. The terrain turned to gravel and scree. She slid, lurched forward, and scrambled up on all fours. A lone tuft of grass became a handhold. Hauling her aching limbs up the slope, Bobbie crested the rise. The arrow showed she had a short downhill jaunt to reach the place where she had stashed her parcel. With a fresh burst of energy, Bobbie jogged and skidded down to the GPS position.

The brush had been pushed aside, the rocks scattered. The bag wasn't there.

She stared at the spot as if that might make the parcel materialize in front of her. There was nothing but a damp circle of soil and flakes of plastic snagged on a nearby bush. A line of darkened earth ran downhill from the main patch and disappeared beneath the splayed leaves of a stand of giant hogweed.

"Wee bastards," Bobbie hissed. She had hidden the bag from people, but the aroma of freshly-thawed human head must have attracted some mountain critter.

She eyed the hogweed. Physical contact with its sap would sensitize her skin to ultraviolet radiation, causing irritation and blistering. She yanked the neckline of her tunic up to her chin and tugged her sleeves over her hands and dove into the stand, following the trail of ribboned plastic and the dark line in the dirt.

She almost cheered when she saw human hair. The thieving critter – a ferret or a polecat by the size of the bite marks – had chewed at the neck, going for the easy meat. The skin on the corpse's face was tattered from where it had broken through the plastic bag when dragged over gravel. Most of the bag was intact. Bobbie grabbed it and searched inside.

No butterflies.

She felt like weeping. To think all this planning could be unraveled because she hadn't considered interference from a fucking weasel. Bobbie bent and gathered the head into the remains of the bag. Skin on her forehead tingled where she'd brushed against hogweed. She searched the ground. "Please God, don't let those fucking ferrets, or foxes, or whatever the fuck–"

"Bobbie?" Joy's voice made Bobbie jump, so she nearly dropped Gustav's head.

"Where the fuck have you been?"

"I can't explain now. Don't... Okay?"

"Don't what, Joy?" Bobbie said, backing out from under the hogweed, searching the ground. "Joy? Come in. Can you hear me? Joy?"

"The place Gracie loved... there..."

"Say again. You're breaking up."

Nothing.

Dad, did you get that? Bobbie blinked to Luke.

Some words here and there. Did she mention Gracie?

But it didn't make sense. What's going on?

Comms playing up. Hovercar here. Nearly there.

Out from under the hogweed leaves, Bobbie straightened up, but her eyes still raked the ground. A sparkle of sunlight reflected.

"Yes!" Bobbie pounced on the butterfly and spotted the other one six inches from it. She felt like dancing, but the sudden thrum of multiple hovercrafts pulled her attention skyward.

She froze.

High overhead, a fleet of a dozen Belus Hovercraft flew in formation like malignant geese.

Her instinct was to run back to the hogweed for cover. Then she realized that the hovercrafts were too high to be searching these hills. Her forehead stung as the sun's rays burned where sap from the giant hogweed had sensitized her skin, but she kept her face lifted, watching. Were the hovercrafts chasing someone? Bobbie searched the skies for a lone craft. Her father was a skilled pilot, but could he outrun military crafts in a civilian hovercar?

A blink from Luke *You see that?*

Yes, what does it mean?

It means I can't take off until they're gone. Can you make it to me?

Bobbie eyed the ridge. Her legs ached. Her forehead burned. Fatigue clawed at her. One mile – only one mile. *Think so.*

Good girl, take it steady. Those crafts have bigger fish to fry.

Bobbie reset the m-app with the new coordinates. It wasn't that far away, on the other side of the ridge from her. She took stock of the gradient with a sinking heart and set off at a stumbling jog.

A fifteen-minute heart-bursting climb took her to the ridge top. Looking back the way she'd come, she saw guards milling around the perimeter of the research facility. She ducked behind a rock. On the other side of the ridge, she spotted the vent where they'd left the shaft to escape Belus Corp headquarters.

Below her, the research security seemed to be in chaos. They ran randomly from the facility into the brush, then back to the buildings. She didn't spot any Belus guards, and gave thanks for small mercies. On wobbly legs, she dropped down on the other side, hugging the contour of the hill until she rounded an outcrop of rocks. There was the hovercar, with her father at the helm.

She climbed in, winded, but grateful to give her body a rest. She greeted Jinko and Patient 17. Her heart skidded at seeing Hicks' face, the familiar expression devoid of connection as he seemed to actively ignore her. He wrinkled his nose at the smell coming from her parcel. Would Hicks have done that? He was a doctor, but that didn't

84

mean he was immune to pungent smells. She put the tattered plastic bag, complete with its contents, in an airtight storage bag and secured them in a locker before taking her seat.

"Are they looking for us?" Bobbie asked Luke, nodding skyward.

"I don't think so. If they were, they would have found us. What happened to your face?"

Bobbie caught her reflection in the glass windscreen. A line of yellow blisters, as wide as her pinkie, rose just below her hairline.

"Giant hogweed sap." She winced, but that hurt more. "Any word from Joy?"

"Nothing since that last exchange with you." Luke checked the radar.

"Didn't you think it was a bit weird?"

"Everyone's been up for twenty-four hours straight. We're all a bit wired."

Bobbie stared at him.

He patted her hand. "Look, try not to worry, sweetheart. A storm might have damaged the comms antennae. Joy might have decided to rest while the techies are fixing it."

He was more used to these escapades than she was; maybe he was right. She watched the last of the fleet disappear off the edge of the screen.

Luke started the hovercraft and looked around at his passengers. "Buckle up. We're on the move."

They lifted off and headed east, following the Belus hovercrafts.

"Wouldn't we be safer going a different way? Maybe head north?" Bobbie asked.

"We've no idea where they're going. Better stick to the regular air routes like the rest of the population. We blend in better."

Regular traffic was light. Bobbie wondered where the people in the hovercars passing them were going, what daily commute they were completing. She felt a pang for the banality of their lives, of the life she'd been dragged from only a couple of months ago. But at least she remembered that life.

"There might be a way to find out who you are," Bobbie said, turning to Patient 17.

"How?" He stared at her with Hicks' eyes, fracturing her concentration.

Beside him, Jinko raised an eyebrow – *really?*

Bobbie pulled herself together. "Everyone's biosensors are registered at Succor Tech. The rejuvenation nanobots won't have changed their configuration, since they're only programmed to change DNA. The gentibots target only other nanobots. Right?"

Jinko nodded.

"We have people who might be able to hack into the system and figure out who you are."

"How long will it take?" Patient 17 asked.

Bobbie closed her eyes, drew a breath. "I don't know."

"Great," Patient 17 grunted. "I'll know my name. But unless it sparks something else, am I any better off?"

She opened her eyes again but kept them lowered, shaking her head. "It would be a start."

Luke turned to Bobbie. "You okay?"

"Yes," she lied, returning her gaze to Patient 17. He now watched Luke with brooding eyes, any concern for her absent. Surely Hicks would worry about her? She shivered.

Her father took a long look at her before adding, "You look done in, sweetheart. Try to get some rest. You've done a great job. We'll be back at the Norway base in a couple of hours. I'll be sticking this on autopilot for a bit so I can rest myself."

Bobbie longed to pick Jinko's brains, but hers was fuzzy, having lost a night's sleep. The combined motion and hum of the engine weighed her eyelids. Despite the sting in her forehead, she floated off into hazy scenarios of reuniting with Hicks, only to have him turn away and disappear. She jerked awake.

"Hey, sleepyhead," Luke said. "You were out for the count. We'll be there soon."

"Really? Have you heard from Joy?"

Luke frowned. "No. It's not like her to leave us so long."

"Do the comms often go down like this?"

"Sometimes," Luke said, shrugging. "But it's usually not for this long."

"How worried are you?"

Luke pursed his lips. "Somewhat."

Bobbie watched the Norwegian Sea glitter through the patchy clouds below them. Traffic peeled off the air-route toward the towns tucked into the nooks of the serrated coastline. Other craft joined the air-route, zipping north or south as the autopilots kept them each in line.

"This is our fjord below us," Luke said. "The ship'll be hidden with an electronic screen till I get closer and deploy the anti-masking code."

Bobbie felt the lean as the craft turned into the green jaws of the U-shaped valley. They stayed high, watching the fjord below them. A cloud obscured their view. Luke kept his attention on the control panel.

Bobbie sniffed. "That smells like smoke."

Luke adjusted the controls. They rose higher, out of the cloud. "There hasn't been a forest fire here in years. It's too damp since the climate switched to tropical."

Higher now, they could see the plume of smoke. Bobbie followed its funnel to where it originated.

"Our ship's on fire!" she cried. "Joy! Oh, God, where's Joy?"

"Shit!" Luke pulled the hovercraft into a turn. "They've no electronic screening."

Several smaller hovercraft floated in the water further down the fjord. One had three children, probably preteens, standing on its roof. A Belus craft burst through the smoke and zeroed in on the crafts, blasting them with laser fire.

"No!" Bobbie screamed as the hovercrafts and children disappeared below the water.

"Jesus Christ!" Jinko said. "Belus ... killing children?"

"We're fucked!" Patient 17 screamed at Jinko. "What did you get me into, you fuckers?"

"It's not about you, asshole!" Luke spat as he worked the control panel, turning their hovercraft. Bobbie lost sight of the burning ship. She was plastered against the seat as they sped up, whizzing past Belus crafts as Luke took them manually overland, skimming the contorted landscape.

Bobbie looked back to see the old ship caving in, chugging coils of black smoke through the wafting grey before the whole thing exploded in a fury of orange and black.

CHAPTER 12

Clouds, boulders, lakes sped past. Luke worked the controls like a magician. Every so often, they felt a shudder, and sparks flew as laser fire clipped their fuselage. Luke hugged treetops and river beds. Bobbie hung on, hardly breathing, preparing for bone-breaking impact. She felt useless. Neck rigid, feet pressed to the floor, she gripped her armrests so hard her fingertips hurt.

Luke dropped the craft into a canyon. The laser fire blasted showers of rocks off the canyon sides. They surged forward along the straighter sections, then swung around the bends. Luke pulled up. A white blip appeared on the radar – a craft behind them.

"Shit!" Luke said, plunging them between layers of rock. The canyon narrowed. Bobbie looked back. The Belus craft slung around the corner.

"They're catching up." She faced forward. A cliff face loomed straight ahead. Bobbie raised her arms. Her head snapped to one side as the hovercraft turned. She looked back and saw a Belus craft hit the cliff, swallowed by a fireball that fractured into black clouds and flying metal.

Luke pulled the hovercraft up out of the gully. No more blips showed on their radar screen.

"Have you lost the others?" Bobbie asked, her voice raspy.

"Maybe," Luke said without slacking off speed. "Or they may be flying too low to pick up. I'll know in a few seconds when we're over flat terrain."

Jinko swiveled in his seat, ducking and bobbing to scan the skies around them. He turned to Bobbie and Luke, eyes popping, sweat dripping down his forehead.

"What the fuck just happened? You said you had people who could keep me safe, keep my family safe." Jinko stabbed a finger in the direction they'd come from. "That was not safe. If you can't keep your own people safe, what hope do I have?"

"Look, we don't know what's happened for sure," Luke said. "When we rendezvous with our people, we'll get more information."

"But my family?" Jinko slammed his hand on his armrest. "What about them?"

"Listen, you're not the only one with family in danger," Bobbie snapped. "We're doing our best."

Jinko rubbed his face. He deflated back into his seat. Patient 17 looked from Bobbie to Jinko as though expecting more. Jinko dropped his gaze and rocked, humming a non-tune.

Patient 17 poked Jinko's shoulder and said, "That's it? You gonna let them talk to you like this?"

Jinko shrugged him off and shrank into himself. His hands shook even as he folded them tight against his chest.

"Hey?"

No one answered Patient 17.

"Where are we going?" Patient 17 asked in a louder voice.

Luke threw him a dirty look. "Zip it for now, alright?"

"Just asking–"

"Don't."

Bobbie's stomach swooped as the craft dropped into flat countryside. Below them, dense vegetation pocked with lakes like green lace. They were somewhere over the lowlands of Sweden or Finland – Bobbie wasn't sure. Either way, she knew that the inhabitants of this once densely populated area had succumbed to swamp and fever when the global water-table had risen. If they crashed here, they might never be found.

Jinko sat ashen-faced, humming tunelessly.

Patient 17 jigged his leg. The movement carried into Bobbie's seat, jangling her already frazzled nerves.

"Crazy... fucking crazy. I want answers... It's a fucking war zone. Should have let me be...You're all crazy," Patient 17 muttered in a loop, quietly enough for Bobbie to miss parts of his litany but loud enough for it to grate on her. She gritted her teeth.

The land disappeared, and they swept over water. Luke kept the craft low. The radar remained empty.

"I think we've lost them." Luke didn't lower his speed as he opened a comms intescreen. "Radio backup connector base."

Bobbie raised an eyebrow, felt the blisters on her forehead catch and sting.

"Radio signal," Luke said. "It can be more robust than ONIV based comms."

"Broadcasting signal frequency 318.69," announced the control-panel speaker.

"Blackbird, Blackbird, this is Lost-at-Sea. Come in."

Bobbie cringed at her father's handle. He'd been lost at sea, presumed dead – even by her. It struck deep that he'd chosen this as his radio handle with the Candels. Was Joy Blackbird? She held her breath, waited for a reply, prayed.

Nothing.

"Blackbird, come in."

Silence blared.

Luke repeated the call.

Nothing.

"Oh, God." Bobbie covered her mouth.

"Don't read into it," Luke said, gently taking Bobbie's hand. "No reply only means Joy can't reply, and that can be for a host of reasons. She may have no power. That old ONIV she's using might be playing up. It doesn't necessarily mean anything... bad."

Bobbie swallowed the lump in her throat and squeaked, "I know."

But she didn't know. All she knew was that two of the people she loved most in the world were missing, and she couldn't help either of them.

"In the last communications, Joy was distracted," Bobbie said. "Maybe she was warned about the attack. Maybe they were able to flee the Norway base." She felt sick with her next thought. "But Joy wouldn't have left children behind, would she?"

"Emergency evacuations are messy," Luke said. "We've had them before. Kids are..." His voice wobbled. "They're hard to manage, especially the older ones. They might have been off-ship when the evacuation started."

Bobbie closed her eyes, but still saw the children on the sinking hovercraft being shot to bits by Belus.

She shivered. What were Joy's last broken communications?

Look, probably nothing, but...

That was when they were still in Patients 17's room. Maybe that's when they got the alert.

Was that why Joy hadn't been able to help them slow the self-drive hovercraft's arrival? Maybe she had known the Norway base was in trouble. Perhaps that's why the comms went down. But she'd gotten through one last time. What had she said?

I can't explain now. Don't...

Don't what? Don't come back to the ship?

If that were the case, Joy would have had three hours' notice, at least. Was that enough time to get everyone away? Except for those kids...

"Bobbie?" Luke's voice broke in. "You okay?"

"Yes, yes. I think the Candels knew about the attack about three hours ago."

"When the comms went down?"

Bobbie nodded.

"Makes sense," Luke said, stony-faced. He pushed the hovercraft at top speed, hugging the waves.

"Oh, God." Bobbie felt like crying but gulped it back. "But where did Joy go?"

The place Gracie loved... there...

"We have to go to Segahan Dam." Bobbie sat forward, pointing west and straining against her seat belt.

"In Armagh?" Luke said.

"Yes. Remember, that's the place Gracie loved."

His face brightened. He slapped his hand down on his armrest. "You're not a pretty face, my girl!"

His words plunged Bobbie twenty-five years back to when Gracie had shortened the old saying, "You're not just a pretty face."

"Joy will be there," Bobbie said. Her mind added, *she has to be.*

"For God's sakes, will someone please tell me what is going on?" Patient 17 said through clenched teeth.

"Like Bobbie said, we're doing our best, okay?" Luke said.

"It's not okay," Patient 17 said. "I'm fed up being fobbed off. I need answers, starting with who the fuck am I?"

"I'll tell you," Bobbie said, twisting around to face him. "You are someone who has been right royally fucked over by Belus. You are someone who they injected with nanobots that changed, or may not have changed, your DNA to make you look like someone else. Or you *are* that someone, and you've had your personality completely eradicated. Because I knew that someone, and he sure as hell wouldn't–"

She stopped, drew a breath, and went on in spite of the confusion and shock on Patient 17's face. "Look, you're someone who's now with people who are actually trying to help you. I know you can't remember a thing, but let me tell you this: for all your confusion, you might be the luckiest fucker on the planet, because there are plenty of things all of us want to forget. So, for now, please shut up and, like the rest of us, put up!" Bobbie finished up gasping for breath.

"What she said," Luke added dryly.

They flew in silence for a minute or two before Jinko cleared his throat and asked, "Can you at least tell us where we're going?"

"Ireland," Bobbie answered, tight-lipped.

Jinko raised his eyebrows.

Patient 17 sat sullen, head down, and muttered, "Doesn't narrow it down much."

Bobbie ignored him. How could he be Hicks and be such a dickhead? And yet if he wasn't Hicks... She put her hand into her pocket and felt the butterflies, with the data they'd downloaded from the quantum computer.

"The Candels have had this happen before," Luke said. "And we've come through it."

Bobbie examined his expression. Her father scanned the horizon as they sped across the waves, too low to be in regular traffic. His brow was smooth, his jaw relaxed.

"We'll get through this time too." Luke looked around his passengers, his gaze settling on Bobbie as he smiled.

Ahead, a coastline emerged. Luke adjusted his controls, bringing them higher and merging with an established route across the islands of England and Wales. They passed other hovercraft. Bobbie wondered what it would be like to be like those people, sheep – oblivious to the world controlling their every move with media propaganda. She envied them their ignorance, their lack of conflict about whether they had made the right choices, their dreams that weren't nightmares of killings, beheadings, bodies decomposing in seconds.

All through human history, there were the blessed ignorant and others who answered a call to stand up to the evil that humanity carried by default, or so it seemed to Bobbie. The burden threatened to overwhelm her. Maybe she should let the Candels set off their EMP bombs, kill all the Rejuvenees, send Belus back to the Stone Age. Would that be a win?

They were over the Irish Sea. Afternoon thunderstorms flashed in the distant west where warm, damp air pushed up over the mountains of Mourne. The air routes divided northwest and southwest to avoid the storm. Luke took back control from the self-drive, readying to leave the air route north of the mountains to swing west again for Seagahan Dam.

As they peeled off from the traffic, Bobbie heard Luke swear softly.

"What?"

"The thruster's been damaged. I can't land vertically."

"Shit."

"What now?" Patient 17 asked.

"I'm going to need to do an emergency landing on water." Luke didn't look up from the control panel.

Jinko rocked faster, hummed louder. Patient 17 swore and curled forward to meet his knees.

"Is the reservoir big enough?" Bobbie jumped up, snatched an empty bag from the locker, and grabbed the bag with Gustav's head. She double bagged it and puffed up the outer bag with air. It stayed inflated – if the air couldn't get out, water couldn't get in. Satisfied with that, she placed the butterflies in it and sealed it so it would float. She tied the bag to her wrist.

"Yes, there's time to decelerate before we touch down."

Bobbie knew enough about flying to know that above a certain speed they may as well hit concrete as water. She glanced at Patient 17. If he were Hicks, he wouldn't know how to swim. Should she warn him? If he panicked, that would be worse. Her fingers massaged the bag on her lap. If it were buoyant enough, he'd be able to use that, and she could tow him to shore. The lake was only about eight hundred meters by four hundred meters, but it was deep, and in certain places, near the outflow, she'd been told there were dangerous currents that could pull a person under.

"Try to land as far from the dam as possible," she told Luke.

"Copy that."

Rain drummed on the hovercraft. White clouds enveloped them. Luke navigated using the console.

"Seat belts," he barked. "But be ready to release them as soon as we stop. The craft will float, but don't rely on that. Once I pop the doors, it'll fill up quickly."

Bobbie's heartbeat kept time with the rain hammering the roof. Jinko looked pale. His eyes darted from one window to the next. The clouds were impenetrable.

Luke watched the console and read the data. "Three minutes," he said.

Patient 17 held his head in his hands, rocking a little in his seat. Bobbie didn't see the wild panic of a non-swimmer. Surely if it were Hicks, he'd know deep down that he couldn't swim?

The engine sound changed from a steady hum to a whirr as Luke tried the landing thrusters one last time. His eyes met Bobbie's. He shook his head. The whirr changed to a high-pitched whine that hurt her ears.

The craft went silent.

"We've lost power. Hold tight," Luke said.

Forward motion gave way as the nose of the craft pitched downward. They burst out from the clouds. Bobbie closed her eyes against the sight of metal-grey water rushing toward them. The craft hit. Momentum flung Bobbie hard against her seatbelt. She heard an ear-splitting crack and opened her eyes in time to see the windscreen spider-web, hold for a second, then give way. Water rushed in, shockingly cold.

She gulped down a last lungful of air as she worked to free her seatbelt. Water covered her head. Its muddy taste filled her mouth and nose. Through the beige murk, she saw the doors slide open. Her father grabbed her hand and pulled her up and out of her seat. She looked around, but saw neither Patient 17 nor Jinko. She needed air.

She kicked for the surface. The buoyancy of the bag was negated by its drag as she struck out for the light above her. Air bubbles leaked from her nose and mouth. She longed to inhale. Her head breached the surface. She coughed as she sucked in air and hair and water. She choked and retched, flipping over onto her back to stop waves breaking in her face as she trod water.

"Bobbie!" Her father's voice rushed at her from behind.

"I'm okay." She swung around and saw Luke, but no one else.She coughed from her guts before she managed to say, "Hicks can't swim. We have to—"

"There!" Luke pointed. Halfway between then and the shore, Patient 17 towed Jinko. Bobbie and Luke charged toward them and helped Patient 17 drag Jinko through the reeds to a flat patch of grass.

Jinko's lips were mauve, his eyes half-open. Bobbie felt for a pulse. For the second time that day, Jinko's heart had stopped.

She set to work with compressions and breaths, only one thing on her mind – Hicks couldn't swim, never mind carry out the rescue stroke.

CHAPTER 13

Jinko threw up. Bobbie flipped him onto his side. His body convulsed as he coughed and spluttered. The color returned to his cheeks. He opened his eyes. He retched again. Bobbie rubbed his back, keeping an eye on her father: he was a few meters away, pacing through the knee-high reeds in a heated debate with Patient 17.

"You're going to be okay, Jinko," Bobbie said. Physically Jinko would survive, but mentally? That the man had nearly died twice since they'd met today weighed down on her. She lowered her aching body and lay flat on her back on the grass behind him. Clouds marbled the sky above her. Reeds and woody stems poked into her back, buttocks, and legs. Frogs hiccupped and chirruped from the water's edge, harmonized by birdsong in the trees further back from the banks. Earthy smells of decaying plants and fishy lake water wafted over her.

The wet tunic felt cool where it stuck to her. Muggy air pressed against her exposed skin. Bobbie's face stung. She was sure her blisters had burst.

She was weary of trying, of pushing, of reaching and never grasping. Every time she attempted to fix Rejuvenation, they were beaten back, stalled by setbacks. She'd taken lives instead of saving them, lost nearly everyone she loved. Hicks was gone. Why bother with anything?

She closed her eyes against tears. Blisters burned on her forehead. Jinko's coughs and gags dwindled to a series of sniffs and snuffles, then dropped to a moaning hum. Was he crying? He knew the power Belus had. Belus was too strong for a bunch of well-meaning misfits like the Candels. How could they ever beat such a formidable force?

"Bobbie," a voice called. It sounded for a split second like Gracie, but Gracie's voice had never been that strong or vibrant.

Bobbie sat up, opened her eyes, turning her face toward the voice. Hang, her half brother, bounded over tussocks of reeds and shrubs toward her with the agility and energy only thirteen-year-olds possessed.

Guilt slammed through Bobbie. She'd not thought of this child for one second during the raid on the base and their mad escape. She hadn't even considered Hang when she saw the children killed atop the downed hovercraft. She'd been too engrossed with worry for Joy, too horrified by the attack and too obsessed with Patient 17.

She scrambled to her feet, her emotions a jumble of shame and jubilation at seeing Hang. He flung himself at her. She burst into tears as the child's skinny arms hugged around her waist. After squeezing her in a ferocious grip, he released her and pulled back.

"You okay?" He frowned as his gaze traveled up her face. "That looks so sore. What happened?"

"I'm fine, don't worry. Are you okay?"

Hang nodded. "Joy says I've to bring you back to the new place."

"She's okay?"

"She's been crying a lot." The child pressed his lips together and frowned. "But she's not hurt."

Relief loosened her muscles. Bobbie trembled as she pulled Hang to her in a bear hug. She knew better than to ask where they were going. The Candels' policy of need-to-know was ingrained in young Hang. Head down, watching his step, her father sloshed through the reeds toward her. Patient 17 stood watching his back. Luke reached dryer ground and looked to Bobbie. His face lit up as he saw Hang. He dropped to one knee and opened his arms wide. The boy ran to him.

How had her father remained so stoic after the attack? He must have been worried about Hang. A hot tide of shame splashed over her. What kind of heartless, self-centered bitch had she become?

She glanced over at Jinko. He sat head in hands, possibly crying. He'd be feeling rough for a while. She'd brought this down on him by involving him. What choice did she have? He had the gentibots – technically, Patient 17 had them. And the way she'd talked to Patient 17 before they crash-landed... deep down, she must have known he wasn't Hicks. Her disappointment had made her lash out at him. She watched him by the water's edge. He pivoted in place, one hand shading his eyes, taking in the lake and rolling hills covered in crops.

"That guy's such a jackass," Luke said, joining Bobbie. "I sure as hell hope that's not Hicks."

"He's not."

"You're sure?" His look of concern nearly buckled her.

"Positive. Hicks could never swim. He was terrified of water. The gentibots obliterate memories, but they don't interfere with core skills. Patient 17 never had to relearn to walk or talk...or swim."

Hang looked around. "Is everyone here?"

"This is it, chum. Lead the way," Luke said.

As they started walking, Bobbie took Hang's hand. "I've so many questions for you."

"But Joy says—"

"I know, we'll get the answers back at the new place. Is it far?"

"About fifteen miles, as the crow flies." He stopped. "But we aren't flying. We're taking a tractor."

"A tractor?" Bobbie almost laughed. "Are you driving?"

"No!" Hang drew the word out, his eyes popping at the ridiculous suggestion. "A local farmer guy that Joy knows. Says his name is—"

"Don't worry about his name," Luke said. "Point us in the right direction."

"He's parked up there on the road."

Bobbie looked up the bank, glimpsing bright red through the tangle of vegetation. In rural communities, farmers still used tractors to prepare the fields and harvest crops.

Jinko clambered to his feet as Bobbie turned to him.

"Can you walk?" she asked. From beside Jinko, she lifted the bag with Gustav's head and the butterflies and hoisted it onto her shoulder.

"I think so."

He was pale. As they scaled the slope, his breaths came faster and shallower. Patient 17 had followed them without rancor. He mirrored Luke, giving Jinko a shoulder. Together they carried him up the steepest part of the hill to where a tractor chugged in the lane. A dingy trailer was hooked to the back of the tractor, filled with piles of empty potato sacks. A tall, slender man with shaggy dark hair sat in the tractor's cab. He turned around as Bobbie and her group approached. She recognized his face, but couldn't place him. It wasn't until he hopped down from the cab and approached them saying, "G'in back," that she remembered his name – John, the guy who'd come with Joy to her mother's wake a few months back. His abbreviated speech, like that of so many young people, had aggravated her then, but today she was heartened to see a familiar face.

She smiled at him.

He glowered. Hard bastard to please, he'd taken umbrage at Bobbie working for the government as a doctor last time they met. What was his problem now?

He let down the tailgate and helped them in, a scowl etched into his angular features.

"Put this o'r ye." He threw a pile of beige material at them. The burlap sacks stank of mildew, and the dust made them sneeze as they settled down on the floor of the trailer.

The tractor revved up. The stink of cheap diesel mixed with homemade ethanol gave Bobbie a headache. Jinko coughed beside her. In the gray light beneath the sacking, she mouthed to him, "You okay?"

He nodded, then closed his eyes and smothered another choking cough.

The sway of the trailer, punctuated by bone-jarring thuds, combined with the dank smell of old potato, stirred Bobbie's nausea. When hovercraft travel became the norm after the war, she had been delighted to leave car sickness behind. Air travel could still make her sick, but not so much as traveling by road.

The old tractor engine combined with the rattle of the metal trailer filled her ears, but Bobbie's heart sped up when above that she heard the sharp whirr of a hovercraft. John had tied a tarpaulin over the sacks, but even so, Bobbie hissed a whisper to her co-travelers when she felt the wind from propellers tugging at the burlap. "Hold on tight."

She prayed Jinko wouldn't take another coughing fit as she heard the hovercraft land in the road ahead of them.

"You there," a woman's voice said. "Where are you going?"

"Up fields," John answered. Bobbie didn't catch the next part, and assumed he'd turned away. It was hard enough following what the guy said when she could see and hear him clearly.

"Seen any unusual traffic today?"

"What like?" John asked.

"There's reports of a hovercraft crash."

"Seen n'out n'ere."

"blink the traffic division if you hear anything."

Footsteps diminished.

The whirr of the hovercraft struck up. The tractor's engine revved, drowning it out. The trailer lurched forward, and they were back in motion.

"You think they're looking for us?" Bobbie asked the back of Luke's head.

He wriggled around to face her. Sweat glistened on his forehead, but his eyes looked calm. "Maybe not specifically. Someone must have reported a hovercraft going down. With a bit of luck, it'll take them a while to pull the craft out of the reservoir."

"Cause we've been inundated with luck," Bobbie said. She closed her mouth and clenched her teeth to stop them rattling together now that the tractor had picked up speed. Her traveling companions grunted and gasped as they bounced over rutted ground.

"He's cutting across the fields," Hang told them in a hushed voice. "It's shorter."

After what felt like an hour, the tractor turned up a steep hill. Bobbie's toes touched the tailgate of the trailer as she slid backward. Patient 17 was heavier and slid faster, so that he pressed against her. He scooted away from her as though scorched, apologizing. She hated the warm buzz his contact left on her skin, despite her knowing in her heart he wasn't Hicks.

"Dammit," Luke said as he too struggled to stop piling on top of the others.

"We're nearly there," Hang said. "This bit is the worst."

The tractor stopped. Bobbie listened as the cab door slammed. Footfalls ended at the tailgate. John wrenched back the tarpaulin and sacking, momentarily blinding her with sunlight. He lowered the tailgate as the occupants of the trailer scrambled to their feet and jumped down onto a hillside covered in grassy tussocks, heather, and rocks.

Bobbie rotated on the spot, taking in the view. They were on land higher than everywhere else. To the southwest, the sun punched through clouds and, in spotlights, lit the land ribbed with crops and splotched with lakes that spread out to the west. To the north, the ground rose in a cairn of rocks. Low shafts of sunlight splintered off a vast body of water further to the east, where she recognized the humps of the Mourne Mountains across the Newry Estuary. They were on Slieve Gullion, the highest point in Armagh.

But there was nothing here. Were they going to be picked up from here by hovercraft?

"Wer'on foot from here," John said, and started walking.

"Are you okay?" Bobbie asked Jinko. His color was better, considering the day he'd had.

"I'll manage." He set off after John.

Hang took Luke's hand and followed.

"Ladies first," Patient 17 said with a wave of his hand.

Bobbie walked ahead of him. The gesture struck her as old. That sort of language was considered sexist now, but when she was young, older folk had considered it gentlemanly. That made sense. Even though Patient 17 only looked as old as Hicks, mid-thirties, he must have been much older and rejuvenated.

In all the distraction about this man being or not being Hicks, she'd forgotten to look at the whole point of Jinko taking him in the first place. So far, it seemed that the gentibots had stopped the side effects of Rejuvenation. She needed to ask Jinko more questions.

Determined to get her head back in the game, Bobbie dragged in a breath and looked ahead. They approached piles of rocks and stones heaped in a mound about thirty meters wide and four meters high.

John stopped at an arrangement of flat rocks set into the side of the mound, two tall ones side by side with a gap as wide a man's body between them. A third rock lay across the top like a lintel. He disappeared into the gap. They followed in single file.

Inside was damp. Moss grew over the rocks lining the walls at the opening.

Bobbie hung back to take up the rear. Patient 17 motioned for her to go ahead, but she insisted, and he moved into place in front of her. Bobbie picked her way behind him along the passage, lit by quarter-meter wide square openings at intervals along the walls. It smelled earthy, laced with a sting of ammonia. She heard her father saying from upfront, "I used to come up here with Bobbie's mother long before Bobbie and Gracie were born."

"Wow, was it here way back then?"

Way back then... A smile curled Bobbie's lips. Kids were cruel.

"Oh, it's thousands of years old," Luke said. "Dates back to Neolithic times. It's a passage tomb. I didn't think you could even get inside it. It was closed up when I used to come here."

" 'Twas forgotten during t'e war," John said. "W'use it as a temp'ry base. El'vation is good for comms April's setting up."

The passage opened up into a round, domed room, wide enough for a dozen people to sit down in. The ceiling rose above so they could stand up straight comfortably. The air smelled less stuffy. Light filtered in through a series of slim skylights, and LEDs in the floor cast shadowed patterns up the walls. Piles of wooden crates, electronic boards, black and gray boxes with cables running to and from them, sat in clumps on the floor.

From the furthest recesses of the dome, Joy flew past John and clasped her father in a fierce hug. Bobbie's heart lifted as she ran to them and put her arms around them both.

"Thank God you're okay," Bobbie said, pulling back and looking into her sister's face.

Joy's eyes were red-rimmed, her cheeks raw from tears. She clutched Bobbie's hand.

"The children?" Joy said. "Did you go to the ship?"

Bobbie swallowed and nodded.

Joy's face brightened. She looked past Bobbie, down the passage. "The kids – we had to go without them. They were out on a trip for Tanna's birthday. We couldn't contact them on time."

Bobbie tried not to react, but Joy read her expression. "You saw them, didn't you?"

Bobbie couldn't speak. Her face crumpled as she shook her head.

"No!" Joy threw her head back. Her hand flattened against her chest as she sank to her knees.

Bobbie bent over and cradled Joy in her arms. "I'm so sorry. We couldn't do anything."

"It's all my fault," Joy sobbed.

"Get up!" April yelled.

Bobbie jumped, turned in the direction of April's voice, and said, "Hold on a second."

April stood behind her, hands on hips, face like thunder. "She can't wallow in self-pity. We have no time for that. We've all done what we had to do, and we've all made mistakes. She doesn't know for sure what led Belus to the ship. Debriefing right away." She looked down at Joy, who had curled into a ball of shuddering sobs. "Joy, now."

As Bobbie helped Joy to her feet, Slade entered from the narrow passage. Bobbie's fingers tightened around the bag with Gustav's head. The debriefing wouldn't be pleasant.

CHAPTER 14

April led them to the far end of the room, to where Slade and Niclas were waiting on benches around a rough wooden table. Slade's eyes met Bobbie's, then dropped to the bag. Bobbie recognized in Slade's face the hollow grief that comes with finally knowing that a loved one is gone. Joy would have already told Slade they had found Gustav's body, so she'd know they had his head. Bobbie's fingers curled into the plastic, its weight dragging.

Slade would now have closure.

Closure.

Would Bobbie, one day, yearn to have that for Hicks if they didn't find him? Or would she carry the flame of hope, her heart fanning the embers even when her head told her there was no point? Hadn't she let go of Dad? Her hope for him being alive had floated from her sixteen-year-old grasp as if she had let go of a string to a helium balloon. The rules were permanently broken now that she'd gotten her father back.

All Slade was getting back was her brother's head, defrosting to slime in a bag.

"Let's all sit down," Luke said. "John, please, could you take Hang and our new friend outside?" He tipped his head toward Patient 17, who opened his mouth, but Luke cut him off. "The sooner we're done here, the sooner we can get you your answers."

Patient 17 narrowed his eyes.

"I'll show ye t' Cairn," John said, placing a hand on his shoulder. Patient 17 shrugged it off, hunched his shoulders around his ears, and followed Hang.

"My family. Has anyone heard about them?" Jinko asked.

Joy wiped her eyes and said, "The last reports were that the Candels were on their way. I'm sorry, I don't have more information, but there's no reason to think things didn't go smoothly." She sat at the table next to Niclas.

Crimson blotches flared on Jinko's cheeks. "No reason? After what we saw at that ship? You're fobbing me off again. Christ!"

"Please sit down. We'll get to your business in due course," Niclas said in a low voice. "There's a lot to discuss."

Jinko folded his arms and paced a few steps in each direction, shaking his head.

Niclas' lips compressed and disappeared into his snowy beard. Deep grooves etched between his white eyebrows. He kept his eyes fixed on his hands, clasped together on the table in front of him.

Slade sat across from Niclas, mirroring his posture. She nodded to the empty spot beside her for Bobbie to sit down. Bobbie set the bag on the table. It wobbled. The head shifted inside, rolling the bag a fraction along the table before its center of gravity settled. Everything felt wrong – the gesture too casual, lacking the respect it deserved, but placing Gustav's head on the ground would be worse.

"Sorry," Bobbie muttered.

Slade lowered her eyes, gave a nod.

Jinko stopped pacing and sat beside Bobbie. He looked from face to face around the table, in turn. In a flash of panic, Bobbie wondered if he had blink access. Was he sending this all back to Belus? But she realized he was simply saying hello to all of them. They each acknowledged him by name. He knew everyone around the table except April.

"We haven't met. Who are you?"

"Not important," April said. "I'm security. You guys are the scientists. It's over to you now."

There wasn't room for Luke to sit on either bench, so he dragged a wooden crate over and sat on it at the top end of the table. He leaned forward with his hands on his knees and said, "What happened at the ship? Where is everyone else?"

"Belus found us," Niclas said.

Joy scraped in a short breath.

"We don't know exactly how they got in through Joy's blink," Niclas continued, "or when. But Joy intercepted a communication that alerted us to the attack. We had to evacuate. Everyone has a meetup point, many different places. Local Candels will find our people and take them into their camps. We had to leave before the last group returned to base. We were hoping they got our messages and knew to escape, but the comms were scrambled at the end–"

"Fox traced us through my comms link," Joy said. "I'm still looking for the breach."

"An electronic trace is the most likely," April said, placing her words as if they were made of delicate crystal, "but the breach could have been any one of multiple sources."

"How do you know we're safe here?" Bobbie asked.

"We've closed down all coms except non-directional public broadcasts," April said. "Until we find the breach, we'll be digitally isolated from the other groups."

"Where's Davitt? And the vaccine?" Bobbie scanned the room. "Do we have any resources to work on the gentibots?"

April threw a look to the ceiling. "Davitt is within walking distance. There's a haulage company at the foot of the mountain. One of their cargo crafts is tricked out inside as a mobile labor unit. We were damn lucky it was here. We can use that as a lab. They have another one that they use for temporary living quarters for pregnant women in hiding."

"They're the same company I got the campervan hovercraft from," Joy said. "They're Candels, but they live in Belus land. Like Ori did, before Rejuvenation."

"What does Davitt remember?" Bobbie asked.

"Not a lot, but we told him that Rejuvenation had backfired and that Fox had turned against her employees and kicked him off the project. He was mad about that." April snuffed back a laugh.

"Does he still think we're together?"

Niclas pursed his lips and nodded.

Bobbie gave a long audible sigh. "Okay, we've more important things to deal with. Is he working on the vaccine?"

"Yes." Niclas shifted in his seat and glanced at April.

"But we're working on other plans to combat Rejuvenation," April said. "Another team is developing a targeted electromagnetic pulse."

"But that will kill thousands of Rejuvenees," Bobbie said. "You have to tell them that Jinko has gentibots that will stop the psychosis and render them harmless."

"I–" Jinko began, but Bobbie nudged him with her knee.

"We have no way to contact them right now," April said.

"What's their time frame?" Bobbie asked.

"Three weeks, a month at most."

Bobbie turned to Jinko. "How quickly can you scale up the gentibots?"

Jinko bit his lip, then cleared his throat. "It depends on the resources we have, but with a well-stocked lab, I could make enough for a hundred people in a few days."

"A hundred!" Niclas said. "We'd need to treat thousands. We don't even know how many thousands."

"Production is exponential," Jinko said. "The nanobots make more of themselves until their raw materials run out. In a week, they'd be producing thousands, hundreds of thousands by the end of the month. Numbers aren't the problem."

"So what is?" Niclas asked, placing a hand on April's arm as she moved to interrupt.

"Dispersal, for one," Jinko said.

"We can use a recreational virus, the same way Belus used Davitt's virus as a vector to spread the nanobots," Bobbie said.

Jinko bit his lip. "Yep, that would work, but they could counter with a vaccine."

"So we time-lapse and send out different variations of the recreational virus so they'd have to keep re-engineering their vaccines," Bobbie said.

Slade shook her head. "We don't have the time or the resources. We'll have to use the EMP."

"It's too dangerous," Bobbie said. "Besides, you'll be killing all those innocent people–"

"They're old," Slade said. "They would've died soon anyway if they hadn't been rejuvenated–"

"You can't know that," Jinko jumped in. "You can't decide who dies when."

"Jinko's right," Bobbie said.

"Bleeding fucking hearts," April muttered.

"Seriously?" Jinko shifted to stand up, but the shared bench made it difficult.

Slade raised a hand and kept talking. "Many more people will die, naturally younger people, if Fox uses Rejuvenees as some kind of army, or if they escape the camps and can't be controlled..."

"Or if Fox is sending them off to be slaves for the Melters," Luke added. "Wouldn't they be better off dead?"

Jinko sank to his seat, his eyes huge. "Melters? We beat them. They're gone."

"Dad has some wild conspiracy theories about Fox being in cahoots with them, thinks she didn't defeat them really – just brokered some kind of trade deal with them." Bobbie turned to her father. "Let's not spin off on tangents. Keep to the facts. If we use the EMP incorrectly, it could cause catastrophic damage to our digital existence. Joy, back me up here."

"She's right. It could send us back to the Stone Age." Joy waved a hand at the room. Everyone fell quiet as they looked around at the ancient chamber.

"Looks fine to me," April said. "Better than living with the threat of Rejuvenees."

"Let's try the gentibots," Bobbie urged. "Jinko, what do you say?"

"The gentibots aren't perfect. They wipe out the recipient's memory, and they attack any form of nanoengineering in the body. Plus, I don't know what will happen to the host as they break down. We haven't gotten that far yet. I'd rather send out a strain that has a shelf life, one that will dismantle after a period of time, so they don't remain in the recipient's body forever."

"I understand that," Bobbie said, "but we don't have time to perfect it. We could develop another round of nanobots to clean up after the immediate threat is over. The memory loss is still better than losing their minds or their lives. Can you give it a go?"

"When I hear from my family –"

"We're digitally isolated," Joy said. "I don't –"

"I'll get John to take you to the village. He can set up a non-trackable connection from there," Niclas said.

Jinko shrugged. "In that case, I'll do my best. Once I see the lab setup, I'll have a better idea of how long it will take."

"You have two weeks," April said. "Including dispersal."

"That might not be long –" Jinko began.

"Two weeks. Make it long enough." April turned to Luke. "Next item on the agenda?"

Luke's gaze slid to the bag on the table and then to Slade. Bobbie's heart banged in her chest like a caged animal.

Slade met his gaze. Her face flushed red, her eyes glistened, but her voice came strong and steady. "I'll conduct a formal identification in the lab when Joy extracts his ONIV." She faced Bobbie, and only then did her voice waver. "Thank you for finding him."

Slade stopped, swallowed hard. Hands clasped, her knuckles whitened. "We may even be able to find out how he died, why it was kept a secret, and if Fox had anything to do with it."

Bobbie nodded, her own words tangled in her throat. Fox had been Slade's friend. The betrayal would weigh heavily if Fox had a hand in any of it.

"Bobbie, did you bring back the butterflies?" Joy asked.

"They're in the bag with... with everything else."

Joy smiled. "Good job, big sis. I'll get that downloaded, and we'll work on finding the real Hicks."

"Can you run a trace on Patient 17's biosensors, see if we can find out who he is?" Bobbie asked.

Joy's face clouded over. "I'm not online, but I might be able to do a workaround from the village. It's not a high priority, is it?"

"No," Niclas said.

"Not for us, but for Patient 17–" In the corner of Bobbie's eye, an icon appeared: an envelope with a lock and key superimposed. "Is anyone else getting this?"

"I am," Slade said. "But I've no private key."

The others murmured the same.

Bobbie's scalp prickled. "Does this mean Belus has found us?"

"The opposite, thank God." Joy brought her hands together, prayerlike, bounced them off her chest, and looked up. "It's a public broadcast sent out because they can't find the intended recipient. Ignore it unless you have a lock and key."

"I have it." Bobbie stood up. She wanted to run. "I have the lock and key. What do I do?"

"She hasn't found you, you're okay." Joy stood beside Bobbie and rubbed her back. "Fox has sent the message for you to everyone, but only you have the key to open and read it. Don't open it yet. I'm switching on my eye-cam-di, and when you do read it, read it carefully and out loud. Okay?"

Bobbie clenched her fists to stop the tremor in her hands. She drew in a long breath and on the exhale said, "Okay, ready?"

Joy nodded.

An icon of a flashing camera winked in Bobbie's peripheral vision. Her eye-cam-di was recording.

She blinked on the key, and it entered the lock.

CHAPTER 15

Bobbie's vision flooded bright. Blinded by the blink recording, she stumbled back. The edge of the bench bit into the back of her knees. Her legs folded. She met the bench with a thud. Her hands found the knotted surface of the table. She spread her fingers, pressing her palms against the warm wood.

"It's not a written message. It's footage. A room. Maybe an office." Bobbie shifted her gaze, but the image was static and didn't respond to her eye movement. "There's a desk in front of a window. I can't see through it, with the light coming in. Everything's backlit. Wait, the picture's adjusting. It's Fox. She's sitting on a chair beside the desk."

"You're sure it's her?" Slade's voice connected Bobbie to the world she sat in.

"Yes," Bobbie said. "But she looks ... disheveled."

"How? Describe her."

"Small things – her hair is messy, she's not as groomed and slick as usual. Crumpled tunic. Fidgeting. Clenched teeth. Hang on, she's talking."

Lisette Fox pointed at the camera, lip curled, teeth bared. "I want him back. Bring me back my Gustav. I will trade you something I love for something you love."

Something. Or did Fox mean someone? A swoop of terror eviscerated Bobbie. Had Fox cut off Hicks' head?

It wasn't a two-way conversation. Bobbie couldn't ask, couldn't plead. All she could do was listen and repeat what she heard.

"Bring my Gustav to the coordinates I'm sending, by three AM, and you can have your precious Hicks back," Fox said. "Come alone. This is between you and me, Bobbie. Love is the strongest force in our universe. Don't fuck it up."

Numbers streamed across Bobbie's vision. She called them out to Joy, fearful of missing one. The footage snapped off, dumping Bobbie visually back at the table, with everyone staring at her. The message icon was gone.

"Three AM. The dead hour." Bobbie pressed a hand to her chest. Three in the morning was the time most people died in their sleep in hospitals. Panic blazed up through her neck and throat.

This is between you and me.

Fox was making this personal. Was it because Bobbie had desecrated Gustav's head? It had felt like that long before then. Back at the PARC, Bobbie had felt Fox was taking individual umbrage at Bobbie's actions. It was as if Fox believed she had the answer to ageing in Rejuvenation, and Bobbie was thwarting her benevolence.

Slade stood. "You need to let us deal with this."

"Not this shite again," Bobbie said. Fox didn't say it, but Bobbie knew that if they fucked this up, Fox would kill Hicks...if she hadn't already. "I got us this far. I found Gustav and Jinko. Dad, tell them."

"It could be a trap," Luke said. "Fox isn't going to just present herself without support. She's not going to simply hand over Hicks. She's too smart."

"She's unhinged. She's talking about love. She's agitated – ripe for making mistakes," Bobbie said. "This whole thing is off-kilter. She's off her game. I have to go there."

"Or that's what she wants you to think," said Slade.

Everyone spoke at once. Niclas stood up, rapped the table. They stopped and turned to look at him.

"We're wasting time. Joy, go sort out that ONIV and the butterflies."

Joy stared at him.

"Now!" he shouted, making everyone jump.

Joy got to her feet and lifted the bag, muttering, "Sure thing, boss."

"April, arrange for Jinko to call his family from the village, and find someone who can read the amnesiac's biosensor. Jinko, we need you to start work as soon as you've connected with your family."

"Copy that." April nodded at Jinko. "Follow me."

Jinko murmured, "Thanks," as he passed Niclas, but Niclas ignored him, concentrating instead on Slade.

"After you have identified the ...body." Niclas cleared his throat. "Take the coordinates, find out everything about the location. You'll have to use public channels, so make sure you cover your tracks."

Slade rolled her eyes and sighed.

"Sorry, just thinking aloud here," Niclas said, scratching his beard. "Meet us back here in an hour."

Slade strode from the room, but Bobbie noted the slump in her shoulders and didn't envy her the task of identifying Gustav's head.

"Luke, can you monitor local traffic, see what they think about the hovercraft going down, please?"

When it was just the two of them, Niclas turned to Bobbie. "We've got work to do."

"But–"

"We'll get you there."

Bobbie tweaked her lips into a grateful smile.

"I'll get someone to fuel a cargo craft right now," Niclas continued. "We'll put Gustav's head into it, in a box – respectful, easy to manage – but first, come with me."

Bobbie followed him out of the passage tomb, itching to ask for details. An orange sun skimmed the horizon, peeking out below a layer of cloud, washing the mountain in bronze light. At this time of year, the sun set around six. It didn't give them much time to get to wherever Fox was. Bobbie clenched her fists. She caught Niclas looking at her hands, and flexed her fingers.

"Your father tells me a witch used to live here," Niclas said.

Bobbie felt a softening in her face as she gave in to a smile. "My sister loved the old legends."

"I'm surprised. Joy doesn't seem the type."

"No, Gracie. She... she died when she was thirteen. She read a lot. I suppose it's what you do if you can't go outside and play with the other kids."

Bobbie shadowed Niclas as he picked his way over boulders, keeping to tussocks of grass, stepping clear of the muddy hollows in the blanket bog covering the mountain. Droplets of water glistened amber in the low sun.

"You can get lost in a thousand worlds if you follow your imagination," Niclas said.

"Gracie certainly did." The memories glowed, beckoning Bobbie to a safe, familiar place. "She knew all the stories of this place, but the one she loved the most was of how the old witch, the Calliagh Berra, tricked Fionn Mc Cool."

"You'll have to elaborate. I'm not familiar with your legends." Niclas hopped over a marshy spot. "Mind your step there."

They were halfway down the mountain, the blur of lights ahead sharpening into distinct orbs. Bobbie liked the old man's style. The reminiscing had calmed her.

"Fionn Mc Cool was a hero. He found a young woman crying by the lake at the top of the mountain. Have you seen it?"

"Yes, we've been drinking from it."

"Ha, well, you might not after you hear what happened."

Niclas chuckled.

"Fionn found the girl crying," Bobbie said. "And when he asked her why, she said she'd dropped her gold ring in the lake. Being the hero he was, he jumped in after it."

"As you do."

"Well, turns out the girl was the old witch, and she'd put a spell on the lake so that when Fionn came out, he had aged. He was a withered old man with white hair."

"Why did she do that?"

Bobbie lifted her gaze. They were near the bottom of the mountain. An old castle, recently restored by the look of the fresh pointing on the brickwork, towered over a flat area of tarmac edged by rows of cargo crafts. "I think it was something to do with pissing off her sister."

"Imagine that." Niclas turned to look at her as they reached the tarmac.

Bobbie raised an eyebrow.

"So what happened to poor old Fionn?"

"Fionn's followers made the witch reverse the spell, and he became young again. Gracie loved that part," Bobbie said. "She had progeria."

Niclas gave a sad smile. "I can see why she loved it."

As they crossed the tarmac, Bobbie made out pullbots arranging pallets into the cargo holds of some ships, and unloading others. Niclas walked her to a metal container sitting against the wall of the castle. Rust patches broke through the white paint. This container looked older than the others. Being metal, it was too heavy to be used with the cargo craft.

Niclas heaved on the handle, and the door squealed open. Inside, taking up a quarter of the space, lay metal tubes, as long as the container and as thick as Bobbie's wrist. They were stacked in racks from floor to ceiling.

"Those pipes, when they're put together, will be a twenty-meter high antenna." Niclas pointed to a grey box with knobs and dials. "This is a high-power longwave radio transmitter."

"But hasn't Fox blocked all transmissions?"

"She controls broadcasts that can be received by ONIV," Niclas said. "But we can't broadcast to the masses on longwave radio, because ONIV doesn't pick it up."

"So what's the point?"

"This is what April has been working on. This transmitter will send a signal that propagates worldwide to synchronize the detonation of EMPs around the planet. To be effective, the EMP bombs must be triggered within milliseconds of each other for maximum effect. She wants a global reach. Even one Rejuvenee surviving is one too many for April."

"She can't do that–"

"I agree with you, Bobbie, but it's our last resort. I'm showing you this so you understand that you must get Davitt on board with the gentibot program. He's holding something back. I can't prove it. It's just that I... and I hate saying this – it sounds so hocus pocus... but I just sense it."

"How close is she to having the bombs in place?" Bobbie asked.

"They're in place."

"Jesus! How? She said three weeks."

"She lied – that's what prompted me to involve you. I never thought I'd see the day I couldn't trust April."

"But you trust me?"

Niclas peered from under bushy white eyebrows. "I do."

A shiver tingled up the back of Bobbie's scalp. "Why?"

"We've been watching you for a long time. You value life more than most people."

In the silence that followed, Bobbie's heart dragged as she replayed the lives she'd taken. She swallowed hard and met Niclas' eyes, unable to speak.

"I'm sorry to put this on you, Bobbie," he said. "But you need to know this. We have Candels all over the world with EMP bombs strategically positioned, ready to go. They have radio receivers connected to their EMP bombs. All it will take is this."

He handed her a black plastic cube composed of smaller cubes with square colored stickers.

Bobbie held it on her palm. "I've seen pictures of these. I thought they were antique toys."

"Good Lord, you're making me feel old! But yes, it's a Rubik's cube, at least on the outside. You arm it by pressing these three buttons."

He pointed to the center squares. "Green, then orange, then yellow. If you press the red square in the center, you'll trigger the signal from here. April made this so she could carry it with her, use it remotely from wherever she finds herself."

"Don't give it to me. You hardly know me." The plastic device was light in her hand, but Bobbie felt the true weight of it.

"I've known your father for decades."

"So give it to him."

"I fear that he agrees too strongly with April at the moment. He doesn't see the Rejuvenees as people anymore. I know that you and I are of the same mind on this matter." Niclas looked old, weary. "I trust that if you need to use it, you will, but only if it's absolutely necessary. April wants to erect the antenna tonight. Even though she promised to give you time, I fear that after what happened at the ship in Norway, vengeance has gotten the better of her."

"Surely she wouldn't go against your orders," Bobbie said.

Fear crossed the old man's face. "Her grandson was killed in the attack on the ship. She's bottled it up. Thinks she's a warrior. I'm worried she'll use this from a place of anger." He cupped his hand below Bobbie's and closed her fingers around the edges of the cube.

"Can't she trigger a signal from here without this cube?"

"She could, but here, I'd have help to stop her." A bleak expression shrouded his face as he added, "If we needed to."

"I can't take this with me. What if it fell into Fox's hands?"

"She won't know what it is, and she doesn't know how to arm it. Besides, why would she use it? A worldwide EMP would wipe out every electronic circuit: destroy everything she's built, including all those Rejuvenees."

"But I–"

"Take it." Niclas released her hand and stepped back. "Now, you'll talk to Davitt?"

"Yes." Bobbie put the cube in her pocket. The folds of her tunic hid the bulge, but the cube's corners made its presence felt against her skin.

A meadow lay along the side of the castle, edged on three sides by oak and beech trees. Many of the oaks had died, and the sun edged their twisted branches. Nestled into the grass, two giant cargo crafts sat with their loading bays closed. Discreet personnel doors had been added to their sides.

"How is he?" Bobbie asked.

"He says he remembers things, but he wants a guarantee that he won't be hurt and will be protected from Fox if he talks. Even if we give him that guarantee, he said he'll only talk to you," Niclas said. "We gave him our word we'll protect him."

A man stood outside the door. Niclas greeted him, and he opened the door. Niclas looked in and said, "I have a visitor for you."

"Who is it?" Davitt's voice filled Bobbie with gloom.

She followed Niclas into the cargo craft. Inside, Davitt had all the intepanels on. They covered every interior wall. He'd set up a couple of portable intepanels on the central worktop. They displayed equations, texts of papers, diagrams, and datasheets. The countertops along the walls were strewn with glassware – flasks, test tubes, and a rack of Petri dishes sat in an incubator at the far end of the room. A gurney with stirrups had been pushed into the corner and had a blanket thrown over it. She liked the idea that Davitt had to sleep there.

"Bobbie?" Davitt sounded genuinely pleased to see her. He reached for her, arms wide open. She stepped back. He dropped his arms, his eyes searching hers. His teeth caught his bottom lip and his face flushed. "It's confusing."

He turned and paced away from her. Her breath caught as the sight of the scar tissue slashing through the dark stubble at the crown of his head reminded her of that awful night she'd had to piece his smashed skull together. He turned, and she saw his balance was off, his co-ordination clumsy. His injury had taken its toll, but in his eyes, she saw something new, something alien to Davitt – humility. His lostness pulled at her. She put her hand on his arm. "What do you remember?"

"That you..." His voice caught. "...You hate me."

Heat flooded her cheeks. Bobbie looked at Niclas. He shrugged. "I'll wait for you outside."

"Thanks," she said, and watched him leave. She waited until she heard the electronics hum in the door-closing mechanism. Then she turned to Davitt and said, "You understand why? You remember what you did?"

"I– I can't decide what's real and what's some horrible dream." He backed up to a stool and slumped against it. He hung his head and stared at his knees.

"When we last spoke, you knew you were working on Rejuvenation," Bobbie said.

"Yes."

"What else has come to you since then? Just tell me, simply."

He gave a long sigh, then started at the beginning, telling Bobbie about how he and Jinko had been picked for the project, how they'd chosen the sample subjects, adding, "When your grandmother was chosen, I nearly told you. I was so excited about the project."

Excited? His naivety was infuriating.

"Why didn't you?" Bobbie kept her tone civil.

"The NDA, for one. Fox had changed from supportive to menacing. And then your grandmother. She was so–"

"Oh, this better be good!" Bobbie said.

"Manipulative...after she rejuvenated, she was so manipulative... and I was so lonely. I love you." Davitt looked up. Sadness dragged in his dark eyes.

Bobbie was glad of her anger. It stopped the pity forming. She shook her head and turned away.

"I do love you, really, Bobbie. I wanted to ask you to marry me, but you... you always held something back."

That triggered a fresh spike of guilt, but she couldn't dismiss the sense she that was being played, that Davitt was spinning this out to have time with her.

"I'm sorry." It was the truth. She had never loved Davitt. She'd kept that for Hicks.

"So you understand? Me and Gloria?"

"Fuck, no! You slept with my grandmother. Fuck, no!"

Davitt rose to his feet.

Two taps on the wall from Niclas outside echoed through the room.

"Look," Bobbie said, her hand out, staying him. "That's all done, and in the grand scheme, not important."

Davitt shriveled in on himself. He leaned back against the countertop.

Bobbie folded her arms. "We need to put that aside, focus on Rejuvenation. What happened?"

"It had been going well until we discovered a few problems."

"Problems? People *died*, Davitt. People went insane. Why didn't you call a halt? Review the data again?"

"I... We hadn't a chance. Fox was impossible to negotiate with, put us under terrible pressure. She talked about running out of time."

"Time? In what way?"

"I'm not sure, but I think she was talking about her own aging. She's about seventy, right? Maybe she wanted this sorted out before she got too much older."

"That makes sense. So the psychosis... did you get anywhere close to figuring that out?"

"The structure and function of the brain involves a complex neural construct, shaped by genetics and early developmental experiences. The nanobots can shore up the DNA in the brain, but these new cells are malformed, and this interferes with the brain's neuroplasticity. Simply put, subjects suffer damage to their brain chemistry, and when the brain tries to adapt, it develops the psychosis."

"So you needed more research before you deployed the nanobots on a larger scale?"

Davitt shrugged, stared at the floor. "Except that Fox wanted a larger sample size and decided that the ultra-elderly were expendable."

Bobbie allowed the anger to flare. He'd done nothing to protect these people.

"But that's not the worst problem," Davitt said in a low voice. "The nanobots screw up the development of eggs, sperm, and embryos."

"Yes," Bobbie said tersely. "So we've seen."

"If the nanobots are deployed to the general population, everyone would be rendered infertile and crazy."

"But I thought the recreational virus you used to deploy them could only be caught by those with a weak immune system." Bobbie didn't think that was ethical either, but there was neither point nor time to go into that. She wanted to meet with Fox and get Hicks back.

"Well, this is the thing." Davitt looked scared. "Fox had also been talking about adding it to the matter streamer mix, introducing it to the general public via the food chain."

"Christ Almighty! Why the hell would she want to do that?" Bobbie was on her feet, backing toward the door. Was Fox so crazy that she'd put the human species at risk of extinction? Bobbie had to do something, anything.

Davitt shrank back. His breath came in sharp pants. Bobbie stared into his face, but he averted his eyes.

"Why would she do that, Davitt? Why does Fox think putting the entire future of our race at risk is a good idea?" Bobbie put her hands on his shoulders, but held back from shaking the answers out of him.

"It's all so muddled," he stammered. "How many days has it been since you took me from the research lab in Ireland?"

Bobbie had to count the days mentally. She'd lost track of some time herself at the park. "That was five or six weeks ago."

"Shit!" Davitt put his hands over his face and moaned, leaning against the counter.

"Just tell me!" Bobbie shouted, pulling his hands from his face.

"She thought I'd fixed the psychotic glitch in the third-generation nanobots."

"Christ Almighty!" Bobbie grabbed his shoulders, stopping herself from shaking him by twisting the material of his tunic in her hands.

Davitt screwed his face up, then looked at Bobbie with despair in his eyes, saying, "She didn't mind that the vaccine carried second-generation nanobots."

"So she knew they would turn the elderly crazy," Bobbie said, letting go of Davitt and taking a step back.

"Her army, she called them," Davitt said in a voice that made Bobbie shiver.

"Why did she think you'd fixed the... glitch?" The word seemed too innocuous to Bobbie.

"I thought I *had* fixed it. Then I discovered the psychosis was still affecting the subjects; at the same time, I realized the effect Rejuvenation would have on the reproductive system. Remember I wanted to take you out for dinner, but then I had to cancel?"

Bobbie swallowed hard and nodded. She remembered like it was an old movie or a vivid dream. That life hardly seemed real any more. Davitt had cancelled, and she had been glad because she'd been going with Joy, Hicks, and Jimmy to rescue Granny from the research facility. Except she hadn't rescued Granny at all...

She snapped her thoughts back to Davitt. Enough time had been wasted. "So what the fuck happened, Davitt? Why didn't you tell Fox Rejuvenation was still not right?"

Davitt recoiled and cast his eyes to the floor. "I was scared of her," he said in a small voice. "Then you came and made me go with you to Yosemite, and I didn't get to tell Fox. I thought I'd have time to test the new formula at the lab in Yosemite, but then Jimmy did this to me." Davitt pointed to the wound on his head.

"So to be clear," Bobbie said through gritted teeth. "Fox is due to roll out the Rejuvenation nanobots into the food chain any day now? They're still faulty, and Fox thinks they're working perfectly without the psychotic side effects?"

"Yes," Davitt said with certainty before a haunted look flitted across his face and he added, "But you have to make sure Belus doesn't get me for telling you. And that the Candels don't string me up!"

"Yes, okay, yes." Bobbie tried to think straight. "Where did Fox plan to deploy the nanobots from?"

"I don't know. I only remembered it yesterday, and you'd already left. Then Niclas moved me here during the evacuation. For a while, I thought I'd dreamt it. My head – it gets so sore sometimes...and I can't tell what's a dream and what's –"

"Think hard, Davitt, any detail will help. Please tell me you locked away the mixture once you discovered it wasn't working?"

Desolation darkened his features. He shook his head. "This morning, I clearly remembered making the mixture and giving it to Fox."

"Did you dream it? Are you sure you didn't dream it?"

"I didn't dream it," he said.

CHAPTER 16

Bobbie raced up the mountain to the Cairn. Niclas struggled to keep up with her. She heard him wheezing close behind. At the opening to the passage tomb, Bobbie bent at the waist, leaned her hands on her knees, and panted. From the corner of her eye, she saw Niclas do the same, his face flushed red, stark against his white facial hair.

Joy met them as they entered the central atrium of the tomb.

"Christ, what now?" she said, rushing to Niclas' side.

Niclas pointed at Bobbie.

"Don't eat from the matter streamers," Bobbie said, straightening up and rubbing a stitch in her side.

"Why not?"

"Fox has contaminated the matter streamer mix with nanobots."

Joy's hand went to her abdomen as Bobbie told her Davitt's newest memory.

"I have to get to Fox. I need to tell her Davitt was lying to her about fixing the glitches."

Joy's eyes widened, her mouth an 'o' of surprise.

"She doesn't know what Rejuvenation does to the reproductive system."

"Oh shit!" She had experienced the damage Rejuvenation could do.

Wishing she hadn't been so brusque, Bobbie scanned the room. "Where's Slade?"

Joy looked pale. "She's just identified Gustav."

"That's hard."

"She's meeting me here. I've extracted Gustav's ONIV footage, and I'm waiting for her to get here to watch it." Joy nodded to a portable intepanel behind her.

"Is it long? Do we have to watch it right away?"

"About fifteen minutes," Joy said, pulling a bench in front of the intepanel. "I haven't seen it, but I'm guessing it will tell us how Gustav died."

"It might give us something we can use as leverage with Fox," Niclas said, settling down on the bench. "I sent a blink to the village about the matter streamer when we were down the mountain. They'll spread the word."

"But for so many people, matter streamers are the only food source," Bobbie said. "Not everyone has access to fresh food."

"Look, we don't know if or when Fox plans to roll that out. All we can do is warn the Candels, and hope they can get food to those who need it," Niclas said.

"You're right," Bobbie said. "I just wish we had an encryption key to access the media broadcasting system. You could connect my eye-cam-di to public broadcast what I say to her – let the public hear what she's done, hear for themselves what she really thinks of the elderly, and close her down on this Rejuvenation thing once and for all."

Joy bit the color from her bottom lip, her eyes resting on the butterflies. "No-one has ever broken into the quantum computer before now, but you... oh...Ori!" Joy's bright greeting sounded splintered.

Bobbie turned to the door to watch Slade arrive. Despite the lines etched into the downturned corners of her mouth and the graying at the temples, Slade carried an air of resilience in her straight back and rigid shoulders.

"Let's get on with it," Slade said, passing Bobbie and sitting beside Niclas.

As Joy fired up the portable intepanel, Slade listened to Bobbie's update – her only reaction the flex of tiny muscles in her jawline.

April and Luke entered, engaged in easy conversation.

"Hang on," Slade said, stopping Bobbie mid-sentence. She beckoned April and Luke over and sat them down on seats next to the bench, facing the intepanels. Slade said to Bobbie, "Start again."

Bobbie began again, and watched their expressions darken as she told them what she had learned about the matter streamers. Luke shook his head and punched one clenched hand into the palm of the other. He stood up and paced a few steps. Slade jumped up beside him and caught his elbow and directed him back to his seat. He sat beside Bobbie with elbows on his knees, head in hands. Bobbie put her hand between his shoulder blades. At her touch, he turned to her. Lips pressed together, he gave her a sad smile.

"So it's worse than we thought," April said. "I suggest we take immediate action."

April's tone scared Bobbie. She ran her hand over her pocket, felt the edges of the cube press against her thigh.

"Now, April, let's not be hasty," Niclas said. "Let's get as much information as we can before we make our move."

"We have a weapon, and I believe it's the only way forward." April held eye contact with Niclas. Bobbie worried about his blood pressure as veins stood out above his temple, and his skin flushed.

"Davitt and Jinko will be working on the gentibots," Bobbie said. "And Hicks and I will be helping when we return."

"If you return." April swung her gaze to Bobbie, sending chills racing over Bobbie's scalp.

"April! Jesus!" Luke's anger made Bobbie heart heavy. How hard must it be for a parent to watch their child carry such a responsibility as she did today?

Had Niclas given her the trigger in the hopes that Bobbie would take it away, permanently out of reach? She watched him, but Niclas had drawn a mask down. His color returned to normal, and his gaze followed Joy's movements in front of the intepanel. It flickered with light, then went blank.

"Shit!" Joy disappeared around the back of the intepanel. After some rattling and tapping, she poked her head around the side and said, "I think it got damaged in the move. Sorry. I can cast this directly to your Foureyes from our intranet. Is that okay?"

"Just hurry up." Slade crossed her legs and folded her arms.

Bobbie didn't relish using the Foureyes app. Unlike the footage she'd viewed earlier, which was static, they'd experience everything as seen from Gustav's eyes. The nausea and disorientation would be nasty, but she was onboard with Slade's sentiment – the sooner, the better.

The image stuttered between her reality and Gustav's so rapidly for the first few seconds that Bobbie struggled to figure out what she was seeing. The warmth of her father's arm, pressed against hers as they sat side by side on the bench, brought her some comfort.

When the staccato of images settled, she saw old computers along a countertop in a variety of sizes, with lights flashing – some with a black screen and white text, others green with circles and dots. A series of LED screens hung on the wall – five, Bobbie counted, but Gustav's point of view didn't take in the whole wall. Each screen showed something different. Gustav's view stayed with the display in the middle. It showed a black background behind a metallic spherical structure, with metal rods protruding from the surface at right angles. Each rod ended in a flat panel like a paddle. When Gustav's gaze flicked to another screen, Bobbie saw the contraption silhouetted against bright light. All the paddles squared to the light, arranged so that none blocked any of the others, like leaves on a tree. Protruding from the side, nearly twice the length of the sphere, was a spike. An antenna, maybe?

What the hell was that? A Melters' ship?

Gustav's gaze swung to a computer screen. When he spoke, Bobbie thought she heard Slade gasp. Bobbie could imagine what it must be like for her to hear his voice after all these years.

"Solar collection at capacity."

So it wasn't a Melters' ship. Bobbie felt relieved.

The picture blurred. Bobbie figured Gustav was swinging around to look at something behind him. The visuals processed more slowly through Foureyes, with a lag-time that real vision didn't inflict upon the brain. The picture steadied on a waist-high model of the apparatus on the screen, set into a well in the ground with a little knee-high wall around it. Was it a scaled-down version of what they saw on the screen? Was the real thing in space?

"Ready to receive energy download," said a tinny voice.

Gustav swung his head to a different LED screen that showed a map of Africa. A red circle with crosshairs appeared in the middle of the continent. The map zoomed closer. The crosshairs pulsed.

Bobbie hadn't time to process the details as a siren blasted three times.

An automated voice said, "Solar energy overload."

Gustav looked at Fox. She stood beside him, frowning and shaking her head as she took in the screens. "It's failing to buffer."

"We have to release it," Gustav said, turning to another monitor with streams of data. "We can't send it downstream. The energy harvest is far higher than we calculated."

In the background, the alarm continued, three blasts of what sounded like a foghorn and interspersed with the message, "Solar energy overload."

"Let's siphon this off and start again."

"Copy that," the tinny voice said. "Shutting down receptors."

Gustav's view flicked between his fingers rapidly typing and a screen with commands that Bobbie couldn't decipher. A different alarm sounded, a shrill harmony against the menacing timbre of the first alarm.

"Shit!" Gustav said as his screen flashed in red the words, "Siphon malfunction."

"Initiating emergency shutdown," Fox said, typing.

Gustav watched the screen, but it continued to flash the same warning.

"It should have shut down," Fox said. "I'll try again."

Gustav's view swung between Fox punching commands into a keyboard, the picture of the solar collector on the LED screen, and his monitor. "Why isn't it shutting down?" he asked.

"Fuck! I don't know."

"We have to shut it down if we can't siphon off the energy."

"I fucking know that!" Fox said through clenched teeth.

Gustav turned to Fox. "Let the collector explode in space."

"What? And lose decades of work? We're on the brink of controlling the best, cleanest energy source humanity has ever had." She turned her back to him and typed on a keyboard, glancing up to check the data from several screens.

"Its thermal energy is too high," Gustav said, putting a hand on her shoulder.

Fox shrugged it off and kept working. "The solar collector will give us control of the earth's economy. I'm not going to let this just become space garbage."

"If it discharges, it's going to destroy the battery station and take the whole city with it."

"Not if I rotate the downstream conductor – send it into space."

Gustav's view flicked to the screen with the solar collector silhouette. The protruding antenna was moving. He looked at the screen with the map of Africa. The target slid slowly south over the vast landmass.

"Come on, come on!" Fox's voice urged.

Bobbie held her breath, positive that nothing good was going to happen. The target crept over the South African coastline and across the ocean.

Bobbie breathed out, but Fox still looked concerned. Whatever the risk was, it hadn't passed yet.

The alarm halted. An automated voice announced, "Solar harvest deployed."

"Jesus Christ!" Gustav's eyes went back to the map.

With horror, Bobbie realized that it wasn't a graphic. There were clouds and weather systems and parts in shadow where night had fallen. It was a view of Earth from the solar collector. The antenna hadn't moved fast enough, and the target was still over Antarctica. A beam of dazzling white light flashed from the solar collector. It hit the snowy landmass. A mushroom cloud rose that was so colossal, it showed as a bulge on the outline of the planet.

"Jesus Christ! Jesus Christ!" Gustav said.

Fox stood motionless, staring at the screen.

Bobbie was paralyzed, too stunned to react.

"No," Luke said. Her arm felt cold where his had been. The bench flexed beneath her. Air moved in the space where her father had been sitting beside her and wafted in front of her. Was he up and walking? She heard him, further from her now, still repeating the one word, "No!"

Bobbie felt tears wet her face, heard Joy sobbing, but it was all too much to process.

Gustav's eyes scanned the screens and monitors, too quickly for Bobbie to figure out what he was searching for. The visual snapped to a hand on a remote control. Another view of a screen with a CNN news anchor showed him jovial and smiling. It switched to a BBC broadcast of a sports team celebrating. There was no "breaking news" here either.

Gustav's voice sounded thick and flat. "Lisette, we need to warn the governments–"

"No!" she hissed, "No, no, no! This has been a secret mission. Only a small team of us knew this trial was happening. We can make this go away."

"Go away? Jesus Christ, Lisette, we blew up a continent!"

"Shut up!"

119

"You think no-one will notice? The ice is melting – fast. We have to get coastal populations to safety."

"Let me think."

"But the media?"

"You fool." Fox clicked on a tab and brought up more code. "We have the Beysil Shield."

Gustav scanned the code and said, "Block the media channels?"

"Redirect them through our central channel." She hit the return button. "There. We own the media – I tell it what to think. Control the media, and you control what the people think."

"And the team in the Congo?"

Fox punched commands into a keyboard. A yellow bar rose on a screen. Numbers counted up. Gustav watched the solar collector rotate.

"What are you doing?" His voice had the high pitch of a man confused and panicked. "Lisette?" He put his hand on her shoulders.

She shrugged him off roughly and turned to face him, wild-eyed. "They're the only other people who know about this project. There's no evidence this was us. We have to do this."

"We?"

On the screen, the cross-hairs lined up in the middle of Africa.

"You love me, don't you? If they catch us, we'll be sent to jail for the rest of our lives. Separated forever. I can't have that."

She turned back to the keyboard.

"No!" Gustav leaped after her.

She spun back toward him, hands outstretched, and shoved him hard.

A gap sprang open between them.

There was a squelching, sucking noise.

Gustav's view dropped. The tip of the antenna from the solar collector model protruded from his chest. Blood squirted, fast and far, for a couple of beats, then slowed. A rasping hiss of sloshing air – rhythmical yet diminishing, like a pendulum slowing down – filled the audio of the ONIV. The noise stuttered, punctuated with silence. The view shifted up, tilted to one side.

A hush settled as the audio signal gave up, but the visual continued.

Lisette's mouth opened in a soundless scream as she approached. The focus of Gustav's viewpoint stayed long, the ciliary muscles no longer varying the focal length of his eyes, Bobbie guessed, so that as Lisette came closer, her features blurred. She backed away, shaking her head, a bloodied hand clasped over her mouth.

Around her, Bobbie heard the muffled sobs of her companions, or perhaps they were her own cries. Gustav's view greyed out in patches at the edges as cells in his retina broke down. Enough cells fired to build an image even after his death. In front of him, Lisette threw her head back, her hands out and her mouth wide open.

A keening rose from the end of the bench where Slade had been sitting. The noise tore at Bobbie. She put her hands over her ears, but closing her eyes didn't take away the image of the demented woman in front of her. Fox stood like that for a split second longer, then snapped to attention and stepped in front of the screen with the view of the earth.

Fox pressed a key. A blast took out the team in the Congo. She threw her head back, like she was howling, and sank to her knees. She cried, violent body-convulsing sobs as she hauled herself to half-standing over the console and keyed in more commands.

Time stood still for Bobbie as the memories of that day, twenty years ago, crashed in on her – the terror, the news reports, the call to war. This was all Lisette Fox, their supposed savior, and not Melters?

Gustav's death-gaze settled on the screen in front of Fox. Patches lost color as the retina's cones died. But his ONIV still received enough neural stimulation for Bobbie to see the cross-hairs moving to the East Coast of the United States. The target settled over Washington DC. Another blast of white light flew from the solar collector. Fox keyed in more commands as the image became tattered and fragmented. It was still possible to make out the target lining up over the San Francisco Bay Area before the picture winked out completely, dropping Bobbie back into the gloom of the tomb, with retina ghosts drifting in orange blotches before her eyes.

CHAPTER 17

Was this what insanity felt like? Bobbie wondered. She sat welded to the bench as if she and it were carved from a block of marble. Sitting heavy, cold, immobile, she saw herself as if from above – her red hair dulling, her skin solidifying, her hands fused to the bench.

Silence fractured around her. Bedlam broke out. The cacophony was excruciating.

Slade lay on the floor at the end of the bench, curled into a fetal position. She sawed air back and forth through her vocal cords in a wail that pulled Bobbie's skin into goosebumps. Bobbie welcomed the sensation. It meant she hadn't turned to stone. She still couldn't lift her hands from the bench, but she could turn her head.

She scanned the room, glancing over Slade keening, past Niclas rising from beside April, checked in on Joy – on her feet but shaken – and finally, Bobbie focused on her father. He was punching the portable intepanel, screaming, "No," with every impact, over and over until the screen shattered. Bloodied splinters of plastic flew from his fists. He pummeled until the intepanel clattered to the ground. That seemed to feed his fury. He kicked it until he reduced it to rubble. Only when it lay in shards did he stop. He stood staring at the damage, breathing heavily through flared nostrils, blood dripping from his knuckles.

His loss of control scared Bobbie. She watched him rein himself in, bubble down, and flex his bleeding hands. Had his reaction frightened her sister? Bobbie turned to Joy. She stood with her hands clasped over her face, peering through her splayed fingertips, her eyes darting between Slade and her father. She looked young and lost.

Bobbie wriggled her fingers. Sensation flooded her extremities.

On the other bench, April rocked back and forth. Bobbie's body responded to the visual cadence. Her shoulders moved forward and back in time with April swaying. The movement, odd yet comforting, fastened Bobbie's thoughts back to her body.

Niclas reached Luke and placed his hand on his shoulder. They exchanged a dark glance, the space between them so charged, Bobbie could swear she saw the air pulse with energy.

It was as if Bobbie had reached the outer boundaries, the furthermost point her spirit could travel without leaving her body altogether, and then she snapped back into herself.

In two strides, she was by Slade's side.

"Shush, now," Bobbie crooned, rubbing Slade's shoulder with one hand, checking her pulse with the other. She stopped short of her usual doctor's mantra of, "You're okay."

Nothing was okay.

"What happened?" Jinko said, arriving through the passageway and skidding to a stop. He stared at Slade as she continued to keen.

"Shock," Bobbie said over the noise of Slade's sobs. "We've all had a shock. Go get John. Bring blankets and tea, warm and sweet."

"Are you serious?" He took in the devastated people in the room. "How?"

"Please, help me. Go quickly."

Jinko left.

He and she were on different sides of a rip in the universe. Jinko still believed that the Melters had wreaked havoc on their planet. Bobbie couldn't decide if she envied him his ignorance or not. Which was an easier reality to bear? That an alien race had done this to them, or that it had been the result of one accident and a deranged human?

There were no Melters!

Bobbie could hardly believe it. Most of her life had been lived beneath a lie. She had trusted Lisette Fox, had admired the woman. Yet the reality was so convoluted... Bobbie did a double-take as if she'd jolted awake. She'd been staring at the wall, with her hand on Slade's shoulder. Slade's weeping had stopped.

Niclas came over and hunkered beside Bobbie, his old knees cracking with the effort. "Is she okay?"

"She will be," Bobbie said, more for Slade's sake than Niclas', and not entirely believing her own words. "Ori, can you hear me?"

Slade didn't respond.

"Niclas, get Dad to help you bring the benches around the table, please. Let's get everyone seated there." It wasn't much of a plan, but Bobbie needed to distract them, help them pull themselves together, build a life-raft, so each didn't flounder alone in their own quagmire of grief, or horror, or rage, or lethargy – the options were far-ranging and all terrible.

Niclas lumbered to his feet and shuffled off toward Luke. Bobbie heard them exchange words, and to her relief, Luke sounded like himself. They moved the first bench, leaving April rocking on the other one.

"Joy," Bobbie called.

Joy startled, stepped back, then turned to face Bobbie, her forehead wrinkled in bewilderment.

"Give me a hand here?" Bobbie said, then more gently, "Please?"

Joy came forward and dropped to one knee.

"Ori," Bobbie said, keeping her voice soft. "Joy and I are going to help you. Do you think you can stand?"

Slade stared off over Bobbie's shoulder with an expression that carried the desolation of a derelict house. It creeped Bobbie out. She took Slade's hand and gave it a jiggle, saying, "Ori?"

Slade's expression didn't change.

Bobbie drew her hand back and slapped Slade's face so hard her fingers stung.

Joy flinched.

Slade inhaled. Her eyes focused. She grunted out her next breath, then said to Bobbie, "You get to do that only once."

Despite her hammering heart, Bobbie smiled. Slade was back. She sat up.

Joy and Bobbie helped Slade to her feet. Joy went with her to the table.

"Are you okay?" Bobbie asked Joy.

"Something Fox said, Bobbie. I've seen it before." Joy's forehead puckered.

"What?"

"I'm not even sure I have words to explain it – it's something I should have paid attention to. I need to think." She sat down at the table beside Slade, chewing her lip. "Fuck, I'll have to watch the ONIV footage again."

"Right now?" Bobbie asked.

"Yes – it's important – if I can just get a handle on it." Joy's eyes zoned out. Bobbie knew she was rerunning the footage. She didn't envy her.

Bobbie went to April and took her hand. April stopped rocking and looked at Bobbie with fiery eyes. This woman was fully present, Bobbie thought – home with all the lights on.

"I'm not going to ask you if you're okay," Bobbie said. "But we're here now. That's all that matters."

The skin on April's chin dimpled. She shook her head, then switched to a slow nod. Bobbie felt the burn in her throat and couldn't trust herself to speak either. Their clasped hands tightened as they fought the urge to cry. They sat together, let the moment pass, and drew on each other's strength.

When Bobbie could speak, she whispered, "Will we join the others?"

"Too damn right we will." April's voice came loud and strong. She stood up and lifted one end of the bench, and waited for Bobbie to take the other. In the same way that Luke's outburst had frightened Bobbie, she felt unnerved by April's cool exterior. Bobbie sensed that somewhere deep down in April there had been a detonation, but April had suppressed it. What would happen if it roiled to the surface?

Jinko and John arrived back, laden down with flasks and blankets. Bobbie insisted that each of the six who had seen the footage take a blanket, even if they didn't feel cold. Jinko poured the tea and handed out the steaming beakers.

"Waz this about?" John asked, directing his question primarily at Joy.

"We've come across intel that's very disturbing," Niclas said. "We need to be careful about how we break this news to everyone else. You've seen our reaction."

Jinko looked scared.

"It's information about the past," Bobbie said. "It doesn't change anything about what needs to be done now." Like get to Fox, get Hicks back, and stop Rejuvenation.

"After we've made a copy—" April began.

"Already done," Joy said. "Several copies."

"Good. Then we have to broadcast this footage," April said.

"No – people can't cope–"

"Niclas," Luke said. "I understand your concerns, but we have to. We'll set the context, post trigger warnings–"

"Like that will help," Joy said.

Luke turned to her. "Can you set that up?"

Joy nodded.

"There will be riots, violence in the streets," Niclas said. "We need to control the fallout–"

"We can't. There's been too much control already. There's no kid-gloving this," Luke said. "People have seen worse, more graphic, more shocking footage. At least this is the truth."

Niclas frowned and stroked his bread. He looked around the group and cleared his throat. "Am I the only one against this idea?"

"I'm with Luke and April," Slade said.

Joy stepped forward. "Me too."

Niclas sighed. "Okay, democracy rules, but democracy isn't always smart. We need to split up, take multiple copies with us in case there's another attack."

"How do we show the footage?" Bobbie said. "We have no access to the broadcasting system. If we sent it out P2P, people will dismiss it as some whacko fake. Belus – no, Fox – will discredit it. She owns the media. Let's first decide how I'm going to confront her. I have to go there tonight. We need to record the encounter, and then we can figure out a way to break into her broadcasting system."

"Like you're going to just walk in there and hand over the head and get your man back? The woman is a fucking whack job," April said. "Fox's not going to listen to you. You saw what she's capable of."

"I'm out of options. Maybe I'll get through to Fox when I reveal that Davitt lied – when she realizes that nanobots make people sterile."

"The women blasted half the planet to hell to cover up a mistake," April spat. "Do you really think she's going to develop a conscience now?"

"I don't need to make her listen," Bobbie said. "I need to make everyone else listen."

"How will that get Hicks back?" Joy's question turned Bobbie to ice.

"I'm hoping to have him back by then," Bobbie said.

"And I'm going with you to kill her," Slade said.

For a beat, everyone went quiet.

The bench creaked as Slade stood up. "The coordinates Fox gave us are Belus Headquarters."

"Why didn't she just say so?" Bobbie asked. "Fucking nutjob! She invited me. I'm going. I have no alternative." She sounded braver than she felt. Would Fox honor the deal? Was Hicks even alive? God, she couldn't bear to think he wasn't. She had to go. Hopefully, Fox was crazy enough that she'd keep her end of the bargain. Fox had nothing to lose and, Bobbie realized, neither had she. Without Hicks, her world was empty, and living on it with the guilt of not trying to get him would be hell.

"After what you've just seen, you expect the woman to be rational?" April said. "You think she's just going to let you walk into her lair?"

"If I have Gustav's head with me, then yes, I think she will. Maybe she realizes we can take out the old ONIV, and wants it back before we figure out how to do that. Too late for that now, but Fox doesn't know that …yet." After what she'd just seen, Bobbie wanted more than ever to confront Fox, look her in the eye, and ask her what gave her the right to play God. It might be a death sentence, but she had to go back there. "I have to go now," she said.

"How? We've no hovercrafts," Luke said. "Take the tractor?"

Bobbie moved to the door. "There's a cargo craft ready at the foot of the mountain."

"And you've already talked to Davitt?" Slade said.

"Yes, and we're wasting time. Let's get on that cargo craft to Switzerland. I'll update you on the way."

Bobbie left. She heard the scuffle of benches and feet and knew they were right behind her.

* * *

As Niclas had promised, a cargo craft waited, fueled and ready to go. She climbed in and went to the back of the cab. A plain wooden box sat in the corner, strapped to the floor. She lifted the lid. Gustav's head lay face up, barely recognizable as a face. Bobbie didn't think this would bring Fox any comfort. Fear uncoiled in her so quickly she felt dizzy. She could abort the mission, run far away, but if there was any chance that Hicks was still alive, she'd as good as killed him herself if she didn't go. But why would Fox give her anything back?

Slade sat upfront. She hadn't tried to talk Bobbie out of going. Perhaps Slade realized Bobbie had nothing to lose either. With Jinko and Davitt both working on the vaccine and the gentibots, was Bobbie expendable?

Luke took a seat at the controls. Bobbie had a view of their faces in the reflections of the glass because of the darkness outside.

Joy pulled herself into the cab.

"Where do you think you're going?" Bobbie asked.

"I need to be close to the ops mainframe at Belus HQ." Joy smiled. Her eyes sparkled. "Something Fox said in that footage..."

Bobbie shook her head. Joy would be safer here.

"Please, Bobbie. We need to do this... together."

Their mother's last words caught in Bobbie's heart – *Together Joy and you, together you can do anything.*

"I need to be there to help you." Joy's eyes bored into Bobbie's with burning ferocity."It's too complicated to explain quickly."

Dammit, Bobbie didn't have time to argue. Joy could stay with Luke, stay safe that way.

"Get in. We'll talk on the way." Bobbie looked out the windscreen and raised a hand as Joy settled into the seat at the back beside Bobbie.

Niclas waved back from the yard.

April had her back turned, already walking toward the radio transmitter container. Bobbie felt for the Rubik's cube and locked eyes with Niclas. He gave one slow nod before the engines whirled a dust cloud between them.

They rose into the night. The crescent moon slipped behind a cloud. Lights of the people living in ignorance sprinkled the darkness below. Bobbie looked up at the stars and thought about the fact that the heavens were safe, always had been. So much made sense now. She'd always wondered why the authorities hadn't tried to capture a Melter, why the policy had been to blow them up instead. Fox had unleashed the bogey man. Then she'd protected him by scaring everyone with the prospect of space viruses.

"How did Fox pull it off? Why didn't anyone know about the solar collector?" Bobbie asked.

"Back then governments, even private companies, were testing rockets to go into space," Slade said. "Everyone was afraid that someone would steal their tech. Fox and Gustav were very wary about it. They never talked about their projects."

"But surely there were powerful enough telescopes to see the solar collector? Why didn't anyone see what they'd done?" Joy asked.

"I think people did see it," Bobbie said. "Remember the sequence of events? Antarctica melted. Then Fox hit their own station in the Congo next so they couldn't raise the alarm. Meanwhile, tsunamis rolled out across the oceans, nature in chaos, flooding and mudslides. No-one knew where to look or what hit them. It was her news channel that suggested an extraterrestrial attack. That was easier to believe than–"

"Yeah, then she blasted NASA, New York, Washington, Silicon Valley, and various sites in China, India, Russia, and the Middle East," Luke said. "The war department thought that the Melters had really done their research. Europe was largely unscathed, apart from the floods and climatic devastation."

"So she could pick up the pieces, come to the rescue with her technology," Slade said through gritted teeth. "Fox made us all think that Belus Corp were the heroes and that she was the savior. Christ, no wonder she has a God complex now. How the fuck did I fall for it?"

"We all believed it," Bobbie said. The memories of the celebrations on Peace Day made her stomach burn with acid. "How were we so easy to fool?"

"It's par for the course with us humans," Luke said, turning his head and flinging the words over his shoulder to her. "We always want to believe what we're told."

"But didn't someone, anyone, ask for evidence?" Bobbie felt a surge of anger at those who had been adults at the time. She'd only been sixteen, had taken everything at face value, but she'd still had the wit to wonder what a Melter looked like.

Slade cracked a bitter laugh but didn't turn to face the girls. "I was Fox's friend. She lied to me the most, and I believed everything she said. Humans propagate untruths all the time. There's Santa Claus, and the tooth fairy, and the fucking Easter Bunny."

"I never believed in the Easter Bunny," Joy said.

"You didn't?" Luke asked, keeping his focus on the control panel.

"Nah, Dad, a rabbit laying eggs? It didn't make sense."

"But a fat man coming down the blocked-off chimney with presents did?" Luke said.

"We're talking about the merits of Santa Claus and the Easter Bunny," Bobbie said. "When what I can't get my head around is that we all believed in Melters! They terrified the entire planet. How the fuck did that happen? You went to war against them, Dad."

Her father's face dropped in the reflection of the window.

Bobbie wished she hadn't said that. "I'm sorry, I'm just trying to process this."

"It's okay, love, we all are. You're just one step ahead of us. You were always faster to the gate," Luke said, turning and patting Bobbie's arm. "Don't beat yourself up about believing the propaganda. Humans all through history have done it."

"He's right," Slade said. "Look at all the wars about religion. People had no proof there was a God, yet they believed enough to fight for one."

"But you know that those wars were never about God. They were a vehicle for some people to gain resources, wield power over others," Joy said.

"Isn't that what Fox did?" Bobbie said. "Except instead of holding God and the Devil and damnation over our heads, she wheeled out different demons."

"We humans are foolish," Luke said. "We didn't believe in climate change, despite all the evidence, because the world leaders didn't tell us to."

"I knew it was happening, I believed," Bobbie said. "All of us youngsters believed. But it became a moot point after the Melters– after Fox attacked."

"Even Fox believed that something needed to be done about our energy generation," Slade said. The anger seemed to evaporate from her and leave behind sadness. "She was trying. Gustav was..." Her face flushed red. She looked down and covered her mouth with her hand.

"It was a terrible mistake," Bobbie said with sudden sympathy for Fox. How would that moment when the beam hit Antarctica have felt to Fox? Maybe Bobbie could make Fox see that by stopping the spread of the nanobots, she could avert a disaster this time around. Could Bobbie offer Fox a form of salvation? Fox had been trying so hard to help humanity in both instances, and it had all gone. Bobbie pushed her compassion away. Facing the facts was horrifying enough. She couldn't deal with empathizing too.

"It nearly happened with Chernobyl," Luke said.

Joy looked at Bobbie and raised an eyebrow. Bobbie shrugged, shaking her head. It happened way before their time.

"I know it was a nuclear accident, but not the details," Bobbie said. "How was it similar?"

"When the accident first occurred, no-one knew what was happening or what was going to happen next. The Russian government tried to play it down. A couple of the scientists realized they were in danger of a larger explosion if the radioactive core wasn't secured. They fought to get that information to the people in power. Thankfully they did, and saved a lot of lives."

"Fox has probably killed their descendants," Joy said.

"Yes, but the point is, it could have been as big a disaster as Fox's initial mistake. But it wasn't," Slade said. "The government cover-up was exposed, eventually."

"Remember the whole "Fake News" movement too?" Luke said.

Slade nodded. "Oh, God, yes. It was getting impossible to know what to believe."

"So why believe Fox's story?" Joy asked.

Slade and Luke exchanged a long glance.

"The news reports," Slade said; she twisted in her seat to face Bobbie. "You would have seen them too, right? The footage was so convincing and no-one, absolutely no-one called it out. Usually, if there was any doubt someone would have – even the moon landings in the last century were getting scrutinized. We were too bamboozled by the Melters attack."

"Except it wasn't a Melters attack." Joy's voice held a bitter edge.

"I know," Bobbie said. "But I remember the news footage. It was so huge – so horrific – so inhuman, that perhaps that was why it was easier to make us believe it was aliens." Bobbie realized they needed to exonerate themselves for believing the whole con. It was their path through the madness.

"We have to get this truth out there too," she said, sitting forward. "I didn't know what the world will make of it, but once they're shown the lies Fox has already told them, perhaps they'll accept that Rejuvenation too is a lie."

Slade faced forward in her seat, nodding.

We have limited blink, April messaged from Armagh, *Keep sending, some will get picked up.*

"How?" Bobbie asked Joy.

"They can bounce the messages through village servers and relay them, but that can take a few seconds. If we do too much, it will raise flags. Last thing we want is the village to be attacked," Joy said.

"Are you back online?"

A shadow felt across Joy's face. "No. Belus knows my signal. I'm certain that's how they found the ship. As soon as I go online, I'll be found."

"So stay offline."

Joy frowned. Bobbie snuggled against her, slung her arm around her shoulders and hugged her close. Joy nestled her head between Bobbie's shoulder and ear. Bobbie inhaled the scent of Joy's hair, heather and wood smoke. She thought of the times she and Gracie had sat cuddled together, just being sisters. Gracie would never have been such an asshole to Joy as Bobbie had been through the years, yet Bobbie loved Joy, and knew Joy loved her. Did Joy expect Bobbie to die in this encounter with Fox? Was this her goodbye? Bobbie kissed the top of Joy's head. She wanted to say, "Hang in there, I'll be back," but she couldn't guarantee it. All the things she really wanted to say, all her truths, all her love, jammed up in her throat.

CHAPTER 18

The clouds swallowed them as they rose in the hovercar. Bobbie wished she could see the night sky. For the first time since she was sixteen, she could look at the stars without fear of what lay beyond. What a stunning hoodwink, Bobbie thought. Fox had convinced people that aliens had attacked, but humanity had believed lies from less skilled, more under-resourced liars than Fox, many of whom had been equally crazy.

And now she was on her way to confront Fox. Rich, powerful, insane Fox.

It made Bobbie question if she was sane herself. She couldn't rely on anything Fox said. Hicks might not be alive. But if he was, Christ Almighty, Bobbie had no other choice. She had to go do this.

Bobbie settled into her seat behind Luke and Slade while beside her, Joy explained how she would break into the quantum computer system to stop Fox from jamming all broadcasts except those by Belus Corp.

"How did you know where to look for the encryption key code?" Bobbie asked.

"When Fox said she was going to use the jamming system, she called it the 'Beysil' Shield. I'd seen that word a half-hour earlier in the decrypted files you gave me on the butterflies. It's on every one of them, like a header. We've never been able to take anything off the quantum computer before. Part of the answer was there all along, but only part of it. The Beysil Shield key needs a specific code to turn it on or off. When Fox set it up the first time, she looked at the code on a monitor. Fortunately for us, Gustav looked at it at the same time. I'm re-running the footage again now to extract the code..." Joy held up her pinkie finger with the embedded electrode. "Literally, the answer will be at my fingertips any minute."

"So why do you need to be at Belus headquarters? Couldn't you have hacked into the broadcasting system from anywhere?" Bobbie asked.

Joy down looked at the console in her lap. Her hair fell forward. Bobbie couldn't see her face as she said, "The key is specific to this site. This is where all the broadcasts originate. I don't need to be inside the building, just close enough to fool it into thinking that the command is coming from a local ONIV or console."

"You can't use your ONIV," Slade said.

"I know, I know." Joy held up a console. "That's why I brought this clunk with me."

"Are you sure it even works?" Luke asked.

Joy blushed. "Of course it does."

An uncomfortable quiet settled over them. Outside, the marine layer wrapped them in blackness, flinging a film of condensation over the windows.

Joy rubbed her arms. "Look, even if I don't manage to break into the system tonight, we're still going to record Bobbie's interaction with Fox. It would be much better if we could send it out live. It's irrefutable evidence then, and Bobbie stands a better chance if this footage goes out. I can't imagine any of the Belus staff following orders from Fox once they know the truth."

"How will I know that you're sending it live? You can't blink to tell me."

"The solid red recording eye-con will change to flashing red when it's live broadcasting," Joy said.

"Flashing red for live. Got it." If only it were that easy, Bobbie thought. "And audio will work even if–" Bobbie couldn't lay that scenario on Joy. She changed tack. "Even if I'm turned the other way, or my eyes are... shut?"

Joy locked onto Bobbie's gaze. "Yes, even then."

The look on Joy's face nearly broke Bobbie's resolve, but they were out of time. She was out of time. Why had she wasted so much time? She wanted more time, a do-over on the times she'd already spent. The years she'd held Hicks at arm's length, been Hicks' friend when she could have been his lover, wife, mother to their children. And Joy, dear God! Why hadn't she savored those days playing with Joy as a toddler in their garden before the so-called Melters' War? Instead, all Bobbie had done was resent and scold the child. All the fighting throughout Joy's teens, and now when they'd found their true connection...

Bobbie hadn't been a good big sister, not in the way Gracie had been to her. Gracie. Always remembered with love and pain in equal measure. How would Joy remember Bobbie—with a fistful of regrets if—?

"Bobbie, can you watch out for the drop-off?" Luke's words snapped her mind back to the task at hand. They were over the Swiss Alps, flying in and out of patchy cloud. Luke dropped the craft to fly low to the ground.

"It's too dark," Bobbie said. "I can't see a thing."

"I'll use the coordinates where we were picked up yesterday. We'll hot-foot it to the ventilation shaft exit from there."

"Don't you think they'll have that secured somehow?" Bobbie hadn't liked the idea of Luke and Slade going in the same way they'd escaped. Fox would have figured out it was their escape route once she'd found Gustav's head missing. But, Bobbie had to admit, this was the best plan they had been able to come up with in the short time they had. At least Joy had agreed to stay out of the facility. She'd hide out on the mountain and wait for them to rendezvous.

"We'll sort it out," Slade said. "Shouldn't be more than one or two guards, easier than shooting our way in through the front door." Slade placed the strap to her laser gun across her shoulder. She'd had to remove her sling to accommodate the weapon. She passed Luke another firearm. "We'll find you inside. I have a good idea where Fox will be. Once Joy gets your footage broadcasting, I'll be able to see for certain – if we haven't already reached you by then."

"Sure," Bobbie said but thought, *What the fuck am I doing? I'm a geriatrician...*

"I'll wait at the top of the shaft," Joy said.

"We'll pick you up there, then," Bobbie said, but she might never get that far. She wanted to formulate a plan B – but if Bobbie didn't make it back, Luke and Slade would need to send out a call for help. They'd know what to do if they had to. She couldn't dwell on that.

The cargo craft landed on a flat grassy patch. Large rocks scattered over the ground, and Bobbie considered replacing Gustav's head in the box with one of them. She could check that Hicks was still alive, and tell Fox the location of the head only when she'd let Hicks go and they were safely away. Play that one bargaining chip to the max. But what if it sent Fox into a rage? Better to pretend she was playing straight, get her talking, record as much incriminating footage as possible. Getting the truth out to the masses was the ultimate goal now.

Her fear was hard to control, but she knew if she let it take hold, it would get the better of her. Back when she was telling patients bad news at the hospital, she would break it down into pieces and focus on one step at a time; getting them comfortable, saying the words, answering each question. If she had looked at the whole situation, her emotions would have overcome her, and she'd have been no use to anyone.

Get to the front door of Belus – she wouldn't think about the next step until then.

There were more weapons in the back of the cargo craft. Bobbie didn't take one. She was going in by the front door, and the guards would take it from her. She watched as Luke and Slade strapped weapons on and filled their backpacks with ammunition and batteries.

"Okay, ready?" Luke asked Slade.

"Yup." Slade raised a hand and saluted Bobbie. "Catch you inside, kiddo."

Joy had a laser gun in a holster under one arm and carried the console under her other arm, like a child carrying a book she never intended to read. She came up to Bobbie and slipped her arm around her waist.

"Stand strong, big sis," Joy said, leaning in to kiss Bobbie's cheek. "Dad will look after you."

"Stay safe," Bobbie said. "I love you." It felt too much like goodbye.

Joy's eyes watered. She seemed about to speak, but instead, her face crumpled. She nodded and stepped back.

Bobbie climbed back into the cargo craft.

"Press the green button," Luke called after her.

"I know, Dad!" Despite the drag at her heart, Bobbie smiled. He'd already told her a dozen times how to initiate the self-drive. If she didn't survive this, he'd remember those as her last words to him – in years to come, it would make him smile too.

The three-minute flight to the Belus Headquarters parking area felt like the longest journey Bobbie had ever made. She felt overexposed in the parking area floodlights. Like a one-woman procession, she carried the wooden box with Gustav's head in both arms, held out in front of her. She imagined a thousand eyes on her, and Fox waiting for her. Forcing each lift of a foot, each bend of a knee, each step felt like a work of art, a work of endurance. She had to keep going forward – no turning back now.

Last time she was here, she'd snuck in through the side entrance. Now she approached the front door and met her reflection mirrored in the dark glass. With her hair wild and fiery, the blisters on her forehead raw and angry, she looked unhinged. Above the door hung the Belus Corporation's crest, a man with butterfly wings – supposed to represent the God of War, and as their propaganda had gone, the War that truly had ended all wars. Of course, Bobbie knew now, it had never been a war; it had been a wipeout.

Before Bobbie could worry about how she'd gain access, the doors slid open with a whisper. A uniformed Belus guard stepped forward, stern-faced, tall, and broad-shouldered.

Bobbie stepped back. Her heart hammered.

"Ms. Fox has been expecting you," he said.

Bobbie checked his eyes: brown without any trace of orange. He might be a Belus guard, but he wasn't Rejuvenated and ignorant of the ultimate truth about Fox. What would he do when he knew?

"Can I carry that for you?" he asked.

"Eh, no thanks." Bobbie clasped the box to her chest. The cube in her pocket dug into her hip.

The foyer felt opulent. The vast space had a real white marble floor and marble-effect intepaneled walls. A spotlight shone on a pedestal holding a model of the first commercial hovercar – the Mini-zoom. Other spotlights shone on artwork, paintings, and sculptures. She recognized Klimt's "Lovers Kiss" taking pride of place in the center of the lobby. Fox's message floated back to her: *Love is the strongest force in our universe. Don't fuck it up.*

Even in the dead of night, people scurried about. Few talked. The only sounds were the blipping of keypads and the swishing of doors. Some workers stared at her; others sent sidelong glances her way, seemingly fearful she would catch them looking.

The guard led her to a table with scanning equipment just on the inside of the door. A woman stepped forward and gave Bobbie a nervous smile.

"Please put the box on the counter." The woman returned to the other side of the table and seemed to relax a little.

"Do you want me to open it?" Bobbie reached for it.

"No, no – it's fine," the woman said with a brittle smile. Her gaze darted toward the guard.

He stepped forward and lowered Bobbie's arm and said, "Ms. Fox has instructed us not to open this box. A scan will suffice."

He watched the numbers scrolling on an intepanel set into the table. Even upside down, Bobbie recognized the formatting. They were reading her biosensors.

The heart rate increased on the screen.

"You can't do that," Bobbie said. "That information is private medical data."

The woman's smile flattened. She dropped her eyes and concentrated on the data.

"Civilians' data is protected. You're a criminal," the guard said. There was no malice in his tone. Bobbie could see he was simply stating the facts as he saw them. "Are you carrying explosives?" he asked.

"No. And if I was, would I tell you?"

He looked at the biosensor data. Bobbie's output was steady. Belus was using her biosensors as a cursory lie detector. The irony of it made her want to laugh, or cry, or both. She was the only one in the entire building, apart from Fox, who knew the truth.

"Please just answer the questions," the guard said, giving her a funny look. "Empty your pockets."

She set the cube on the table.

"What is that?"

"It's a toy."

"A toy?"

"From the last century. A Rubik's cube. You can look it up."

"Why do you have it?"

"I'm keeping it safe for someone." Bobbie read the data, saw it hold, and met the guard's eye. "I'm not a criminal."

The guard's expression stayed flinty as he watched the data remain steady. He looked at the woman behind the table. She raised her eyebrows, as if answering a question with, "Maybe?" Bobbie figured they were blinking each other. The woman picked up a scanner wand and passed it over the box. Nothing. But when she waved it over the cube, the wand blipped.

"It's got magnets, I think," Bobbie said. She kept her breathing level. Her heart rate rose, but only for a few beats and settled. She was pretty sure the guard didn't trust the data anymore, and so long as April didn't get her hands on the cube, Bobbie was happy to let it go. "You want to keep the toy?"

The guard gave her a dirty look. "Take your belongings. Ms. Fox will see you now, come this way."

"Wow, oversensitive," Bobbie said in a stage whisper. The woman behind the table dropped her gaze, puckering her lips together as though fighting a smile.

I'm in. Bobbie blinked, hoping her Dad, Slade, or April might pick it up. A reply might ward off the crushing loneliness she felt.

No-one answered.

Bobbie followed the guard through several sets of sliding doors. Each time a set swooshed closed behind her, the air contracted around her. She had the feeling these doors wouldn't open so easily should she turn around and try to leave. Her tunic felt damp. Perspiration stung the scabs on her forehead. She pulled her elbows in tight to stop the trickle of sweat down her sides.

Focus on the next step – present the box to Fox.

Nothing looked to Bobbie as it had the first time she'd had come through here, in disguise with her father. She thought she might recognize the way to the quantum computer, but the guard led her to a different part of the building. When she'd come with her father to break into the quantum computer, they had gone deep into the bowels of the complex. Now the guard stopped in front of an elevator, which they rode all the way to the top.

She stepped out into a small lobby area. The walls, ceiling, and even the floor were made of intepanels, similar to the ones they had in the hospital. They could be set to transparent like the ceiling, allowing a view of the crescent moon, or opaque – design optional – like the walls in the lobby. These were set to pale grey so that they gave off a low light. The floor was bright white, illuminating Bobbie and the guard from below, casting their faces into eerie shadows. Her mind's eye brought up an image of Gracie telling ghost stores with a torch under her chin. Had she known back then how terrifying real life would be, perhaps they wouldn't have spent so many hours trying to scare the wits out of each other.

Bobbie stepped closer to the wall, leaning in so her nose almost touched the intepanel. Could these walls function as one-way mirrors? Was Fox standing in the next room watching her?

Bobbie guessed these intepanels were a higher-grade toughened glass than they used in the hospital. She didn't imagine Fox would sit up here atop her tower without adequate protection. But perhaps the woman was so secure in her domination that she didn't think anyone would try to kill her. Bobbie's mind swung to Slade, once Fox's best friend, creeping through the building, trying to find her, full of vengeance.

The guard cleared his throat. She startled back from the intepanel, realizing with a fizzle of embarrassment that he'd been watching her. What he must think of her weird behavior? What did it matter now?

He escorted her along a corridor. On her left, the wall's intepanels were set to opaque and glowed oyster-white. The intepanels on the right were set to transparent and looked out into the black night. Her reflection in the glass was brutal. She tried not to look at the stranger carrying the box clasped to her stomach. It smelled of spoiled meat; the seal at the seams and around the lid didn't do enough to keep the odor in. But if this got Hicks back, she could put up with the stench.

The guard stopped and touched his pinkie finger to a panel a couple of meters from the end of the corridor. "Go through this door and follow the corridor." He stepped back.

"You're not coming with me?" Bobbie asked, turning on her eye-cam-di. The eye-con came on with a steady red light – recording only.

The guard didn't answer. Instead he looked past Bobbie's shoulder, probably getting his next set of instructions. She waited for the door to slide back, wondering if the guard would remain here for her until she came out. *If* she came out. He had a laser gun in a holster on his hip. Would she be quick enough to grab it when the door opened? Why wasn't the door opening?

Bobbie cleared her throat loudly.

The guard frowned, then touched the panel again.

It slid open.

The walls were matte black behind the door, sucking up the white light given off by the intepanels that made up the floor. Faint moonlight shone through the ceiling. Golden light glowed from further along the corridor. Bobbie couldn't determine how far away it was. She edged forward, heard the swish of the door closing behind her, but didn't turn around.

Blood pounded in her head. She wished the guard were still with her. Having anyone beside her right now would be better than walking alone into this void. The steady red eye-con added to her sense of isolation. If she disappeared like Gustav had, this footage might never be viewed.

The light ahead changed from golden to purple, pulsed a few beats, then changed again, switching randomly through green, magenta, violet, and finally back to purple. It came from one intepanel at the end of the corridor. Was it malfunctioning, or was Fox doing this on purpose? Was this some new high-tech gadget Bobbie couldn't fathom? What was it doing? Scanning her?

As Bobbie approached, an intepanel swung open to her left, and light spilled into the black corridor. She squinted against the glare and stepped into the room. Flare-spots floated in her vision as she focused on the figure standing in the middle of the room. The intepanels on the ceiling and two exterior sides of the room were set to transparent. The remaining walls and floor were set to white. Faint reflections on the glass extended the image of the white room into the blackness, giving the sense that they stood on a white platform suspended over the dark mountainside. Fox had taken the time since sending her message to fix her hair and change into a white sheath dress that skimmed the floor. Her image floated in ghosting reflections on the glass of the two transparent intepanels – three representations of the one person – an unholy Trinity.

"Bobbie, I would say, 'Good to see you,'" Fox said, "but it's not."

"I brought you what you asked for. Now, give me what I came for."

CHAPTER 19

The room was furnished with an intedesk, white office chairs, and nothing else. No models of spacecrafts or solar collectors – nothing Fox could impale her on. What would blood look like splashed across this white expanse? Bobbie closed her eyes, calmed her nerves, then looked at Fox – the eye-con steady, recording everything.

"You can put that down now." Fox patted the desk beside her.

Bobbie clutched the box to her. "Not until I see Hicks."

"He's been very helpful with Rejuvenation." Fox moved to the chair and waved a hand at the other one. "Come, sit down. Let's have a little chat, woman to woman."

"I'd rather stand," Bobbie said, thinking if she played out enough rope, maybe Fox would hang herself. "So talk."

"How is Slade?"

"She's been better. We all have." Bobbie drummed her fingers on the wooden box. Fox's eye narrowed. Her jaw clenched. She stared at Bobbie's hand as though trying to stop her by sheer willpower. Bobbie tapped a rhythmical beat and took satisfaction from the flare in Fox's nostrils.

Fox inhaled through her nose and released the breath. Calm descended over her.

"I'd imagine she has questions for me." Fox lifted the corner of her mouth in a half-smile and opened a screen on the intepanel on the wall beside her. "She'll be joining us shortly."

The footage on the screen showed two Belus guards walking in single file, with Slade between them. The guard behind Slade poked her in the back with his laser gun as they walked. Slade's nose bled. One eye was swollen shut. Both guards had orange eyes.

Bobbie fought hard to show no reaction. The effort of clamping her jaws tight stretched into her shoulder muscles. She gripped the box to her chest, no longer beating their tune.

"She's your friend, Lisette," Bobbie said, sitting down as casually as she could before her knees gave way. Her mind tumbled. Where was her father? She had to assume he was still free. If Fox had caught him, she'd show her.

He got away, Bobbie decided. It kept her from falling apart... *He got away, and he's coming for her.*

"She *was* my friend," Fox said. "She betrayed me. I should just kill her, but... she is Gustav's sister."

"She betrayed you!" Bobbie said sarcastically, lifting the box. "You have her brother's body in a fridge—have had it for decades, and she betrayed you?"

A snarl flashed across Fox's face, but was quickly replaced with a condescending smile.

Bobbie would confront Fox with the footage they had taken from Gustav's ONIV when the eye-con was flashing, and she was certain that they were broadcasting live. But there was no reason she couldn't have a go at Fox about Gustav's body in the freezer while they were recording. His murder was minuscule in the grand scheme of things.

Why was it taking so long to broadcast live? Had Joy's plan to get past the Beysil Sheild failed? Had they found her too? No, Bobbie thought, no way – Fox would have shown her that first.

"So tell me, how did Slade betray you? I want to understand, I really do."

Fox tilted her head to one side and gave a soft smile. "You're a good girl, Bobbie. You think you're helping. I see that in your actions. Others won't." Another intepanel popped up, a news channel.

"The fugitive Doctor Bobbie Chan was captured today amid speculation that she was behind the raids on the shelter for displaced persons in Norway yesterday. Twenty-three children were killed in the raid."

Bile rose in Bobbie's throat. She looked away from the images of her being escorted by the Belus guard.

In the next screen, Slade stood in a cell, head bowed.

Bobbie wanted to put her hands over her ears to block out the lies the news anchor was telling. "Doctor Chan was wanted for attacking the elderly and murdering her own grandmother at a facility in Ireland. Psychiatric experts have determined that she is suffering from a psychotic condition triggered by feeling overwhelmed with having to care for so many dependents in her post as a geriatrician. Belus Corp authorities say this syndrome is surfacing in the population as too many people place their lives on hold while they care for dependants. It is another reason why the Rejuvenation Programme that Belus Corp is rolling out is so important."

"That's bullshit!" Bobbie cried. She was about to stand up, then stopped. Her eye-con blinked red. Live broadcasting. Christ, where did she begin?

Bobbie turned away from the screens and focused entirely on Fox, ignoring the news report as it rattled on. She had to get Fox talking.

"We know you –" Bobbie changed tack as the eye-con stopped flashing and returned to a steady red.

Fuck!

"...Rejuvenation gives the ultra-elderly a new lease on life..." The news anchor's voice cut in on Bobbie's thoughts again.

Footage – Bobbie needed to gather footage on everything she could.

"Davitt lied," she said.

Fox's eyes narrowed.

"Oh, that's right, your boyfriend," Fox sneered. "The one you shared with your grandmother! Ha!" She threw her head back.

"He lied to you about fixing the glitch." Bobbie studied Fox. The woman didn't flinch, and waved her hand airily.

"I can manage that. More minions for me." Fox smiled.

"Did he tell you that when young, healthy people get infected with the nanobots, there are dire consequences?" Bobbie asked.

Fox tilted her head to one side, her smile frosted. "What consequences would that be?"

"They can't reproduce. The nanobots destroy the eggs and sperm."

Fox drew herself up to her full height. "I don't believe you."

"Have you added them to the food chain?" Bobbie couldn't tell if Fox was angry at Davitt or at being told something she didn't know. Wait until she heard that Bobbie knew Fox had been the Melters.

"I don't have to answer to you." Fox turned her back on Bobbie and took a few steps toward the screen showing Slade pacing the length of a small cell.

"If you've added the nanobots to the food, warn the people, own up to your mistake."

Fox ignored Bobbie, keeping her back to her.

Bobbie pushed for a reaction. "It would be idiotic to annihilate the entire human race because you're getting old and wrinkled," she said with venom.

Fox swung to face Bobbie. It was like Bobbie had tipped liquid nitrogen over the woman. Fox's expression froze in a snarl. She ground her teeth.

"How dare you! You're the liar. Davitt wouldn't lie to me. He knew he was playing for the winning team but you...you tried to stop Rejuvenation right from the word go," Fox snarled.

"Only because it harms people. Even you can see that," Bobbie said.

"Bullshit! You just don't want to lose your job."

Bobbie nearly laughed at the ridiculous suggestion. She put her hand to her mouth and shook her head, feeling a rush of hysteria. She had to keep herself together, not give in to the madness that threatened to engulf her.

"I'm not telling you to stop, I'm asking you to postpone," Bobbie said, modulating her tone, reaching for calm.

"Who are you to ask me anything? I created all of this. I saved us from the Melters. I remade the world. And now I've ended old age." Fox flung a hand at the opaque intepanels. Several turned transparent. Behind them, a fully equipped lab beavered away, even though it was the middle of the night. Bobbie recognized a couple of doctors from the medical board meeting, when she had tried to warn them about Rejuvenation.

Bobbie caught her breath. Doctor Coughlin, her old mentor at med school, shuffled down the lab. He had tried to help her when she had first discovered Rejuvenation in her patients only a couple of months beforehand. Then he'd disappeared. Bobbie thought they might have kept him locked up in the PARC indefinitely or killed him. He was stooped now, skin grey, eyes sunken, his white hair wispy. He walked along, barely lifting his feet.

"Ah, you see, even Octavio came around to my way of thinking," Fox said, raising an eyebrow. "Eventually."

Fox had called him by his first name, stripping away his title and status, but Bobbie recognized the tactic. The bitch was goading her, but Bobbie knew too much to let that irk her.

No-one looked into Fox's office. Maybe they couldn't see through the intepanel from their side.

Slade stepped away from the screen, giving Bobbie a clear view of her again. Blood smeared across Slade's face where she had wiped her face with her sleeve. She appeared to be calm, pacing with head held high.

"Slade is Gustav's sister," Bobbie said, nodding to the screen, projecting self-confidence. "She shares his genetic code. I understand his DNA is..." She dropped her eyes to the box in her arms. "Compromised."

"Good point, my dear." Fox narrowed her eyes, hitched up one corner of her lips. "Perhaps we can ask her to give us a hand."

Bobbie's mind flashed to the corpse in the freezer with its hand missing. She swallowed hard. Fox was insane.

"You know," Bobbie said, lowering her voice to match Fox's menacing tone, "it doesn't matter how many people you inject with Gustav's DNA. How many you rejuvenate to look just like him. They will never *be* him."

Fox bared her teeth, then pulled her lips closed tight over them, her face a mask of fury. She closed her eyes and, as if a switch had flipped, muscles flexed in her jaws, her forehead smoothed, and she drew her eyes open on a calm demeanor.

Chills coiled over Bobbie's skin.

Fox smiled and looked at the screen.

The news had moved on to another item about the release of a new brand of matter streamer formula. Was it the one Davitt told her about? Were they too late to stop the spread of the nanobots?

"What have you done with Hicks?" Bobbie asked, trying to keep focused, trying not to think about Hicks suffering, but for one terrible moment, she thought it possible that Fox had amputated his hands to get DNA samples from him. She pushed the idea away.

"He was much more forthcoming in the PARC than you were. He wanted to help us."

She's lying, Bobbie told herself, *don't believe her*. She hugged the box tighter, welcoming the discomfort of its angles digging into her flesh, and said, "Take me to him now."

Why did Fox toy with her like this? She could just have a guard take the box from her. She could kill any one of them at any time. Bobbie thought of how Gracie's kittens had played with mice before they killed them outright.

Fox twisted her lips as if trying not to laugh. "I believe you've seen lots of him."

Bobbie glared at Fox. "You know what I mean. You haven't answered my question. We had a deal," she said. "I kept up my end. Do you keep your word?"

Fox sighed loudly. "You are tedious. Don't you know when you're beaten?"

"You don't keep your word?"

"Hicks, Hicks, Hicks...Bor-ring!" Fox fake-yawned.

Three more intepanels in the wall turned transparent, revealing three cubicles with a naked man sitting on the floor in each one. From the back, they all looked like Hicks.

The eye-cam-di icon remained solid red, recording but not broadcasting. If one of these men was Hicks, did Bobbie really want this to be broadcast?

"One of these men is not like the others," Fox said in a sing-song voice. "But which one, Bobbie? How well do you know your man?"

Two of the men stood up; one covered his crotch with his hands and kept his head down. The other smiled at Fox, standing tall, hands on his hips, unashamed of his nakedness. Bobbie met his orange eyes and knew he wasn't Hicks. Or if he had been, he no longer was.

The third stayed curled on the floor, knees to chin, wrists clasped over shins, back to the glass. The man standing covering his crotch lifted a hand and pounded on the panel.

"Get me out of here, you bitch," he yelled. The sound came through vents in the corner of the panel. He didn't acknowledge Bobbie at all. She knew he wasn't Hicks either.

Bobbie ran to the third man and hammered on the glass.

The man turned his head. When he saw her, he uncoiled, twisting himself to put his hands on the glass. He kept his lower half turned away in an effort at modesty.

"Bobbie?" he said, so softly that it barely made it through the vents.

The tone of his voice, the sound him saying her name was enough to convince Bobbie even before she looked into his eyes – grey eyes. He smiled softly; then his eyes drifted closed.

Bobbie sank to her knees, placed the box on the ground beside her, and knocked on the panel. Hicks jolted. His eyes opened wide.

"Are you hurt?" Bobbie asked.

He looked confused. "Are you really there?" He reached for her, but his hand met the glass. He frowned and curled back over his knees.

"Get him out of there," Bobbie hissed. "Keep your damn word!"

Fox sat down and folded her arms.

"Hicks." Bobbie pounded the glass. "I'm here. It's me." She wanted to cry with frustration. How was she going to get him out of there? Fox was impossible.

On the intepanel on the adjacent wall, the news recapped the headlines, summarizing Bobbie's capture.

Hicks turned back to face her, his expression brighter. He put a hand to the intepanel and said, "I thought you were dead."

CHAPTER 20

Hicks was alive and, as far as Bobbie could see, uncontaminated. Kneeling, she put her hands to the glass. Hicks rested his forehead against the other side of the glass. Old bruises yellowed his temple and jaw. A bald patch on his eyebrow suggested a newly healed cut. His skin stretched over his cheekbones and joints, sagged in the softer parts between bones. Tears spilled over and ran down his face.

"I'll get you out," Bobbie said, hoarse with emotion.

Hicks' expression was bleak. "There's no way out. She won't let you go."

"She?" Fox said, behind Bobbie. "Who's 'she'? The cat's mother?"

Hicks met Bobbie's eyes and mouthed, "She's mad!"

Bobbie nodded. She stood, faced Fox, held out the box. "We had a deal. Release Hicks."

"Oh dear, you really aren't the brightest laser in the arsenal. That's a pity." Fox walked over and put her hands on the box.

Bobbie snatched the box from Fox's grasp and stepped back. She clenched her teeth and said, "Let him go."

Fox cast her eyes to the ceiling and expelled a long sigh. "Why don't you just set the box on the desk? I can easily get my guards to take it from you and throw you in that cage with Hicks. But think about it; where would that get you?"

Bobbie had to play her role carefully. If she were too confident, Fox would suspect she had a backup plan. At least she'd found Hicks. If Bobbie could convince Fox that she trusted her to keep her word, Luke would spring them both when he got there.

Bobbie stepped forward, allowing a nervous smile to show, and set the box on the desk beside Fox.

Fox leaned against the desk, folding her arms, and said, "Good girl. You see, I like intelligent people. I tend to keep them alive. Like your boyfriend here."

The recording light in Bobbie's eye-con displayed a continuous glow. Joy hadn't managed to get the live broadcast back yet, but Bobbie wanted to give them as much recorded material as possible.

"Why didn't you infect Hicks with Rejuvenation nanobots against his will – like all the others?" Bobbie said. If she could get Fox talking, she could record it on her ONIV.

Fox rolled her eyes as if it were tedious to explain all this to someone so stupid. "My dear, he's the sample source. You keep those pure. He's a great sample. Handsome, intelligent, strong genes–"

The eye-con blinked. It was broadcasting live. Bobbie drew in a deep breath. "We read Gustav's ONIV."

"That's impossible!" Fox stood up. "I wiped his ONIV."

Bobbie had her.

The blinking icon returned to a steady red light. Shit! Bobbie would have to carry on and hope that Joy got her back online fast.

"You might have wiped his updated ONIV, but you forgot about the old one."

Fox's eyes widened as the realization dawned. "No, no. That one was extracted."

Bobbie shook her head. "That one was left behind, and we were able to access it."

Fox covered her hand with her mouth.

Bobbie softened her tone. "Even brilliant people make terrible mistakes. Leaving the old ONIV in Gustav showed us another mistake you made."

"You don't know what you're talking about." Fox backed up. Hand out, she grappled her way to the edge of the desk and leaned against it.

"I know you didn't mean for it to happen, but it did. Then you took advantage," Bobbie said.

"What I did, I did for the greater good. I brought peace to the planet."

"You obliterated nations!"

"I ended war. You saw what was happening back then. The world leaders were out of hand. China was on the brink of war with Britain. Britain and Europe fighting over unity. It was only a matter of time before that became bloody. India and Pakistan, at it again. And the USA and the Middle East – Christ, where do I start with that? It was going to be the same thing over and over and over." Fox drew a breath. "I united humanity when I presented a different enemy."

"You killed billions of people."

"The planet was overrun. The high population was sending the climate haywire. It was a cull. It had to happen for the survival of the species." Fox stood with her arms out, her eyes bright and her cheeks flushed. Fox believed every word she said. It made Bobbie's skin crawl.

"The Dependency Law," Bobbie said. "Was that to keep the population low too?"

"Absolutely," Fox said. "Humanity is selfish. People were spouting on about saving the planet and cutting emissions, but they wanted someone else to make the sacrifices for them. Each person blamed everyone else but themselves. We had to break the cycle. That's the beauty of Rejuvenation. A stable population – no need to reproduce to replace those who get old and die. Work with me, Bobbie." Fox extended her hand. "We can inherit the earth. Look after it, keep it beautiful."

Bobbie stared at Fox's outstretched arm, but didn't move.

Fox looked from her hand to Bobbie and twisted her face into a wry smile. She folded her arms. The eye-con was still not flashing, but Bobbie had to keep Fox talking.

"Perhaps you would have gotten away with it, if you hadn't continued to play God with Rejuvenation," Bobbie said, saving the main feature for the live broadcast.

"Play God?" Fox laughed. "God was never this smart, never this measured. The planet's leaders were destroying the earth; the population was out of control. I reset that. I took out the predator nations, left the pacifists. It was working fine until you came along."

"You pushed thousands of people underground with the Dependency Law" Bobbie said. "You made people choose between their unborn children and their grandparents."

The red eye-con flashed again. *Go, go, go!*

"Would you like to see what we have?" Bobbie asked. "I'll show you the footage."

Fox's eyes narrowed. "Why?"

"Because I want you to explain it to me." Bobbie's guts churned as she tempered her voice to sound sympathetic and play on Fox's ego. "I want to understand. I know I'm not as smart as you, but if you explain it, maybe I can understand, and if I understood, maybe I could help."

Fox's eyes bored into Bobbie's, and Bobbie felt as if her soul were being probed. But she held Fox's gaze, frozen in place with her heart thumping in her ears.

Fox tilted her head to the side, tapped her fingers against her chin, then glanced at the men in the cubicles. The glass darkened. Hicks curled up on the floor again. The other two stood still, staring into space. Bobbie reckoned it was a one-way mirror setting.

Fox flapped a hand at a wall near Bobbie. "Use that intepanel."

Bobbie placed her pinkie finger on the intepanel and transferred a copy of the footage. The screen flickered, then filled with the image of the old lab.

Fox winced as Gustav's voice came through the room's speakers. She covered her face with her hands, watching through her fingers.

"I was helping humanity," she said on a tattered breath. "The solar collector would have provided the planet with energy for as long as we had a sun."

Bobbie checked the eye-con was still flashing. "Why was it a secret?"

Fox huffed a sigh. "The permits would have taken months, maybe years. Fucking red tape. The Russians would only sign if the Americans signed first. Korea wouldn't sign unless the US signed. Europe was faffing about over member states voting, leaving, frigging about. The British prime minister, fucker, I don't even think he could read!" She cast her eyes downards and sighed again. "Believe me, we tried."

"It's hard to know what to believe," Bobbie said. "Other than concrete evidence."

She let Fox watch more of Gustav's ONIV footage.

Joy was sending this out live to every ONIV in the world except Fox's. It would wake those sleeping, take priority over any other blink they were watching or reading. The public was watching. Bobbie wanted Fox to lay out her crazy rationale so the world would see the truth behind Belus Corp.

On screen, the solar collector beam hit Antarctica, and Fox doubled over as if punched. Her breathing ragged, she straightened up, clasping her hands together at her chest.

"It was an error in the calculations. We missed a factor!" She buried her face in her hands. Bobbie listened to her sobs with a hard heart. Forgiveness would be a long time coming – if it ever came.

"Stop!" Fox said just before the part where she impaled Gustav.

Bobbie let it run.

This was the moment, Bobbie decided, the unforgivable act, when Fox took control of the solar collector and turned it on her team. This was the start of all the cover-ups and lies and destruction. The true point of no return. The what-ifs scalded Bobbie's heart. So much death and destruction could have been avoided if this moment, so many years ago, had swung in a different direction.

Fox turned her back on the screen and faced Bobbie with the footage streaming behind her. Tears ran down Fox's face. "From the moment Gustav died, I worked to make this a better world."

"You killed him so that you wouldn't have to face trial for the mass murder of billions of people." Bobbie checked the broadcast was holding. She glanced at Hicks curled up in his cell, then pulled her eyes away, realizing that the public was receiving whatever Bobbie was seeing and recording now, with Joy's transmission of Gustav's ONIV footage as live feeds simultaneously side by side. Bobbie focused on Fox. Would she surrender now that the world knew her secret?

"It was an accident," Fox said through gritted teeth. "But it had its advantages. The world needed a reset, still does." She threw her arms up. "Gustav and I will be the new Adam and Eve –"

"Gustav is dead."

Fox surged toward Bobbie, glaring. Bobbie backed against the wall.

"I can bring him back with rejuvenation. Look at how many Hicks I made – and all better than that wretch there." She stomped to the intepanel Hicks sat behind and slammed her palm against it.

Hicks jumped up and overbalanced. Bobbie's heart broke. She wanted to run to him and hold him. But first, she had to see this through – she had to somehow show the world Fox's insanity.

Fox sneered as Hicks scrambled to the furthest corner. His reaction seemed to ignite her strength. She drew herself up and turned to Bobbie and said, "Once I have perfected Rejuvenation... Those subjects would have died anyway. But Gustav was young, brilliant... He didn't deserve to die... I'll give him back his life, and together we will rebuild a plant worth having. Repopulate –"

"How about we let the world decide?" Bobbie interrupted.

"What are you talking about? You can't access our broadcasting–"

Bobbie opened a public broadcast channel on the screen beside Gustav's ONIV footage. This screen was seconds behind what was being said between Bobbie and Fox, but it was clear that Joy had hacked into the Belus broadcasting system. Below the footage, a ticker stream announced in yellow writing on a black background, "Belus certified verified live untampered footage." Bobbie enjoyed the irony of it – Belus had brought this in to stamp out fake news and attempts at propaganda in news items before the MelterWar. They had become the gold standard of fact-checking, and during the Melter War, they hadn't been questioned. Joy was still broadcasting Bobbie's footage live. No-one, not even Fox, could refute it.

The anchor on the news channel on the other wall announced, "News just in..."

They rolled the footage there too. Fox stood before multiple open screens – one showed the raw footage from Gustav's ONIV that Bobbie had opened for Fox; another ran Joy's hacked broadcast, verified by Belus and beamed into ONIVs around the planet; another showed the news reports of the footage from the screen Fox had opened originally to show Bobbie what the news was reporting on her; another showed Slade standing in her cell, banging the door.

Fox looked from one screen to the next. She pivoted and took a step toward Bobbie and hissed through clenched teeth, "That was not smart."

Bobbie backed up. "Truth is out. You need to step down."

Fox's lips curled. "What are you hoping to achieve? I have the only army on the planet. One billion Rejuvenees all over the world. I'm in charge here."

One billion!

"I'm declaring martial law," Fox said, walking up to stand in front of Bobbie.

Bobbie was still broadcasting live, and Fox's face appeared on the screen behind her. Fox turned to check and swung back to Bobbie with confident eyes, her chin lifted.

"Everyone, go home and stay there until further notice," Fox said. "Anyone outside will be arrested or killed."

Bobbie felt for the cube in her pocket. Sweat trickled down her back. Fox wasn't going to back down.

"The Candels can wipe out your army at the push of a button. They've set up a system of EMP bombs across the planet," Bobbie said.

"They don't have the technology."

"I have it here in my hand." Bobbie held up the cube.

"A Rubik's cube? Are you fucking kidding? They set you up, Bobbie. That's an antique toy."

Bobbie ignored the scorn. "We don't have to go down that path. We can use gentibots–"

Fox snorted. "Gentibots? Why would anyone want that?"

"I don't want to kill Rejuvenees, but–" Bobbie held up the Rubik's cube.

"How about you hand that over, and no-one gets hurt?"

"How about you stand down and face trial for your crimes against humanity and let us treat the Rejuvenees with gentibots?" Bobbie watched her request repeat on the screens behind Fox.

Fox's attention drifted. A smile stretched her face. Her fingers flicked ONIV commands. She pulled her gaze back to Bobbie and said in a soft voice that gave Bobbie the shivers, "Don't be a fool. It's bad enough that your sister is a fool."

Bobbie's heart iced over.

Fox muted all the screens and opened a new one. It showed Joy, off in the distance, running across the mountainside. Her blue-tipped black hair streamed behind her. She sprang over a clump of vegetation, landed, wobbled, and then took off again. The camera was catching up with her. When Joy turned to look at the drone, Bobbie could see her tunic was ripped, and blood ran from a gash on her knee. Her sister was bleeding. Bobbie couldn't bear it.

Joy pulled her laser and shot at the camera. As the drone was snagged by laser fire, the viewpoint swung around and captured the image of a swarm of drones converging on Joy – Melter drones. Fox had unleashed the fake foe again. Joy's laser fire hit several. They lurched sideways, dropped out of formation, and crashed in a shower of sparks, taking another couple of drones out with them. It wasn't enough. The picture was replaced by a camera on a different drone. This was one closer.

Joy fired wildly around her, then took off again, zig-zagging as she ran. Laser fire flashed off the ground she had just run over. Smoke plumed, flames danced from the ignited vegetation. Joy must be terrified. Bobbie couldn't imagine what was going through her head, but she felt the heart-bursting panic, the frenzied terror as she watched Joy skid, nearly fall, recover, and launch back into the sprint.

"Stop it!" Bobbie screamed. "Call them off."

Fox sniggered. "Hacking's not so much fun now, is it?"

"You don't need to do this," Bobbie cried. "Please, leave her alone."

The drones were close enough for Bobbie to hear Joy's labored breathing as she ran. She pointed the gun behind her, but nothing happened. Joy stopped, turned, and threw the laser gun at the camera. The picture fizzed out.

"Oh, nice shot," Fox said.

Another camera took over. This drone was further out, but gaining ground.

"Please," Bobbie said. Her mind screamed, *don't hurt her, she's my sister, please, don't hurt her!*

"She could be a great asset to you. Please," Bobbie said, as she held up the Rubik's cube. *The EMP could take out all the drones. I can save Joy.*

Yes, her mind countered, *but can you kill all those people – 1 billion Rejuvenees, when you have gentibots?*

The drones seemed to be close enough for the kill shot, but they hovered, keeping pace but not shooting anymore. Maybe Fox was going to show mercy. Bobbie lowered the cube, leaned forward.

Time stalled.

Joy looked straight at the camera. Her dark eyes showed no fear. Had Joy hacked the drone too? Was she going to be able to control these drones through her connection to ONIV? Bobbie felt a surge of pride for this strong, beautiful woman on the screen.

Joy lifted her hands in surrender. Her ribcage heaved. Sweat ran down her face. A breeze wafted her hair behind her.

"Thank you," Bobbie whispered.

Fox's laugh froze Bobbie's heart.

A message appeared in Bobbie's blink from Joy.

A flare of laser fire tore Joy's chest open in a diagonal slash from shoulder to waist. Charred flesh gaped open, showing rounded orbs of organs and the tangle of intestines in shades of pink to deep red. Blood oozed into the fabric of Joy's tunic. White nubs of broken ribs sat like pearls in scarlet tissue. She stumbled, crumpled to the ground, falling onto her back. Her eyes stared at the sky, a soft smile on her lips.

A scream ripped from Bobbie as she fell to her knees. She closed her eyes. Pain tightened her chest. She couldn't breathe. The blink from Joy opened.

I love you, big sis. It was all worth it.

CHAPTER 21

The screen froze on the image of Joy lying dead. Bobbie couldn't tear her eyes away. Joy's face looked peaceful despite splashes of blood on her neck and cheek and the rip through her chest, exposing frothy lung tissue. Bobbie held her breath, frozen, waiting. Any minute now, movement would ignite in the picture. Joy would blink and sit up laughing. She'd be okay. She always was. Joy had gotten them out of tight corners before. It was a trick. Another one of Fox's cons. An inhalation – Bobbie's body on autopilot – brought her mind crashing into reality. Pain tore through her chest. She bent forward, clawed at her tunic, and howled.

Bobbie turned to Fox.

Fox stood behind her desk. She raised a hand. "Don't move, Bobbie. My guards are right outside the door."

Rage surged. Bobbie lunged, slammed into the desk, and drove forward, pinning Fox against the glass overlooking the mountain. Fox pushed back. Bobbie pulled herself up onto the desk with one hand, snatching at Fox's face with the other. Bobbie's nails dug into flesh. She tore three strips of red down Fox's cheek.

Fox grabbed the hair on Bobbie's crown and slammed her head into the desk.

Pain rocketed through Bobbie's skull. Black dots bloomed in her vision. She pressed her knees down on the desk and slammed her shoulder into Fox's ribcage.

"Stop," Fox grunted, and shoved Bobbie off the desk.

A crash turned both their heads in the direction of the lab. The intepanel turned transparent. Doctor Coughlin swung a retort stand at the equipment on the desk in the middle of the lab. Broken glass flew in all directions. The other lab workers kicked at the machines, pulled incubators off the walls. A door opened and several Belus guards piled into the lab, laser guns raised, shouting though Bobbie couldn't make out what they were saying. Every guard had orange eyes.

Coughlin looked straight at Bobbie, his dark eyes connected with hers, and he mouthed, "Sorry."

Despair drenched Bobbie. They'd lost so much, and were still no closer to beating this monster Fox had become. They'd only freed Fox from any pretense at compassion and justice. They'd created a wilder monster.

Doctor Coughlin and his staff raised their hands and interlaced their fingers, placing their hands behind their heads. The guards forced them to kneel in the broken glass. Some of the workers sobbed. One young woman crumpled over. A guard kicked her in the gut before pulling her to a kneeling position by the hair.

The guards stood over the people in the lab, their eyes zoned out as if reading a blink.

Bobbie's knees gave way. She slumped to the floor, sitting with her back against the desk.

"Any more fuckwittery from you, my dear, and I will kill them," Fox said. "I don't want to. They are very valuable." She pushed her bottom lip into an exaggerated pout. "Joy was valuable too, but so hard to control. We'll be better off without her."

...without her.

Bobbie fought the surge of grief. Joy would hate it if she cried for her in front of Fox. She felt a tickle on the side of her face and wiped it. Her hand came away covered in blood. A head wound? Hopefully, just a burst scab on her forehead, but the dizziness made her suspect a concussion.

A tap on glass made Bobbie turn her head to Hicks' cell. He knelt with the side of his body pressed against the glass, his face peering out as though waiting for her to look his way. His eyebrows pulled together as Hicks locked into her gaze. He dipped his head but didn't lose eye contact. His right palm pressed against the glass.

She wanted to run to him, fold into his arms and sob her heart out, but she couldn't move.

The two rejuvenated Hicks clones stood as if suspended in time, waiting for something to happen.

Bobbie's gazed drifted back to Joy's face on the screen. The pain in Bobbie's heart snatched her breath away, stole the strength from her limbs, and buzzed through her skull. She couldn't stand up yet.

The screen below Joy's showed footage of Slade banging on her cell door. Bobbie squinted to focus, to push away the gray patches that threatened to fog her vision. Slade stepped back and took a run at the door, rebounding hard, landing on her back on the floor. She got up and ran at the door, kicking it.

On another screen, the news report was still going. The footage from Gustav's ONIV played on a split-screen with the footage from Bobbie challenging Fox a few minutes before Joy was killed. The anchor looked stricken as he linked to a new interviewee. Niclas appeared with a face like thunder.

"It's time to give control to the people, take back the media, hold democratic elections," Niclas said. He took a deep breath, looked down for a second, then lifted his gaze and stared into the camera. "We, the people of Planet Earth, reject Belus Corp and its management of our lives. We want democracy and truth. It is time that the heinous lies this corporation is built upon come to light and Lisette Fox is held to account in a humanitarian court of law."

Gustav's ONIV footage began again from the beginning. Other screens popped open. The ticker along the bottom of one identified Anchorage, Alaska. Thousands of people filled the streets.

"...People are striking, walking out of work to gather on the streets," the voice-over said. "Cities across the globe have come to a standstill. The protesters are demanding the same thing, 'Give us the truth.' 'Give us democracy.'" The camera turned to the anchor sitting at his news desk, and he continued the report, asking, "Where is Lisette Fox? What does Belus know about the solar collector malfunction? According to the footage still coming from the Candels source, Fox is in Belus Headquarters with Doctor Chan."

Fox paced before the screens, her eyes were unfocused, and her fingers flickered. Someone somewhere was receiving instructions. Bobbie hoped to hell whoever it was, they were ignoring those directions.

The camera angle changed, and the anchor turned to face it before continuing his report. "Previous news reports from Belus cast Doctor Chan as a violent criminal, but in the light of new information..." He paused. "Verified new information, it seems that Belus broadcasts cannot be trusted...we..." He frowned, put his hand to his ear and nodded. "News just in, Belus guards have attacked a crowd of protesters in Ladak..."

New pictures from overhead drones populated the screen. Hundreds of Rejuvenees dressed as Belus guards walked toward thousands of people on the streets. They lifted laser guns and shot, cutting protesters in the front row in half. The crowd retreated like an anemone withdrawing tentacles. A split second later they surged forward, toward the guards. The guards continued to fire. Bodies piled up between the protesters and the guards. The guards walked forward and climbed over the bodies. The protesters at the front tried to run back, but the ones behind them were still surging ahead.

"Stop them!" Bobbie screamed, getting to all fours, the pain in her head piercing and dizzying.

"I will not do that," Fox said, slowly. "This is your fault, Bobbie. You forced me to do this."

Slade had stopped moving in her cell. She seemed to be conversing with someone through the door. She stood flat against the wall. Laser fire slashed past her. She ran out of view; the screen showed only an empty cell.

Another screen opened with screenshots of blinks scrolling past.

"What the fuck?" Fox hissed.

Kill any civilian on the streets. Your lives depend on it.

Shut off the live broadcast – NOW.

Hold ranks until further notice.

Medical support will be withdrawn for noncompliance.

Gentibots will be used against any soldier not obeying orders.

Bobbie realized they were Fox's commands to the Rejuvenees. She'd been hacked. Bobbie tried to keep up with reading the blinks as they whizzed by. Some she could follow. She sat back on her heels and read them.

"Fox is controlling Rejuvenees with drugs, and they'd do anything to ensure their supply lines stay open," Bobbie shouted as loud as she could to get the words recorded and broadcast.

Fox ran toward Bobbie. "You shut your mouth."

"They'll obey her as long as they think she can help them," Bobbie yelled for the broadcast, scrambling backward. "They don't want to be treated with gentibots and lose their youth. You have to fight them."

The guard who had escorted Bobbie earlier appeared at the door. He aimed a gun at Fox. "Let Doctor Chan go."

"Not going to happen." Fox rotated toward the lab, smiling. "This one's for you, Bobbie."

Inside the lab, a Rejuvenee shot a laser and a young woman kneeling before them slumped over.

"No more!" Bobbie scrambled to her feet. Grey splotches flared in her vision. She pulled the cube from her pocket, held it up. "Call them off."

Fox laughed. "You're holding me up with a fucking Rubik's cube."

The guard kept his gun on Fox, but looked at Bobbie like she was insane.

Bobbie felt insane. "It's the trigger for an EMP blast."

"I don't believe you. If it worked, why didn't you use it to take out the drones to save your sister?"

Fuck!

Why hadn't she? Bobbie's heart tore at the thought of it. She'd really believed Fox was going to let Joy live. Bobbie hadn't pressed the button then because, despite the evidence against Fox, Bobbie believed Fox had some humanity left. Killing billions of people had permanently altered Fox's idea of right and wrong.

"No-one supports you anymore, Lisette," Bobbie said. "How many of your people are not rejuvenated? None of them will help you. If I press this button, you're completely on your own." And if Bobbie pressed the button, if she killed billions, would she become inured to killing like Fox had? Bobbie's hand froze around the Rubik's cube.

"I know you won't do it. Your little bleeding heart would never kill so many geriatrics," Fox said, smearing the blood across her face from where Bobbie had scratched her.

"They're not geriatrics anymore."

"You're a doctor. You want to cure them. You want to use gentibots. You press that button, there's no going back for any of them."

Bobbie knew there'd be no going back for her either. Her pulse pounded. Pressure built in her head.

The crowd in Anchorage was under fire. What was happening in other places around the world? How many people were dying at the hands of the Rejuvenees?

"This is on you," Bobbie said. "You can stop this. Call them in. Face what you've done."

"Never!" Fox said. "I will not surrender."

"Do you want to go back to the Stone Age?"

"You don't have the balls."

Bobbie didn't want to press the button. Everything about it repulsed her. Yet if she'd pressed the button ten minutes ago, Joy would still be alive.

Fuck!

If she didn't press it now, Fox would be unstoppable. How many more would die?

Bobbie held her thumb over the button, but couldn't press it. One billion people. She'd be just like Fox.

Fuck!

"Lower your gun," Fox said to the guard, "and we can overlook your little moment of weakness."

The guard closed his eyes and dropped his arm.

"Clever boy," Fox said. "Now shoot her."

Tears streamed down his face. He lifted the gun and aimed it at Bobbie.

Fox gave a triumphant laugh. "You can't do it, Bobbie. You can't kill all those people. You're a dove... and us hawks eat you doves every single day!"

The guard swung the gun back to Fox.

"Bad choice," Fox said.

A female Rejuvenee appeared at the door and shot the guard, watched as he dropped, then turned the gun on Bobbie.

"I can help you," Bobbie said, holding out a hand to the Fox look-alike.

The rejuvenated woman looked like Fox had in the footage with Gustav, full of youth and fire. But there was confusion in her orange eyes. She lowered her gun.

"No, she can't, you idiot," Fox spat. "Just kill her."

The Rejuvenee turned to Bobbie, smiled, and said, "Sorry... not sorry."

Bobbie's hand curled; her thumb pushed the button. It depressed with a loud click. Nothing.

Bobbie stared at the device in her hand. She clicked the red square again, rapidly, several times.

Fox threw her head back, dropped her jaw, her mouth opening in an obscene laugh.

The Rejuvenee aimed her gun at Bobbie's head.

Bobbie threw the Rubik's cube at the Rejuvenee and dived to the floor.

Then the lights went out.

CHAPTER 22

Bobbie lay panting on her side, curled on the floor, her back to the glass. She picked out the square edges of the desk in the gloom as her eyes adjusted to the darkness. A sticky wheeze came from a mound on the floor near the door. Was it the guard, or the Rejuvenee who had shot him? The EMP had worked. It must have destroyed the Rejuvenee's nanobots. Bobbie hadn't seen a Rejuvenee survive having their nanobots fried unless they had been young to start with, like Joy.

Joy...

Bobbie felt like her lungs had turned to concrete. She squeezed her eyes shut, pulled in a breath to the count of three, and released it. The pain stayed, but she could breathe again. Where was Hicks? Her father? Slade?

In the lab, someone was screaming. People shouted.

Bobbie crawled toward the lumps on the floor – she could see two of them now. She twisted around to look out the window behind her. The sky had brightened, the craggy horizon highlighted with a yellow glow.

On hands and knees, she reached the Rejuvenee first. The smell hit her. Bobbie reared back and covered her face with one arm, taking shallow breaths through her mouth. The woman's skin, flesh, and bone had broken down. There was nothing left but a puddle of grey pulp where her head had been.

A raspy inhale made Bobbie turn her head to the next mound. The guard was alive – a chest injury, she reckoned, based on his breathing.

A golden beam lit up the room as the tip of the rising sun came into view between the peaks on the horizon. Bobbie dragged herself to her feet. Her eyes had adjusted, and she could see enough to walk. There was no sign of Fox. Had she slunk away in the darkness?

Hicks' cell had doors into both the lab and the room Bobbie was in. Without electricity, the doors swung open.

"Bobbie!" Hicks pushed the door and stumbled to her, stooped over, covering himself.

She embraced him quickly. "Are you hurt?"

He shook his head.

"Thank God." Her hands framed his face, and she pulled him to her, touching her lips gently to his swollen mouth. Having him back safe gave a glimmer of solace to her fractured heart. He was her home, the center of her compass, but they'd both be lost without Joy.

His arms wrapped around her, and he held her to him in a brief hug before letting her go.

"Quick. Take this." She tore at her tunic, taking a swath from the bottom of it and tying it around Hicks like a loincloth. "We have to help him." Bobbie nodded to the injured guard.

They knelt on either side of the guard. The laser had burned a hole through the right side of his chest. Hicks placed his hands to seal the entrance wound on the guard's chest and the exit wound at his back. The guard seemed to breathe a bit easier, or perhaps he was slipping away.

"There might be a first aid kit in the lab," Bobbie said.

"Go."

Bobbie stood up. The rising sun gave her light to see that all the intepanels were turned off. They were transparent with no electricity to power their display. Bobbie could see into and past the lab, clear through to the other side of the building. Where was Fox? In the lab next door, Doctor Coughlin stood over the bodies of the Rejuvenees who had been holding them at gunpoint. One of the scientists sat rocking on the floor; another was rubbing his back. The rest stood in a group, shaking their heads and looking lost.

The easiest way to the lab was through Hicks' old cell, since the other two compartments were full of decomposing Rejuvenees. Bobbie stepped through the first door, but Hicks called her back.

"No need for the first aid kit." Hicks closed the guard's eyes and wiped his bloody hands on the end of the guard's tunic.

"Shit!" But a part of Bobbie was relieved for the guard's sake. Without any electricity, they had few resources to help him. Field medicine would only prolong his suffering.

She was responsible for this. It had been her only choice, but Christ Almighty, what a choice. How many had died? How could she carry that for the rest of her life and, worse still, the thought that if only she'd done it sooner... Joy... Bobbie's hand clutched at her chest. It felt like shards of glass tore through her heart.

It wasn't until she opened her eyes that she realized she'd been standing for a few seconds with them closed. Sunlight reflected off intepanels at different angles across the top floor. It felt like a rooftop. People moved about freely now that they could see, now that the initial shock had worn off. Most seemed to be converging on what appeared to be a central corridor, and all in the corridor moved the same direction – toward stairs? The heat was picking up. The gut-churning stench of rotting flesh rose from the dead Rejuvenees, making the air rank and oppressive. Between the heat and the cloying stink, this glass cage would be unbearable in full sunlight.

Hicks came and stood beside her, slipped an arm around her shoulders, and pulled her to him. She breathed him in.

"You did the right thing," he said. "You saved all these people."

"But I killed–"

"Shhh!" He bent and kissed her. Bobbie pulled back to look into his face. He didn't hold her gaze. Instead, his focus drifted over her head and he said, "Luke?"

"Look at what?" Bobbie turned.

Luke and Slade pushed their way along the corridor in the opposite direction to the people leaving the top floor.

Bobbie jumped to the nearest intepanel, hammered on it, and waved. "Dad! Over here!"

Doctor Coughlin knocked on the intepanel wall from the lab and pointed at something in the room. Bobbie followed his gaze and saw Fox peek out from under the desk. Bobbie and Fox's gazes fused. Fox sprang for the door. Bobbie sprinted after her, connected, and knocked Fox off her feet. Bobbie sprawled on the floor, her hand inches from Fox's foot.

Fox was on her feet. She bolted for the door.

Bobbie threw herself after her. She grabbed the back of Fox's tunic and yanked, pulling Fox backward on top of her. Both of them lay on the floor, winded. Bobbie pushed Fox off and realized that Fox had quit struggling because Hicks had barred the door.

Fox looked at the holding cells.

Avoiding the two containing the decomposing corpses of Rejuvenees, Doctor Coughlin entered Hicks' old cell, making his way toward Bobbie.

"On your knees, Fox, hands behind your head," Bobbie said, getting to her feet.

"Fuck off." Fox leaned back on her elbows, knees bent. She could have been sitting on the grass at a picnic.

Hicks pulled the trousers from the puddle that had been the Rejuvenee. The stench made Bobbie gag, but Hicks showed no reaction. He pulled Fox to her feet. She wriggled, but he shook the woman hard by the shoulders. Fox glared at him but stopped struggling. He tied her hands behind her back with the trousers.

"Kneel." He pushed down on Fox's shoulder with one hand. She bent at the knees. He took one of the long ends of the trousers he'd used to tie her up and looped it around her ankles. "I have no problem gagging you with this material if you fuck around, do you understand?"

Fox stared back, flinty-eyed, and gave a fraction of a nod.

Hicks stepped back into the doorway, placed his hands on his hips. He looked like some terrible Greek statue, with the loincloth, his skin covered in fading bruises, and his hands and forearms bloodstained. He staggered forward, pushed off balance.

Slade flew in past Hicks and kicked Fox in the stomach. Fox bent forward, straining against the binding. Slade crouched over Fox, her hands around Fox's throat.

"No!" Bobbie grabbed Slade's arm to pull her off Fox.

In Slade's fury, she felt no pain. Her fingers tightened on Fox's neck. Fox's lips turned blue. Her eyes rolled in her head.

Bobbie's arms wrapped around Slade, yanking on her. "Stop, stop!" Bobbie roared.

"Kill her! Kill her!" a scientist screeched from the lab, slamming her hands on the intepanels.

When the world had processed what Bobbie setting off the EMP meant, would they bay for her death too? No power to run any machines, no matter streamers, no access to food and clean water, no transport, no medical help – how many more would die?

Luke appeared beside Hicks, and the two of them pulled Slade off Fox.

"I have to kill her," Slade said, sobbing.

"We all want to kill her," Bobbie said. "But she has to stand trial. We have to do this right. There's been enough killing. We can't even injure her, because I don't want to waste time and resources doctoring her. We need her to testify. She has to stand trial."

"Bobbie's right, Ori. Don't make this harder than it has to be," Luke said. "Let's get off the top floor. With the intepanels off, there's no shade. It's getting hot, and there'll be no air conditioning."

Not for a long time, Bobbie thought, and it was all her fault.

Doctor Coughlin had made his way from the lab. He walked to Bobbie and put out his hand. Bobbie looked down at it, confused.

"I want to shake your hand," he said. "I know what pushing that button cost you."

Bobbie's hand drifted to his as if of its own accord.

"Thank you," he said.

Dr Coughlin's simple words filled Bobbie's eyes with tears. She blinked, unable to find her voice. Pushing that button had cost them all, but not pushing it was more than they could afford, pushing it sooner... No, she had to stop thinking about that, or she'd go crazy.

"How can I help?" he asked, his gaze shifting to Luke.

"I need an around-the-clock guard on Fox," Luke said. "She cannot be harmed, and she cannot escape. You understand why we need her?"

"I do. My team can take care of that." Doctor Coughlin looked back at the people in the lab.

"Are you sure?" Luke looked past Doctor Coughlin toward the woman who had screamed for them to kill Fox.

"They trust me, and I them," the doctor said. "They'll do as I ask."

"I wouldn't leave you with this, but I have to go find my daughter," Luke said, his voice hollow.

Bobbie thought her heart would burst. "Dad…"

Luke stared at the ground, sucked in a long breath, and then met Bobbie's eyes. His devastated look left her speechless. He pressed his lips tightly together and looked up, blinking hard. "She knew the risks, as we all did."

Bobbie chewed the insides of her cheeks. If her father cried, she'd unravel. She felt Hicks' hand on her shoulder.

"I have to bring Joy back," Luke said.

"I know, Dad." Bobbie thought of the scavenging animals out on the mountain. "We're coming too."

She looked at Hicks.

He nodded.

Bobbie couldn't help the thoughts that sprang unbidden to her mind.

Maybe Joy survived. The guard didn't die right away. Maybe Joy is lying there, bleeding, waiting…

CHAPTER 23

But the guard did die, Bobbie told herself, wanting to embrace the hopeful thoughts yet hating them. She knew in her heart that Joy was gone. False hope was a torture she didn't need.

Most people had left the top floor, but the stairs were slow going. Bobbie wanted to push people out of her way. She needed to get to her sister, but causing a crowd crush wasn't going to help anyone. They made a sorry procession at the back, Luke and Hicks supporting Slade, with Doctor Coughlin's team forming a circle around Fox. Bobbie led them downstairs. The light from the roof only reached a couple of floors, and they had to feel their way in the dark. Voices floated up to them. The people below were appealing for calm. Someone was directing everyone to gather in the parking lot.

"Don't run. There's no rush," people passed back up the line.

"Treat it like an evac drill."

"What do we do now?"

No-one asked, "What happened?" and Bobbie realized just what a good job Joy had done in getting the broadcast out. People seemed informed but shocked, too stunned to panic.

"How will we find..." Bobbie faltered. "We'll have to find the shaft and work from there."

"The easiest thing to do would be to climb up from the quantum computer rather than try to navigate outside," Luke said.

The stairwell ended at a mezzanine that flowed into a grand staircase leading to the foyer Bobbie had walked through earlier. A couple of hundred Belus Corp employees streamed down the staircase and filled the lobby. Bobbie went to the metal and glass railing that edged the mezzanine, and looked over. Was there a faster way to the quantum computer room? How would they see in the dark underground corridors?

She expected to see more remains of Rejuvenees, but realized that Fox must have kept them behind the scenes, doing her dirty work. Bobbie found it hard to discern what was and wasn't dirty work where Fox was concerned.

Below, a couple of women looked up and saw Bobbie. They stopped walking, causing people behind them to bump into them and also look up. Someone pointed and shouted, "It's Doctor Chan."

Bobbie tried to step back, but a press of people behind kept her in place, in full view of the people below. Frightened, she looked around for Hicks and Luke. They were off to her left.

A polite but firm clap began on the level below her, too quick to be menacing, too slow to be jubilant – controlled and respectful. Others joined in until most stood facing Bobbie, clapping. Sprinkled through the crowd, some employees folded their arms. Some of their faces were hostile, but most had closed, wary expressions.

Bobbie's heart pounded. These people either looked to her or blamed her, yet she was broken and in no fit state to lead. She was still reeling from witnessing her sister dying. She had pushed the button that took humanity backward to a time before electricity. Bobbie closed her eyes. Her hands moved to cover her face, but only got as far as being clasped in front of her chest.

Gracie's voice whispered in her head, "Be strong for them."

She thought of Joy's blink.

I love you, big sis. It was all worth it.

Bobbie had to make Joy's sacrifice worthwhile. This was not the end, but a beginning. And as if from outside her body, she saw herself open her arms to the crowd below. A silence fell over the people gathered.

"Thank you," she said. "Today, our world changed irreversibly. It's going to be hard moving forward, but if we work together, we honor the people who ..." Bobbie's voice caught.

A murmur rippled through the crowd and settled.

Bobbie cleared her throat. "What I'm trying to say is that we have lost so, so much. Let's never forget that. Let every act of kindness, every compromise, honor the sacrifices made today."

Soft sobbing in the crowd tore at Bobbie. She kept going. "I'm so sorry that I had to deploy the EMP."

"We understand, honey," an older man called.

"I sure don't! She's fucked everything up," a woman in a Belus guard's uniform said, jabbing a finger at Bobbie.

"She'd no choice!" came a chorus of voices.

Bobbie looked around for Hicks.

"You can do this," he whispered in her ear.

Knowing he was right behind her helped. She directed her gaze at the angry woman and said, "You're right. Perhaps there were better ways. The only way to ascertain that is by an investigation, and I'm turning myself in to comply with that."

A burble broke out, but one voice came louder than the others.

"Kill Fox!"

A babble of agreement rumbled through in an angry bluster.

"No!" Bobbie shouted over the crowd. "That's not the right way. Lisette Fox—"

Booing and hissing broke out. Bobbie raised her hand again, waited for silence. "Lisette Fox needs to account for and atone for her actions."

"Damn right!"

"String 'er up!"

"But what about us?" The woman in a Belus guard uniform stepped forward. "The world will think we're part of this. We'll be hunted down."

A melee of voices yelled over one another.

"Wait," Bobbie shouted. Someone below gave a high-pitched finger-in-lips whistle that bought a terse silence.

Bobbie cleared her throat and said, "When Fox testifies, and we need her to do that, we need to know who else knew about this – who else was involved. Questions have to be answered, and those of you not involved need to be exonerated. She can do that. Then I believe the world will see that no-one else was responsible for the so-called Melters War. That's important, especially for you. If you kill her, it's all hearsay, and the truth will never come out."

A rumble spread through the crowd.

Bobbie lifted her voice above the noise. "Yes, we have the footage, but Fox needs to account for every detail." The crowd settled, paying attention. She went on. "We the people need to see that. Please don't think that her guards were involved. We need to show compassion toward one another. Help where you can, give what you can, take only what you really must."

Bobbie waited while the people clapped and shuffled forward as more joined the throng.

"Who are the Candels?" someone shouted.

"Will they help us?"

Chatter broke out through the crowd. Some people were nodding and waving their arms.

Luke stepped forward and clapped his hands above his head. The people turned their attention to him.

"For those who don't already know, the Candels are, were an underground group set up initially to help expectant mothers sidestep the dependency laws. There are groups of them all over the world, and they'll work with us to establish communications and to rebuild a democratic society." Luke took Bobbie's hand. "Right now, I suggest you all go home and regroup around your families."

"How will we get home? Will the hovercrafts work?" voices asked.

Slade stepped forward. "If home is inaccessible right now, go to the canteen. We'll set up an emergency command center there. No-one is in this alone."

Bobbie stepped back from the edge of the mezzanine and saw a man passing a bundle of clothes to Hicks, who shook his hand.

"Spare uniform in his locker," Hicks said, turning to Bobbie.

"Thanks," Bobbie said, looking past Hicks to the man. He looked around the same age as her dad, and wore a janitor's uniform. A prosthetic limb hung by his side. The EMP would have rendered it useless – he'd lost his arm all over again. "I'm so sorry," she said.

"Melters War," he said. "Not your fault."

Bobbie would have to work hard to fully accept that. She pressed her lips together, blinking hard, and nodded.

The janitor's expression softened. "I'd like you to have this."

He dug into a bag slung over one shoulder and took out a white blanket in woven cotton.

"It's a family heirloom," the man said. "I had it in my locker. I was to go straight after this shift to my granddaughter's christening in Italy."

How long would it take him to get to Italy now? How long would it take them to get back to Ireland, to Hang?

The man pressed the soft material into Bobbie's hands. "Take this for Joy. To wrap her–"

Bobbie screwed her face up hard, but couldn't stem the tears. "Thank you," she whispered, and gave the man a quick hug. He backed away, wiping his eyes.

The crowd thinned as people moved on, clearing the stairs. Luke stopped Doctor Coughlin and indicated an office off the mezzanine. "Can you keep Fox here until we get back?"

"Good idea," Doctor Coughlin said. "Best not to inflame the crowd."

"When I return, we'll figure out how to move forward. I just need–"

"I know. Go." Doctor Coughlin patted Luke's shoulder and met Bobbie's gaze with sad, dark eyes.

Slade appeared, carrying a red rescue services bag. "I'll show you to the quantum computer room," she said.

She led Luke, Hicks, and Bobbie out of the foyer. When it became too dark to see, she gave them each a green chemical light-stick.

"Let's light these one at a time. They're supposed to last for twelve hours," Slade said, cracking one open and casting an eerie green light.

They descended stairs, so many that Bobbie lost count. Slade took them along a corridor – the place seemed bigger than ever, so many dark corridors. Bobbie knew she'd revisit this in her nightmares, heart heavy with dread, knowing what they'd face when they found Joy. It felt like it would never end.

They turned a corner, and ahead a light spilled through an open door at the end of the corridor.

"What is that?" Bobbie asked, terrified at the unexpectedness of it.

"The quantum computer room was surrounded by a Faraday cage," Luke said. "It was protected from the EMP."

Bobbie thought of the Hicks clones. "Wait," she whispered. "Any Rejuvenees inside that room would have survived."

"She's right," Slade said. "You two wait here. Luke, take this and come with me." Slade took a crowbar and a bush knife from the rescue bag.

They crept along the corridor and flattened themselves against the wall. Slade threw something that rattled against the wall beyond the doorway loudly enough to entice someone inside to come out to investigate.

Bobbie held her breath, hoping that no-one appeared at the door, yet hoping too that they did, so this torture would be over.

Slade peeked into the room, pulled back quickly, waited, then ran forward, swallowed up by the doorway.

"Clear," she called from inside.

Bobbie felt wobbly with relief.

The quantum computer hummed and twinkled as if nothing had happened.

"It will help us rebuild," Luke said, pulling a stool to the ventilation shaft and removing the hatch.

"Can you manage this?" Bobbie asked Hicks, remembering his panic attack as they'd crept through the maintenance duct in the research facility in Ireland where they'd gone to rescue Granny.

"Fox kept me in the dark in a box too small to stretch out in, never mind stand up in for... I don't know, a week, maybe. This..." Hicks pointed into the shaft. "This is massive by comparison."

The horrible psychological torture for someone with claustrophobia to be forced into a dark box made Bobbie's gut twist. Hatred for Fox engulfed her. She clamped down hard on the urge to turn back and strangle the evil bitch with her bare hands. A soft squeeze of Hicks' hand on Bobbie's shoulder dampened the heat of her rage.

"You're with me now," Hicks whispered. "That's all I need."

The climb took them to the vent on the hillside near where Joy had planned to access the servers.

Bobbie blinked in the sunlight. Smoke hung over the mountain. Another plume curled over the horizon. The sight slashed another strip off Bobbie's heart. When the EMP hit, all flying hovercrafts would have dropped from the skies.

She scanned the slopes, but saw nothing. "We need to get higher," Bobbie said, and headed for the ridge.

The view from the ridge looked into the next valley to the research center. The hoverport on top of the building had caught fire. A human chain had formed to carry water and fight the fire.

"There!" Luke pointed at what looked like a bundle of grey and red material halfway down the slope ahead of them.

Bobbie ran, stumbling and skidding, the others keeping pace. They ran past the debris of drones that Joy had managed to shoot, past the spent laser gun, and finally reached the chaos of blood around her sister's body.

Joy lay on her back, her legs straight, her arms flung wide from her sides as if she were flying. Her chest was slashed open, her heart exposed.

"Oh, God, Joy." Bobbie sank to her knees. Hicks knelt beside her and wrapped an arm around her, pulling her against him.

Luke knelt at Joy's head. He stroked her hair, gently untangling knotted strands.

"She was so brave," he said. "She knew the only way was to go online through her ONIV."

"Did you know that before she—"

"I wasn't sure. I hoped she'd figured something else out, but I knew that once they detected her online, they'd open a channel to her. She must have reverse piggy-backed that to get into their system with the key to upload to the public broadcast system."

"She was amazing," Slade said. She handed Bobbie a wad of bandages.

Bobbie wrapped Joy's torso. Luke helped Bobbie while Hicks and Slade assembled the stretcher.

Once Joy's body was securely bound, they laid her on the stretcher. Bobbie arranged the white cotton blanket over Joy, hiding the bandages, disguising the disfigurement from her wounds. Joy looked like she could be sleeping. Her face looked serene. Her lips held a little smile that seemed to say to Bobbie, "We beat them."

They took a corner of the stretcher each. From this far up the mountain, Bobbie could see the way down to the road that led to Belus Headquarters.

A crowd walked up the slope to meet them.

Bobbie kept her eyes on the people as she carried her sister. Her arms were tired, but she embraced the sensation. This was for Joy. This was all about Joy. She'd given the ultimate sacrifice. Bobbie's emotions swung a fierce pendulum between pride and anger, slicing through a pit of loss and regret.

The first of the people reached Bobbie.

"Can we help carry her?" a man asked.

"No, thank you," Bobbie said through her tears. "I'm bringing my sister back."

The man touched his fingers to his lips and gently touched Joy's head. He stepped back and knelt, bowing his head. Two women knelt beside him, and across from them, a young man in a guard's uniform knelt facing the others. People fell into position, standing heads bowed on either side, creating a path, paying homage, all the way to the car park.

CHAPTER 24

The sun rose at six – the spring equinox. Bobbie chose to think of this day as the anniversary of new beginnings, and not of Joy's death. It was five years since Bobbie had carried Joy's body down that hill. Bobbie still missed her little sister, still listened for her voice in her vibro implants, though they hadn't worked since the EMP. In the quiet of evening, after she had the girls in bed, she would sit on the veranda overlooking the reservoir and gaze at the sky. A shooting star could catch her unawares and still raised her pulse, so conditioned was she to fearing invaders from space.

Bobbie set a posy of wildflowers in the middle of the table, then turned her attention to preparing and serving breakfast. She set the table for five – two adult settings dispersed between three smaller ones – all identical, to avoid the squabbles.

Today was their wedding anniversary and the girls' birthdays. Bobbie had packed the day full. The first event planned to honor Joy's memory, and the second... Well, Bobbie liked to think that Joy and Gracie were having their own little joke with their only living sister. Had they enjoyed her terror when the doctor told her she was carrying three babies? They really must have gotten a kick out of Hicks' reaction. He'd almost fainted.

The danger to the babies and Bobbie had been real enough, though. Resources were in short supply, and by the time the babies were due, only battery-operated incubators were up and running. One thing the Candels had plenty of was skilled obstetricians and neonatologists. Bobbie's pregnancy had been no more difficult than any multiples pregnancy. Water retention had caused her to legs to swell so badly, she'd felt like a barrel from the waist down.

She went into labor at thirty-three weeks. The first two babies were big for triplets, weighing in at four pounds each. They'd both demonstrated their working lungs with a hearty cry. Hicks and Bobbie named the first one Gracie and the second Joy. But the third girl was small, weighing only two pounds and twelve ounces – she'd barely cheeped. Her first weeks were precarious. Bobbie had called her Hope, and Hope prevailed.

Laughter drifted down the hallway. The girls had invaded their parents' bed, and Hicks took his vengeance in tickles. Bobbie tucked the happiness the squeals brought her into the folds of her heart. It helped to offset the grief and regrets that still haunted her from that day, that time, five years ago.

Although those were terrible days, Bobbie held the memories close and revisited them often. They'd waked Joy for a week. After the first night, when the family and close friends said their goodbyes, Luke, Bobbie, Hicks, and Slade laid Joy's body out on a platform on the ridge above where she had died. People came from all around to pay their respects. Some walked miles over the mountain; a few arrived on horses and donkeys. A group turned up in vintage cars. A transport museum in Zurich had a fleet of tractors and a truck that worked, and with their help, they were able to bring people to and from the funeral.

They cremated Joy on the mountaintop and let the wind carry her ashes far and wide.

A year to the day later, Hicks and Bobbie married at Seaghan Dam. It had taken them three months to get back to Armagh, walking, cycling, and sailing. Luke had traveled with them, desperate to get back to his son, not knowing if Hang was safe. Slade had stayed in Switzerland to direct Fox's trial under the umbrella of the Truth Commission, and to set up a newly elected government.

The trial took a couple of years. Representatives, like Niclas and April and other principle Candel organizers, as well as leaders from communities all over the globe, traveled by whatever means possible to Switzerland to take part. Fox would never have freedom again. Davitt had faced conspiracy charges in the latter part of the trials pertaining to Rejuvenation. His testimony against Fox had helped his case, but he'd never fully recovered from his brain injury, and had suffered long-term psychiatric problems and lived in an assisted care facility in Wales until his death two years later. Bobbie never saw him again.

The Truth Commission had deliberated on Bobbie's role in uncovering the Melters' hoax and detonating the EMP. Their findings concluded that Fox had started a war in the first instance with the malfunctioning solar collector, and in the second instance by declaring martial law and directing the refugees to attack civilians. Bobbie had ended the war by pressing the button that set off the EMP. Bobbie was declared a war hero. Though she was never able to accept that accolade in her heart, she recognized the importance of that status to her children's future.

The Candels were never accused of any wrongdoing, and were deemed no longer necessary, since the new governing body overturned the dependency laws along with the use of biosensors, and gave people autonomy over their own health needs.

Communications took a while to reestablish. Some high-tech equipment and computers, like the quantum computer in what had been Belus HQ, had survived the EMP. There had been reports of a couple of Rejuvenees surfacing and being viciously beaten to death. People were less inclined to believe everything that was reported to them, and the news was disjointed.

Most of the ultra-elderly had been rejuvenated and killed by the EMP. The remaining population was predominately young, and realized they needed the experience and wisdom of their remaining elders.

A clatter of giggles and chatter brought Hicks and the girls to the kitchen.

"Those are beautiful," he said, pointing at the wildflowers and kissing Bobbie on the cheek. He leaned into her ear. "Hope, seven minutes."

Bobbie smirked. "My money's on Grace, five minutes."

They were both wrong. The flowers lasted ten minutes, and it was Joy who knocked them over.

Hope wailed because the water had splashed her "birthday breakfast cake" – a scone with strawberry jam.

Grace sidled off the end of the bench before the water could spill over onto her lap and came round to stand beside Hicks, ignoring Bobbie, who mopped the mess with a tea towel, wishing she hadn't bothered with the flowers at all.

"Daddy," Grace said. "When is Uncle Hang and Na-nad coming?"

"Soon."

"Today?"

"Yes," Hicks said, lifting Hope and shushing her frazzled crying. She was small compared to the other two, with ginger curls and grey eyes. Grace and Joy looked alike, with dark hair and brown eyes. Hope stuck her thumb in her mouth and snuggled against her daddy's chest, her head coming just under his chin.

"Why don't you go and watch for them?" Bobbie said. "They'll be here any time."

Grace and Joy skipped to the kitchen door, which opened onto the veranda. They sat on the steps for about ten seconds; then Joy came back to the kitchen. She stood by Hicks' knee and put out her hand to Hope.

"Chum on," she said.

A smile split Hope's face. She wriggled down from her daddy's knee and tottered to the front step, settling herself down between Grace and Joy. Hope was always the one in the middle.

Bobbie slid onto the bench beside Hicks. Morning sun streamed through the door and warmed her face. She closed her eyes and leaned back against him. She listened to his heart thudding, felt movement from him as he lifted her hair and let it fall.

"I love the sun in your hair. It looks –"

"Like flames," she finished for him, and squirmed around to kiss his lips.

"They're here! They're here!" The three girls jumped up and down with excitement. Bobbie wondered if it was for the love of their Uncle Hang and Grandad, or if the children knew the arrival of their relatives heralded presents.

Her father and brother were based at the new settlement at Slieve Gullion, but traveled a lot. She never knew how they would arrive. In the early days, they came on foot. Then they acquired bicycles and sometimes horses. But today, the air filled with a whirring sound. Bobbie looked up. A small hovercar swung low over the drumlin countryside. How did the girls know what this was? The children's acceptance of what was in front of them amazed Bobbie.

As the hovercar approached, the noise and bluster from its jets made the girls switch from cheering to screaming. They ran back into the kitchen and climbed up their father's legs and piled into his lap. Bobbie looked from the doorway, shaking her head.

"You'd better hope they're not still doing that as teenagers," she said.

"If their aunties are anything to go by, they'll hate me in their teens." Hicks extracted himself from the tangle of arms and came to stand beside Bobbie.

"It didn't take long to dust the old prototypes off," she said.

"It's been slow progress, but it's progress," Hicks said, stomping through to the veranda with the girls still hanging off his legs.

Three people climbed from the car. Bobbie recognized her father and brother right away, but squinted at the tall figure with flowing white hair. The woman turned around, and Bobbie's hand went to her mouth. She hadn't seen Orinda Slade since she'd left Switzerland five years ago. They'd kept in touch, writing letters that took months to be delivered at the start; now they wrote every couple of weeks. Bobbie had been touched at how Ori had mourned Joy. Back then, Bobbie had lost three very important women in her life within three months. Staying in contact with Ori had been an unexpected balm.

Ori lifted a box from the hovercar. Hang put his hands out, but Ori shook her head, glanced up at Bobbie, and smiled.

The girls ran to Luke and stopped just as they were a few steps from him, red-faced, hanging their heads and twisting their skirts in their hands.

"Oh, come on," Luke said. "Don't go all shy on me." He knelt down and opened his arms, and the three pounced on him. He fell backward, the girls piled on top of him.

Bobbie rolled her eyes. "He'll do himself a mischief," she said, hugging Hang, then releasing him to Luke. She turned to Ori. "It's good to see you," she said. A swell of emotion dampened her eyes. Ori's glittered too.

Ori shook it off and presented the box – a cooler box, Bobbie saw.

"For me?"

"Not exactly, it's on its way to the labs in Armagh, but we wanted to share it with you, show the girls," Ori said as Bobbie showed her where to set it on the kitchen table.

Everyone gathered around. Ori unlatched the lid. Bobbie felt the coldness on her face as they pressed forward together to peer into the box.

"Ice?"

Joy extended a finger, but Hicks wrapped his hand around hers.

"It's snow," Ori said.

"Oh, my goodness! Snow," Bobbie said, feeling the grin on her face. "Where did you get this?"

"We took it from a snowfield near Everest," Ori said. "It fell in September, lasted all winter, and is starting to melt now. We're just running a few tests to see what the chemical content is like. There's more in the hovercraft."

"Seasons again," Hicks said.

The adults shared a smile and nodded.

Ori scooped a ball out with a large spoon. "This you can touch."

Joy's hand flashed to the white mount and pulled back. "It bites," she said with a frown.

"It's alright," Hicks said, kissing the tiny hand. "It's just cold."

"I hear it's a special day today," Ori said.

Three faces grinned. Three heads nodded.

"A big birthday today," Bobbie said.

"How old are you?"

"Free," Hope said.

"Wow, that's very old."

Hope nodded with a gravitas that made Bobbie's mouth twitch.

Ori turned to Bobbie. "They're beautiful."

"They are, and a handful," Bobbie said.

Ori put her arm around Bobbie's shoulder and squeezed. "You made a better world for them," she said softly.

Bobbie shook her head, but before she could open her mouth to argue, Ori raised one finger and placed it gently over Bobbie's lips. "It *is* a better world now," Ori said, "A world fit for Grace, Joy, and Hope."

The End

###

Thank you for reading Rejuvenation, book 3 of The Rejuvenation Trilogy by Byddi Lee. If you enjoyed this book, would you please leave a review?

ABOUT THE AUTHOR

BYDDI LEE IS AN IRISH writer living back in her hometown, Armagh, after having lived abroad for many years. Before she wrote "Rejuvenation", a speculative fiction trilogy, published by Castrum Press, she had success publishing flash fiction, short stories and her novel, "March to November". Byddi co-founded and manages Flash Fiction Armagh, shortlisted as Best Regular Spoken Word Night in the Saboteur Awards. She co-edits "The Bramley – An Anthology of Flash Fiction Armagh".

Along with two other members of the Armagh Theatre Group, Byddi wrote: "IMPACT – Armagh's Train Disaster" which was staged, for the anniversary of the tragedy, in June 2019 in the Abbey Lane Theatre in Armagh and "Zoomeo & Juliet" a live play performed on Zoom, by the Armagh Theatre, during the 2020 UK-wide COVID-19 Pandemic lockdown.

WORKS BY THE AUTHOR

NOVELS
THE REJUVENATION TRILOGY
Rejuvenation, book 1
Rejuvenation, book 2
Rejuvenation, book 3

March To November

PLAYS
IMPACT – Armagh's Train Disaster
Zoomeo & Juliet

Printed in Great Britain
by Amazon

54920660R00106